# *Liberty's* RUN

## Walter G. Esselman

DARK MYTH

www.darkmythpublications.com/

Dark Myth Publications, a division of
The JayZoMon/Dark Myth Company.
21050 Little Beaver Rd, Apple Valley, CA 92308

ISBN: 978-1-7372947-4-0

First Printing September 2021

Dark Myth Publications is a registered trademark of The JayZoMon/Dark Myth Company

10 9 8 7 6 5 4 3 2 1

# Dedications

A huge Thank You to Dave Russell for encouraging me to complete what would be Chapter one.

And dedicated to David K. Montoya because, after he read that story, he wanted to read the rest of it.

Also, special thanks to Diana Rivera for helping to make Uncle Danny sound more authentic. And Rebecca Lynch, an anonymous commenter, and the Great Stephanie Bardy for keeping it going.

# Forward

It's funny, my buddy Dave and I were talking about his book, "The End" when I mentioned something about it. He then asked if I'd read the forward because he talked about it there.

I replied that I never read the Forward. I just dive into the book.

So.... there ain't no Forward here.

Enjoy!

# Dramatis kinda Persona

Liberty [*"Mija"*] Schonhauer
Uncle Danny Ramirez
Colin "Cobayo" Boseman
Dr. Miles "Tagg" McTaggert
Tessy Ramirez (Danny's niece)
"Abuela" Diana Rivera (Danny's grandmother)
Tofh, the King Doctor

Armory: Sergeant Russell Wu
Armory: Candace "Grandma" Rollins
Armory: Mrs. Khapor
Armory: Simon, the tattoo artist
Armory: Giselle
Armory: Stephen, the old entertainer
Armory: Ted

Dyson: Renoir
Dyson: Dr. Milton
Dyson: Fred, the unofficial leader of this group
Dyson: Dr. Hauser
Dyson: Ted
Dyson: Raj
Dyson: Dakarai
Dyson: Mr. Moyta

Aircraft Carrier: Rear Admiral Antony Cirilo

Aircraft Carrier:  Rex Bordeaux

Aircraft Carrier: Brent Smalls, the Navy mechanic.

Aircraft Carrier: Captain Deep Singh

Aircraft Carrier: Private Collins

Aircraft Carrier: Sergeant Victoria Ruiz

Aircraft Carrier: Private Mullins

Aircraft Carrier: Lieutenant Washington the medic

Aircraft Carrier: Private Frankline

Aircraft Carrier: Private Locke

Aircraft Carrier: Private Sondes

Aircraft Carrier: Major Princey

# Liberty's *RUN*

Take care of your friends!
Thanks,
Walter H. Esselman

## Volume One
### Chapter One

**EVEN THROUGH HER** leather gloves, Liberty felt the friction from the rope as she slid down.

Last year, she had been afraid of heights, but that was a lifetime ago.

Now, her big clodhopper boots dropped down hard onto the bed of the pickup.

Startled, a Big Mexican man turned quickly with his shotgun, but Liberty caught the barrel.

"I'm here to help!" she said and pointed up. The man smiled in relief, speaking swiftly.

But Liberty had no idea what he was saying. She gave an exaggerated shrug. "Sorry. I don't understand."

"Sorry, *Mi Mariposa Unicornio* is back here," muttered the

Big Mexican in English. He reached behind him and out came a little girl. She looked worried and confused.

"This is Tessy," said the man.

The little girl looked up at Liberty wearily.

"I'm not supposed to speak with strangers," mumbled the little girl.

Liberty almost did not hear her over the mob of guttural voices, which surrounded the truck. So, she crouched down.

"My name is Liberty Schonhauer," she said gently. "And I'm here to take you to safety."

"There is no safe," murmured the little girl, Tessy.

"Up there is safe," insisted Liberty.

Tessy looked up the side of the old City of Angels Armory; two stories of red brick, going straight up.

"Too high," squeaked the little girl.

"I know," said Liberty quickly. "I used to be afraid of heights too!"

"Why aren't you afraid anymore?" asked Tessy curiously.

Instantly, horrible memories began to bubble up. Memories that made hitting concrete, just a minor concern, maybe even a welcome one.

But Liberty couldn't tell a little girl that.

Gratefully, the Big Mexican saved her. He spoke swiftly in Spanish to Tessy. Liberty noted that he was really sweating, despite the cool breeze from the Pacific Ocean. But it could have been the mob of zombies, which surrounded the truck.

"Uncle Danny told me to go with you," said the little girl, and she reluctantly came closer.

"It'll be fun," promised Liberty as she stood. She took a leather belt, which was attached to her harness, and wrapped it around Tessy's waist. This put the little girl right next to her. The girl briefly touched one of Liberty's bare arms, which were covered in full sleeve tattoos.

"Uncle Danny's got a girl with a sombrero on his chest," commented the little girl. "Are you a soldier? Soldiers usually have tattoos like that."

"Oh, I'm not a soldier," said Liberty.

"Police?" asked the little girl.

"Oh! Definitely not," replied Liberty.

"What're you then?" asked Tessy in concern.

After a moment's hesitation, Liberty smiled. "I'm a librarian."

The little girl nodded thoughtfully at this.

"My Uncle Danny helped keep my Papa's garage open until...," started Tessy, but then her voice fell away.

Liberty offered the other belt to the Big Mexican, Uncle Danny. However, he just shook his head and pulled up the sleeve of his tan coat.

There was a nasty bite on his forearm.

Liberty just nodded. The mob of zoms had not been causing him to sweat.

Looking up, Liberty motioned, and she and the little girl began to rise.

3

"What's Uncle Danny doing?" asked Tessy suddenly with fear.

"Uncle Danny has to stay down there," said Liberty.

"But...he promised he'd stay with me," said the girl, and panic crept into her tiny voice.

"And he did," said Liberty gently. "For as long as he could."

\*\*\*

Liberty heard the roof door opening. Her head snapped around.

Sergeant Wu stepped out into the cool night air.

"The girl?" asked Liberty urgently.

"She's fine! She's fine!" said Wu quickly. The stocky man held up two beers as he walked towards the edge of the roof. "She's with Grandma Rollins; sleeping soundly."

"Thank God," exhaled Liberty in relief.

Wu sat on the edge of the roof, letting his legs dangle over the zoms below. Their moans and noises drifted up. Ignoring them, he put a cold beer beside Liberty.

"Thought you could use a refill," said Wu, but then he glanced at the bottle in her hand. "OR I might just drink it, since you haven't even touched yours."

Liberty looked in surprise at her hand. The bottle was open, but still completely full.

"I guess, I...," began Liberty, but then her voice trailed off.

"Have you seen the uncle?" asked Wu carefully.

Liberty shook her head. "Disappeared. Maybe...maybe he saved the last shell for himself."

Wu gave a bark of laughter, which was a little forced.

"That's crazy," grinned Wu. "I'd go to a gas station and get as many of those things to follow. Then I'd throw a flare into a gas tank of some bigass vehicle and turn it into a bomb. Boom!"

"But would that work?" asked Liberty.

"Why not?" asked Wu.

"It's stoichiometry," wondered Liberty out loud. Her eyebrows knitted. "There has to be enough air in the gas tank to set off the explosion. And if you don't close the lid fast enough, the flame could just vent out through the open gas tank. Pretty, but not lethal...unless you stick your face over it."

"OR" continued Wu gleefully. "I'd start pumping gas, and then shoot a bullet through the stream, an' set it on fire like it was a flamethrower." He made whooshing sounds and mimed using a flamethrower on the zoms below. "Take that!"

"I'm just wondering if the gun has enough...oomph to set off a....," began Liberty, but then suddenly she stilled. Slowly, she turned to glare at him.

"What?" asked Wu, trying to look innocent.

"You're just trying to distract me," grumbled Liberty.

"Nope! I'm doing a great job of distracting you. IfIdosaysomyself," said Wu with a smug tone. "Now, give me your beer."

5

"What? Why?"

"Because I don't mind warm beer. It's a superpower." Wu switched beers, but then stopped to peer through the brown bottle. "Any backwash?"

Despite herself, Liberty chuckled. "Nooo. Ew! I didn't even take a sip."

"Good, I don't wanna get some strange book related disease," nodded Wu. "Like Alphabetitis."

"That's not real," cried Liberty, loosening up.

Wu took a long pull of his warm beer, and not too long after, his face turned bright red. Knowing that it was just a biological reaction, Liberty did not even comment on it.

Instead, she asked in horror. "How can you even drink that?"

"What? The warm beer, or the fact that it's Casper beer?" asked Wu, and then he added brightly. "Hey! You *do* know why it's called Casper, right?"

"Because it's named after someone called Casper?" asked Liberty drily. "Hence the dude on the label."

"Well, yes...but, the real reason is because it has as much body as a ghost," said Wu airily.

Liberty chuckled again, a little more easily. "It's not that bad."

"I saw someone throw themselves off *this very roof*, because we only had Casper beer," said Wu. "He gave up *all* hope at that very moment."

"Now you're just making stuff up," retorted Liberty with mock chilliness.

Wu sniffed. "It's a very true lie."

"A wha...," started Liberty.  But she saw something bright over the policeman's shoulder and twisted to look at it.

A light was moving through the sky, and Wu saw her look of shock.

"What?" asked the policeman.

Turning, he saw the light drifting placidly over what had been the City of Angels.

"The hell?" spat Wu and he almost dropped his beer. Only years of experience saved it.

"I think our life just got more complicated," said the Librarian, almost to herself.

Setting down her beer, Liberty hopped up and snagged her Steyr SSG 69 sniper rifle.  She ran to the other side of the roof and shouldered it.

Through her scope, the light resolved into a shape.

"What're you seeing?" asked Wu from behind her.  His voice professional; cool and assured.

"It...it looks almost like a diamond, but...that's not the right word for it," said Liberty.  And, if she had known the word for octahedron, then she would have been able to describe it exactly.

The Octahedron passed over an apartment complex until it reached an office building close to them.  Since the office building was taller than theirs, the Octahedron was partly obscured as it settled down onto the roof.

Liberty lowered her rifle in shock.

Behind her, Wu suddenly shouted. *"NO!"*

The Librarian nearly jumped out of her skin. She whipped around. "What?"

The Sergeant grimaced, looking apologetic. "Oh! Sorry! I wasn't talking to you!"

"Then…," started Liberty, still concerned.

"No, no, no," said Wu quickly. "I meant 'No! That is not a flying saucer!'."

Turning from him, she looked at the octahedron, and then returned to him.

"Could be a ship from Wakanda," she suggested cheekily.

The Sergeant glared at her, grumbling unhappily. "I'm serious! I'm not going to put up with this nonsense. I mean, zombies are bad enough, but this…". Wu rubbed his face in frustration. "I mean, this is all too weird."

"No one's going to argue that" agreed Liberty calmly. "But, unless Russa is that far more advanced than us…. that doesn't look like anything from our planet, does it?"

Wu did not answer, nor did she need him to.

Liberty continued, gently. "We need to talk to them, whoever they are."

The Sergeant started in surprise. "Reason?"

"Because we need to know if they can help us," explained Liberty patiently.

"You're kidding," started Wu, but then he continued quickly. "I know you're not, but…how're you going to contact them? Smoke signals?"

Liberty looked out over the city. She quickly devised a route that went from the office building, where the aliens were, to atop the roof that she currently stood on. There was a small bridge, which ran from their roof to a building nearby. It was not the studierest though.

"I'm going to have to run over there," she said.

"What?" asked Wu in alarm. "The hell you are!"

"How much food do we have?" asked Liberty.

"We're fine," grumbled Wu.

"Okay, but we just added another mouth to feed," said Liberty.

"A small one," countered Wu quickly.

"And we've saved three people this week alone," said Liberty. "If that keeps up, well...soon, we won't be fine."

A little icily, Wu replied. "We can't turn people away."

"No! No, I'm not suggesting that" said Liberty quickly. "But, even if we did, it wouldn't matter. Eventually, we'd be in the same place. Not enough food."

"Well? What do you suggest?" asked Wu carefully.

"We need to find out what that thing is," said Liberty, pointing towards the other building.

"There's no guarantee that anyone will make it back," said Wu.

"That's why I'm going alone," announced Liberty.

Wu's eyes turned fiery.

Liberty countered. "You know I can run fast." And she was thrilled that her voice stayed even and steady. "And my library was really close to that building, so I know the area."

"But more guns...," countered Wu.

Liberty shook her head. "I don't want to risk anyone else on this trip."

"And what if you don't come back?" asked Wu with a tight voice.

"Then the food will last that much longer," said Liberty gently.

Wu gave her a squint worthy of Clint Eastwood. "You're not going buggy on me, are you?"

Liberty started in surprise. "What?"

"You know. Not caring if you live or die."

"I do care if I live," replied Liberty hotly. She felt stung by the inference. And this made a distant part of her wonder if she was lying to him and herself.

Wu made an unhappy noise. "Okay, I need to think before I authorize this."

In response, Liberty scrunched up her face. "Um...technically, I'm a librarian, not a policewoman. So..."

"So, you can do whatever the hel...heck you want to do?" asked the Sergeant in annoyance.

"I don't work for you," said Liberty finally.

"Oh! So, you're going to play that card?" asked Wu in surprise.

"I'm gonna to play the hell out of it," replied Liberty, but then her voice softened. "I don't want to be zombie food, but I also don't see any big changes coming down the road. At least, none for the better. We NEED to check this out."

"Will you at least take a SAT phone, just in case?" asked Wu.

"They still work?" asked Liberty in surprise.

"For the moment," nodded Wu reluctantly. "So, you really think you can make it there."

Liberty grinned. "Piece of cake."

\*\*\*

Swinging by a rope, a cinder block smashed through an office window. From the roof next door, Liberty's jaw dropped. The cinder block swung back to the flagpole—which it had been tied to—and clattered against the side of her building.

"I can't believe that actually worked," she said in surprise. But the cinder block had followed the arc perfectly. It had built up just enough speed to smash right through.

Carefully leaning over, Liberty looked down. The restaurant which made the best Pad Thai in town backed up into this alley. More than once, while shelving books during the day, she had dreamed of this Pad Thai until quitting time. Today, she had moved right through her favorite eating place without a thought.

Behind her, the door to the roof was shaking violently, knocking her out of her hollow place.

Liberty picked up a thick board, which she had dragged all the way up from the alley below. She grunted at its weight, but it needed to be strong. Distantly, she wondered

11

if she should have brought help. But really, the only one capable of being out here was Sergeant Wu, and the Old Armory needed him.

"No time to test this last bit," she muttered.

Liberty set the thick board between the two buildings.

With a piercing noise, the door to the roof gave. Now, the cook who had made the best Pad Thai in the city led the zombies out onto the roof. They spoke with their usual guttural noises.

"I hate rushing," grumbled Liberty.

Stepping up onto the board, she walked out over a twelve-story drop, but she wasn't scared.

And distantly, Liberty began to wonder if Wu was right about her going 'buggy'. This was an awfully stupid risk as she walked across the board. True, the entrances on the first floor had been blocked up, but maybe she should have tried harder before doing this.

Closing in on the building, she carefully tossed her sniper rifle into the office. If the rifle's previous owner— and her mentor—had seen that, he would've thrown a conniption-fit. But Mr. Jamie wasn't here anymore, thought Liberty blandly, just like all the rest.

The wind picked up and buffeted against her. She immediately reached out for the broken window. The glass only slightly pierced her leather glove. Liberty used the barest amount of pressure, but—as she was righting herself —the glass broke under her hand.

Dangerously unbalanced, Liberty pitched herself forward and fell into the office. Dropping onto the back of her leather coat, she hit the ground and rolled right across the bits of glass.

Stopping just past the debris, she found herself on a hideous green carpet. Despite the sight of that carpet, she seemed okay. However, when Liberty shifted, something sharp poked her in the back.

"Ow," she muttered softly.

Pulling off her leather coat, she saw that the glass had turned it into a pin cushion. It would take an hour to get all the glass out.

"And I liked this coat too," moaned Liberty. As she dropped the ex-coat, she noticed the zoms on the other roof. They were pawing at the board, which still lay between the buildings.

"I'm wondering, are you smart enough to get across?" she asked as she retrieved her rifle. Just as she straightened up, a zom pulled at the edge of the board and sent it tumbling down into the alley below.

"Awww, you are your own worst enemy," said Liberty sympathetically and saw the Thai cook. The knowledge that there was no more Pad Thai echoed throughout her. Unbeknownst to her, Liberty gave a soft sigh.

Slinging the rifle behind her back, she pulled out the Glock 22, which she had taken from a cop after he had fallen. She really wished that it had a silencer, but then— while she was at it—she wished she had a lightsaber too. With a near frictionless energy blade, she could clear a whole town with a lightsaber...eventually. But that was just silly dreaming, she added morosely.

Carefully, she moved out into the corridor. She looked up and down, but the coast was clear. She followed the

'EXIT' signs and found the door to the stairwell. Peeking through the small window in the door, she saw a zombie standing there. She nearly swore out-loud, but—luckily—it was looking away from her.

With careful movements, she put her handgun away and started to draw her knife. The zom turned around and saw her. Hungry noises clambered out of its throat. Liberty kicked the door open, which smacked it, right in the face.

It stumbled backwards as Liberty leapt forward.

As the zombie grabbed for her, the Librarian ducked underneath its arm.

With one hand, she snagged its hair in a tight grip. And, with the other hand, she shoved the long, thin knife through its eye socket, deep into the brain. She then twisted it, just like Mr. Jamie had taught her.

It pawed at her shoulder for a moment, but then quickly went limp.

Below, she heard footsteps. She guided the body gently to the ground. Tugging out the knife, she held it, at the ready.

The first floor had been thoroughly barricaded, which is why she had had to come in through a window. But this meant that she did not know how many zombies were trapped in here with her.

Not even daring to breathe, Liberty watched the stairs going down. But the shuffling soon stopped.

Taking in a gulp of stale stairway air, she moved around the dead zom.

As fast as she dared, she went up the stairs towards the

roof. Suddenly, a distant doubt entered her mind. What if there had been no ship? What if it was all a hallucination? What if she HAD gone buggy? Or, if there is a ship, what if it's already left?

Reaching the top, she sheathed the knife. Unslinging the sniper rifle, she stopped. This building was still drawing power, which meant that the lights were still on. With the butt of her rifle, she smashed the light fixture over the stairs.

For a moment, she held her breath, but it did not sound like anything below was curious about the noise.

Liberty went to the roof door, and cautiously opened it.

On the roof, the Octahedron floated. The bottom point hovered just a foot off the ground. Liberty listened, but she didn't hear any noise, except for a dull, rhythmic sound, emanating from the ship.

A boy cried out and fear flooded through her.

Tossing open the door, she scanned the rest of the rooftop. A small orb—the size of an orange—also hovered above the rooftop. And above that, like an insect stuck in amber, was a boy. Liberty wondered what would happen if she shot the orb. Would it free the boy, or kill him?

"There is no need for the crying," came a strange, mechanical voice. Moving across the rooftop, towards the boy, came...something.

Liberty's mind desperately tried to process it. It looked organic. The creature moved on hundreds of tentacles, which covered its body, if there actually was a body under there. To her, it seemed like a tumbleweed in the old Westerns her grandmother watched.

15

"Let me go!" cried the boy.

"Too dangerous," replied the creature in its strange, mechanical voice.

"I don't wanna be eaten," said the boy, panicking.

"I understand," said the creature, and it's dark purple tentacles shook. "On my world, the Go-Zah treated my people as if WE were some kind of delicacy for them to consume. It was a long time before we bent them to our will."

"What're you going to do to me?" asked the boy.

Before the creature could answer, Liberty spoke up.

"Have they hurt you?" she asked of the boy.

The creature let out a cry of alarm. For a moment, Liberty could see a blue body under all those tentacles.

But then the creature brought up several tentacles, which were covered in metal tips. For a brief moment, there was a flash of green between it and her.

"Who...who are you?" asked the boy of her.

Liberty gave her name, but then she asked again. "Are you hurt?"

"Um, no," said the boy.

"Good," said Liberty. "What's your name?"

"Colin," said the boy. "Can you get me out of here? I can't move."

Liberty turned towards the creature, barely able to contain her anger. "Why is he in there?"

"He is a danger," said the creature.

16

"No, I'm not!" snapped Colin.

"I have to admit, he doesn't look that dangerous to me," said Liberty.

"Who are you?" asked the creature.

"My name is Liberty Schonhauer. I saw your ship. I wondered...I wanted to see...?"

"We have come to save the planet," replied the creature. "I am Tofh. King Doctor."

"King Doctor?" asked Liberty curiously.

The creature, Tofh, grumbled, a bit defensively. "My translator is doing the best it can with your basic language."

"Hey, I'm not complaining," said Liberty quickly. "We could use all the help we can get." She looked over at the boy. "Whoa! What happened to your arm?"

Liberty moved closer to the dark-shinned boy. There was a terrible bite on his arm.

"Oh no," said Liberty with a sinking heart. "You've been bit. How long?"

"Oh, that," said the boy, unconcerned. "Last week."

Liberty looked up in surprise. "A zom bit you last week?"

"My father," said Colin with a sad voice.

"Oh, I'm so sorry sweetie," said Liberty sincerely. But then she looked at the arm again. "But that can't be."

"The child is immune to the virus," explained Tofh. "It must have washed right out of his system, probably in his urine, because there's no trace. With his blood, there might be a way to deal with this virus."

17

Liberty grinned in relief. "Oh my God. That's great. That would be a miracle."

"No miracle," said Tofh. "In a disease, there's always a chance that someone will have a resistance, or even immunity to the virus. I don't know if it is in his generic makeup, or something environmental. But it happens to be him. Took us a few cycles to find him."

"I thought I'd be safe in this building," said Colin sadly.

Something tugged at Liberty's mind. "But wait. You said he was dangerous."

"He is," insisted Tofh.

Liberty stilled. "You said you were here to save the planet."

"Oh, we are," said Tofh. "And we are making significant headway too."

"How?" asked Liberty.

"By removing the planet's biggest problem," said Tofh, and she could feel the alien's full attention on her. "You."

"When you say 'You'...," began Liberty with a cold pit in her stomach.

"The virus will decimate 93.6% of the human population within the next year," said Tofh, and his upper tentacles vibrated. "It is my crowning achievement."

"So, he's gonna kill us all?" asked Colin in a hollow voice.

"Oh no! Not complete extinction. There are laws which prohibit total genocide," said Tofh.

"Lucky us," commented Liberty drily.

"Yes, you should count yourselves lucky...," droned on Tofh.

Out of the corner of her eye, Liberty saw something moving. she ducked aside as another tentacled creature sprang up behind her. It grabbed at her and wrapped its tentacles around her rifle. She twisted the barrel towards the creature and fired.

Two of the new alien's tentacles were immediately severed, but the bullet missed the main body. Another dozen tentacles grabbed the rifle, while more ensnared her arm. However, the creature was not very strong.

Letting go of her rifle, Liberty pulled her knife with her free hand. She cut through the tentacles holding her other arm. The creature let out a piercing scream and dropped the rifle. She dove at the orb holding Colin.

But the first alien, Tofh, snatched it up. It pulled the orb close. The boy drifted above, almost as if he were weightless.

Turning her dive into a roll, Liberty came up on one knee, drawing her sidearm.

Tofh started to raise the tentacles with those metal tips.

Liberty fired. The bullet pierced right through tentacles, and the orb, which set off a small explosion. Colin— thankfully unharmed by the explosion—suddenly fell towards the edge of the roof. He hit the lip of the roof and began to slide off.

Heart lurching, Liberty scrambled forward and grabbed his shirt. With a soft grunt, she hauled him back to safety.

"You...you horrible creature," screeched Tofh as the alien waved its severed tentacles.

19

"Kill it!" cried the second creature.

Liberty did not wait. She pulled Colin to his feet and practically dragged him towards the stairs. The boy stumbled with her.

"Get her!" cried Tofh.

Bending down while they ran, Liberty was just able to grab the strap of her fallen rifle.

Before the second creature could mount an attack, Liberty reached the roof door, still open, and dove inside. As they started down the stairs, a bright beam pierced through the door where she had just been, and the stairs lit up for a moment.

"We're going to die, aren't we?" moaned Colin.

Liberty grinned. "Heck No! We're just getting started!"

# Chapter Two

**AS TWO BULLETS** went through the office window, it shattered. Pieces crashed onto the SUV directly below.

Jumping out, Liberty landed on top of the vehicle. She scanned the alley, but it was thankfully clear of trouble. There were a couple of zoms lurching about, but nothing to worry about as they shambled towards them.

It also did not escape her that this would have been an easier way in, rather than playing Trapeze Artist without a net. Had she been going buggy in the Old Armory?

"You okay?" asked the boy.

Liberty's attention was pulled back. Turning, she holstered her Glock and turned to the African American boy in the broken window.

"I don't want to be lunch," said Colin worriedly. He

looked up and down the alley, and then up.

"I understand, but I'll protect you," said Liberty. "We can't stay here. The second those two aliens are done licking their wounds, they're coming straight for us."

"For Me," corrected Colin.

Liberty shook her head and said in a hard voice. "Us."

Colin was surprised for a moment, but then he nodded. He let Liberty pick him up. He was so skinny; she was able to lift him down onto the SUV.

The moment they reached concrete; Colin called out.

"Up!"

Liberty did not even bother to look. She swiftly pulled him under the protection of an overhang.

"Hey," growled Colin indignantly. He pulled loose, but he did not step away.

Holding her breath, Liberty listened.

Immediately, she heard the distant rhythmic noise of the alien ship.

"Are you sure we're not going to die?" asked Colin, almost casually.

"We're not going to die," replied Liberty with a quick glance.

"Should we run?" whispered Colin.

A blue cone of light appeared from above. It covered the SUV, and then it moved away to light up some zoms. The creatures were lurching towards them as fast as the poor things could manage.

Distantly, she realized that she was against the back door

of her favorite Thai restaurant. She touched it a little sadly. They had been nice people. The ship continued to move down the alley, and then it disappeared around the far corner of the office building.

"Let's go," said Liberty and, aiming for the opposite direction, she took Colin's hand.

But the boy snatched his hand away.

"I'm not a baby," spat Colin.

Liberty whipped around. She was about to snap back-- and hard-- but she managed to stop herself. It was a kid, she reminded herself. A kid who was having a really bad day.

"Can you follow me?" asked Liberty. "Quickly."

After a moment, the boy nodded. "I know how to run."

Stepping out, Liberty went to the mouth of the alley. The streets were relatively clear of zoms. Leading Colin, they started back towards the Old Armory, but the two had not made it more than ten feet when they heard the Octahedron in the distance.

"There," hissed Liberty, and they both ducked into a recessed doorway. She set the boy against the door and then pressed her back against him, facing out.

"Hey!" grumbled Colin.

Liberty was a few feet from the mouth of the doorway, but she still felt too exposed.

The UFO came around the corner of the office building, still searching. The street in front was suddenly awash with blue light, which spilled partway into her doorway. Liberty tried to pull her toes back.

23

"I'm getting squished back here," moaned Colin.

"Sorry," muttered Liberty, and she tried to ease up. But the blue light was right up to the tips of her clodhopper boots. Was it looking for human life, and could they find it through steel-toed boots? She worried. Her heart pounded.

"Go! Go! Go away, come again some other day," whispered Liberty.

"Isn't that rain?" asked Colin grumpily.

Liberty looked over her shoulder with a smile. "It's worth a try."

Despite himself, Colin smiled back, and it made Liberty feel better.

The blue light disappeared, and Liberty let out a long, happy sigh. She moved a little forward to give the boy a little more breathing room. Then Liberty realized that she could still hear the Octahedron.

"Why isn't it moving away?" she wondered out loud.

In the distance, Liberty heard shuffling, but it was still a little way away.

Glancing around, she saw that their recessed doorway was brick on two sides, and a wooden door. Just in case, she tried the doorknob, but it was locked.

"Annnnnnd, I never learned how to pick locks," said Liberty to herself.

Suddenly, she froze. The shuffling was getting closer to their position, from the opposite direction of the ship.

"I think the ship is doing something," whispered Colin.

Liberty blinked at the boy, but then she noticed the low

sound—almost like a musical note. Carefully, she leaned a little forward. She could see the very bottom of the octahedron.

There was no preamble.

A red beam shot straight out of the bottom of the ship. The moment the beam hit the pavement, superheated asphalt splashed up, like pasta boiling over on a stove. And, as she ducked back, something was moving closer to their position. However, the red beam moved into the alley.

"They're trying to flush us out, like birds," said Liberty.

"Do you hear...?" asked Colin softly.

"Company," nodded Liberty.

Colin gestured at her gun. "Can't you just shoot them?"

"We've already made a lot of noise. More sound could wake up the whole neighborhood," replied Liberty with concern.

Suddenly, there was an explosion in the alley.

"The SUV?" wondered Liberty. She pulled her long knife, but it felt inadequate. Right now, she wished she had learned to use a sword, like a cutlass.

Several zoms quickly shambled past them, drawn by the noise of the explosion. One made the mistake of walking on the asphalt. It tried to keep moving, but its feet sank into the molten street. The heat was enough to make the zom's pants start to smolder as it struggled to move.

Liberty pulled back from the horror of it. Her heart ached for the poor thing. Though admittedly, it didn't seem to notice the fact that its feet were certainly burning. The blue beam returned to play over the street again, distracting

25

her from the plight of that poor zom.

There was a dread rumbling sound.

The Librarian blinked and glanced behind her. "Wait...was that your stomach?"

The boy looked stricken, but, before he could respond, another zom suddenly shambled in front of the doorway. The blue light illuminated a former man in a three-piece suit. The light moved away to the other side of the street, but the zom stopped.

The creature turned and saw them. It lurched into the recessed door grasping for Liberty. She backed up into Colin again and pushed the boy into the wooden door, like a duck press.

"Hey!" squeaked Colin.

But Liberty was trying to stab her knife into the zom's eye. However, this zom was mostly bald, so she couldn't grab its hair to steady the head.

Her first stab glanced off its temple. Meanwhile, it snapped its teeth. She managed to shove her other hand under its chin and shut its teeth with a sharp clack. However, the zom was strong and pulled at her. Then, she saw another zom appear in the mouth of the door, following the noise.

Letting out a cry, Liberty shoved the well-dressed zom. She pushed it back into the other one. While the two were trying to keep their footing, Liberty stabbed the well-dressed one in the eye. It slackened and began to fall.

Liberty tried to hold onto her knife, but she lost her grip. As the first zom hit the ground with her knife, the second was already stepping over its fellow creature. However, while it had its foot up though, she shoved it. The zom tripped over the fallen one.

Ducking back into the doorway, Liberty grabbed Colin's hand and pulled him out onto the street. This time, the boy did not complain about being dragged along.

Halfway across the street, she remembered the UFO. The zom in the asphalt was getting stuck in it. Glancing right, she wondered if the red beam would hurt, and for how long.

But the street was empty of alien craft.

Letting go of Colin's hand, she put her hand on his upper back and directed him towards the Old Armory.

"This way for food," she smiled.

"Food?" whispered Colin hopefully.

"And I'm sorry I didn't bring any with me," said Liberty. "I had only planned for a quick run."

"It's okay," replied Colin.

And inside, she admitted that she maybe wasn't planning on surviving long enough to need food.

The density of zoms was not so bad here. They were able to duck around the poor, shambling creatures. Colin followed quietly, perhaps dreaming of food.

Stepping up onto the sidewalk, Liberty led the boy along. She was trying to keep an eye on the zoms but also watch the sky for the UFO. She wondered how long she could keep this up.

Nearing an alleyway, she heard noises coming from down inside it. Liberty skidded to a halt and Colin looked at her curiously. She pointed first towards the alley, and then towards a place to hide.

"Another doorway?" moaned Colin softly, but he followed. The walls and doorway were all glass this time revealing tacky nouveau-riche jewelry in the empty store.

After a long, drawn-out moment, the Librarian saw a group of people leaving the alley. They turned immediately away, towards the Old Armory.

Jumping forward, Liberty called out with a loud whisper.

"Hey! Girl's uncle!"

The group of people turned swiftly, including the Big Mexican at the front.

The girl's uncle hissed. "What're you doing out here?"

With Colin following, Liberty ran up to the big man.

"You...you're Uncle...Danny! Isn't it...?" began the Librarian, but then she saw the fear on his face. "Oh! Your niece is okay! Totally."

And Uncle Danny's shoulders slumped. "¡Hijole! You nearly scared me to death when I saw you out here."

"I can explain all that," promised Liberty. "But, on the go. Please?!" She nodded pointedly towards several zoms lurching towards them.

The group began to move again.

Uncle Danny held his Remington 870 shotgun at the ready and, interestingly, had a cooking cleaver in a holster on his belt. But everyone else was carrying canvas bags. Liberty maneuvered Colin into the middle of the group. Then she took a little hop forward to fall in step beside the Big Mexican.

The Librarian had a ton of questions, but "So you're headed for the Old Armory?" she asked.

"Last time I could only deliver my niece, but this time I wanted to bring some food too," smiled Uncle Danny.

"More food is always good," agreed Liberty fervently. "Your good deed for the day, as my Grandpa always said."

"I guess...," replied Uncle Danny softly.

Liberty felt like something was on his mind. She decided to give him a moment and glanced back to make sure that Colin was okay. One of the women was giving him a power bar, and Liberty smiled with relief.

"Honestly," continued Uncle Danny in that same soft voice. The Liberian turned back to him as he continued. "I was out here, walking, feeling pretty sorry for myself. And I happened upon these people, running out of a burning building." She looked at him with a Questioning Look and he shrugged. "Guess a candle fell over, so they basically had to run out with nothing, or be burnt to a crisp."

"They're lucky that you happened to be passing by," said Liberty earnestly.

"Maybe me too," murmured Uncle Danny.

Despite having been bitten by a zom, Liberty realized that he was still moving pretty well.

She started. "Yeah, I thought you were..." But her voice suddenly trailed off. "I mean...I'm sorry. It's good to see you...you know..."

"I was surprised too," replied Uncle Danny good-naturedly. "Don't know why God is waiting for me. Maybe *mi Abuela* got to him." He gave a sad, little chuckle.

29

"However, it's almost been 2 days for me."

"Huh! That's weird...," began Liberty, but then she added, encouragingly. "But! Still! Good problem to have!"

Uncle Danny smiled at that. "Could be worse."

Starting to feel more comfortable with him, Liberty gave him a look that said, 'Who the heck did he think he was kidding?'.

Uncle Danny's smile grew wider.

"No, seriously. When I was in my 30's, I got cancer. That *chamba*..." he said before a darkness crossed over his face. As Liberty tried to think of some bland words of comfort, the Big Mexican continued. "So, this is bad, but it's still not as bad as that."

"You too?" called out Colin, moving swiftly to walk between them.

Uncle Danny glanced at the boy. "Hey! You beat the C *grande* too?"

"Remission for two years," said Colin. He gave a smile, but it was somewhat brittle.

"*¡Orale!* You must be a tough one," grinned Uncle Danny, and the boy looked up to him in surprise.

The Big Mexican looked back to Liberty.

"So, what're you doing out here?" he asked of her. "Being Batman?"

Liberty blinked in confusion. "Um..."

Uncle Danny nodded his chin at the boy. "That your Robin?"

The boy suddenly exclaimed indignantly. "Hey! If anyone's gonna be Batman, it's me!"

Uncle Danny looked down at the boy with mock seriousness.

"My apologies Mr. Wayne," he said. Then he turned back to Liberty. "So, what're you doing out here with the Dark Knight?"

As the group moved around knots of zoms, Liberty recounted her impromptu rescue mission, from saving Colin to the aliens melting asphalt.

"You're shitting me," said Uncle Danny.

"Aliens," nodded Liberty.

"*Ya te cargó el payaso,*" muttered Uncle Danny.

"Huh?" asked Liberty.

"¡No manches! ...I... I just can't believe it. "

Liberty gave a chuckle, and it felt good. "You think you're having troubles. When we first saw the ship. *Oh Man!* Sergeant Wu's-- that's the policeman who protects the Old Armory. You'll meet him shortly-- he was SO mad about the aliens. It's just too weird for him."

"It *IS* a little hard to swallow," said one of the women, Giselle, with an arch voice.

Liberty was about to be annoyed, but then she realized that this was the same woman who had given Colin a power bar earlier. So, she replied genially.

"I know, but they definitely aren't from around here," she nodded.

"And they look like spaghetti," added Colin, and then he

31

added mournfully. "I used to like spaghetti too."

Liberty patted his shoulder. "I'm sure you will again."

She turned back to Uncle Danny.

"So, we need to get to the Old Armory as soon as possible," said Liberty.

"But...is that the best idea?" mused Uncle Danny.

"What?" asked Liberty.

"Oh! I'm just thinking," said Uncle Danny quickly. "*Disculpe...Mi Abuela* always said I would step into something that wasn't my business."

"No, no," said Liberty quickly, earnestly. "I'd like to hear what you were going to say about the Old Armory."

"Oh, okay, "said Uncle Danny, and he took a second to collect his thoughts. "If these..." And he used the next word with distaste. "*El extraterrestre...aliens* are really pissed, then the Old Armory might not be so safe. Especially for the people inside."

"What does he mean?" asked Colin, who knew there was food at the armory.

"No! No, he's right," whispered Liberty quickly.

"What's right?" asked Colin in annoyance.

"These things might decide to flatten the building that you're in," suggested Uncle Danny gently.

"But they...," started Colin, however he went silent.

"Too bad we can't talk to the Old Armory," said Uncle Danny.

"OH!" chirped Liberty with a grin. "That's a great idea."

And Uncle Danny's eyes grew wide as she took a SAT phone out one of the big pockets in her cargo pants.

Liberty smiled shyly. "Sergeant Wu *really* didn't want me to go in the first place, so this was our little compromise."

Soon, Wu's voice came on, and Liberty filled him in.

"You're shitting me," he said.

"That's what I said," interjected Uncle Danny with a little laugh.

"That look like spaghetti," added Colin loudly.

"You know I wouldn't joke about this," said Liberty seriously.

"Yeah, I know," admitted Wu. "But it's just...a lot."

"The question is, is bringing Colin back to the Old Armory a good idea?" asked Liberty.

In the end, Wu needed time to think, and they still needed to get back to the Old Armory anyway.

"What the hell is that?" cried one of the men, Stephen as he pointed right.

Liberty didn't even look. She took Colin's arm.

"Wha...," started the boy.

Colin looked up and saw the octahedron coming towards them over some buildings. Liberty hustled him towards a storefront, out of sight of the ship.

But there were no recessed doorways on this one, so she took the direct approach. Letting go of Colin, she smashed the butt of her rifle against the plate glass window of a Vintage Clothing shop. The glass spiderwebbed but did not break. She could hear the rythmic sound of the ship getting closer, almost on top of them.

Uncle Danny took a step towards her to help.

Frustration and anger building in her, Liberty let out a guttural shout and hit the glass again.

It shattered and glass fell everywhere.

"What should we do?" asked Uncle Danny.

"I... I don't know. It's us they want," admitted Liberty, and she added earnestly. "Sorry!" She thought furiously. "Maybe try and look harmless?"

The badass Mexican just raised an eyebrow at that.

Liberty grabbed Colin and lifted him over the broken glass, into the shop.

"Hey!" cried the boy indignantly.

Placing the boy past the glass, she stepped inside and moved towards the far wall, watching the racks of vintage clothes. She wished it'd been a nice clean Apple Store, with its clear line of sight.

"This way," she whispered to the boy.

"Why?" asked Colin, and he stuck out his chin indignantly.

Then they heard a noise deeper in the store.

"That's why," replied Liberty.

"'Kay," squeaked Colin nervously and he ran over to her.

Liberty reached for her knife but immediately felt a pang of grief remembering that it was now gone.

"Hey! Help!" cried a voice from outside.

Liberty glanced out the ruined window and saw Uncle Danny frantically waved his arms towards the sky. Now, she could hear the rythmic sound of the UFO right over the store.

"Can you help us?" cried out Uncle Danny.

A blue light covered him, and then it rolled over everyone else.

And Liberty's heart pounded in fear as she watched helplessly. If they got incinerated…, she worried.

There was a hiss to her left. Liberty was already lifting up her rifle when a young girl—dressed like a hippie—tried to gnaw her face off. Liberty tried to push the hippie-girl back.

"Shoot it!" cried Colin, but she did not dare. Not with that ship out there.

Liberty kneed the hippie-girl in the stomach, and—curiously—the zom doubled over. For a second, she wondered if it was in pain, but then she decided it was probably an automatic reaction. With her rifle, Liberty hit the girl in the back of the head.

The zom dropped like a stone, twitched for a brief moment, but then lay still.

"Is...is she dead?" asked Colin.

And oddly, Liberty hoped that the hippie-girl was okay.

"Let's not find out," she said instead. They moved back towards the front of the store.

From the window, Uncle Danny worriedly asked. "You okay in there?"

Liberty looked out and saw with joyous relief that he

and the other people were all right.

She grinned. "Hey! That's my line."

Uncle Danny shrugged. "If we'd run, they'd have thought we were guilty. By asking for help, I figured they'd leave quickly."

Chuckling, the Librarian carried an indignant Colin back over the glass.

"Great thinking," said Liberty to the Big Mexican.

Immediately, they started moving again.

After dodging a knot of zoms, Uncle Danny said. "It's gonna get more crowded, the closer we get. And we need to find a pickup truck, sooner rather than later."

"A pickup?" asked Colin.

"That way you can drive right up to the Armory, and then they'll lower a rope for you," explained Uncle Danny.

"If he's going there," said Liberty.

"*Orale.* If he's going there," admitted Uncle Danny.

"Don't I have a say in this?" asked Colin.

Liberty was about to say 'No', but then she stopped. It was his life too. She glanced up at Uncle Danny, who gave a little nod.

The Librarian regarded the boy. "Okay, what do you think we should do?"

Colin blinked. "Um, what?"

"What do you think we should do?" asked Liberty again, patiently. "We could go back to the Old Armory..."

"You're giving a boy a right to vote?" asked Giselle with

grave disapproval.

"He's in danger too," shrugged Liberty. "And he's survived this long."

"But still, it's not a good idea!" huffed Giselle.

"Excuse me? Who are you?" asked Liberty. Her voice was a little sharper than she had intended, but this lady was getting her annoyed.

"My name is Giselle," said the woman.

"Right," said Liberty. "We're going to get *you* to the Old Armory where you'll be a lot safer."

"Not if we're attacked from above," said Giselle hotly, and other survivors started to nod. Colin looked back and forth between everyone.

"I'm wondering," suggested Uncle Danny curiously. "Could those heat beams really do much to the building? It looked pretty sturdy to me."

Liberty looked up at him. "It melted asphalt right away. So....it wouldn't be good."

Uncle Danny made an unhappy noise.

"Don't we have a say too?" asked Giselle. "Maybe we shouldn't go to the Armory as well."

"That's the best place," said Liberty.

"And I haven't seen any place safer," said Uncle Danny. "Not since the airport fell."

"What about the Fleet?" asked an old man, Stephen.

Gisele huffed immediately with pointed sarcasm. "Do you really believe that there's a bunch of ships out there?"

"It makes sense," replied Stephen.

"Then why haven't you gone out there?" asked Gisele.

"I get seasick," sniffed Stephen. "Like, really, really bad seasick."

Colin looked up. "I vote that we drop these people off and keep going!"

Everyone turned to him, which made the boy more nervous, but Uncle Danny watched the boy lift his little chin in defiance.

"Oh, I'm sorry, we weren't trying to make you feel guilty," said Giselle with an immediate apology.

"But succeeded," muttered Uncle Danny under his breath. Liberty heard it and cast him an amused side-eye. The Big Mexican gave a small smirk in return.

Liberty also noticed silently that no one else was offering to go with Colin.

Half-joking, Uncle Danny barked. "Don't all line up at once to go with the boy,"

Only with great effort did Liberty manage not to laugh out loud.

The others looked away.

Before anyone could say anything, the SAT phone went off.

The moment Sergeant Wu was on, he asked. "What about A.U.?"

"What?" asked Liberty in confusion.

"City of Angels U," amended Wu. "Remember, we got ahold of them...was it last week or the week before?"

"Two months ago," said Liberty.

"What?" asked Wu. "Wow! Time's really starting to blend together up here. Yikes."

"You're not wrong," replied Liberty gently. "And didn't the science department say they had a safe zone."

"Where?" asked Uncle Danny of Liberty as he leaned over to listen in.

Wu heard him and responded.

"Apparently the person who designed the new Physics building, also secretly made it to withstand a zombie siege," said the Sergeant.

"Maybe they'd know what to do with the boy," said Uncle Danny.

"Hey! Don't call me '*boy*'," snapped Colin.

Thoughtfully, the Big Mexican looked at him. "Are you even in High School yet?"

"Um, well, no," started Colin.

"Wait, what's happening?" asked Wu through the phone.

"Nothing," said Liberty to the sergeant at the Old Armory. "So, they…"

"'Nothing'?" asked Colin hotly.

Liberty blinked.

"What's that?" asked Wu, but the Librarian asked him for a moment before turning to Colin.

"What's wrong?" she asked, perplexed.

"Who's 'Nothing'?" asked Colin, and his eye twitched with anger.

"What? I don't...," she sputtered.

"That guy asked what was happening, and you said I was nothing," spat Colin.

"What?" she said again. "What, NO! I wasn't saying that."

"Oh!" said Uncle Danny, understanding. He looked at the boy. "When you and I were talking, the *cabrón* at the Old Armory was worried something was wrong. Something maybe dangerous. She was just telling him that our conversation was 'nothing' for him to worry about."

Colin's mouth opened and closed. "Oh. Okay then." He still didn't look entirely convinced.

Liberty leaned over and quickly rubbed her cheek on the top of the boy's head. "You are definitely 'Someone', and I'm betting someone awesome."

Despite himself, Colin gave a little smile.

Straightening up, Liberty said to Wu. "The science building should have medical equipment too."

"Wait? What?" sputtered Colin worriedly as he stepped closer.

"Don't worry," said Liberty earnestly to the boy. "You'll be okay."

"Guinea pig," smirked Uncle Danny with amusement.

"What do you mean...," started Colin.

Liberty shushed the guys and looked back at the phone.

"Unfortunately, I think that's our best plan," said Liberty sadly.

"You'll be back," said Wu. Despite his bravery, a

sadness crept in. "I should be going with you."

"No," said Liberty flatly. "They need you there. Me and Colin will get to A.U. okay."

"You, Colin and me," corrected Uncle Danny.

"What did he say?" asked Wu.

Unable to answer, she just looked at Uncle Danny in surprise.

"But can he tell little Tessy that her Uncle Danny is still kicking...and trying to help people until...?" asked Uncle Danny, a little shyly. "But..." And he looked at the bite on his forearm.

Liberty continued and told the Sergeant. "Tell her that even though it's not safe for her Uncle Danny to stay with her, he still misses her and loves her very much."

"I can, but...," started Wu. "He was bitten, wasn't he?"

"Yeah," said Liberty softly. "But...so far, so good."

"Okay then," replied Wu. He repeated the combined message from both of them, and—of course—agreed to give it to Danny's niece personally.

"Still, I should be coming with you," grumbled Wu good-naturedly.

"Just be ready for us," said Liberty. "We're dropping off some more people and Danny has them loaded down with canned goods."

"Ooooh! Awesome!" cried Wu with genuine joy.

***

41

The pickup truck jolted when it hit a crowd of zoms. The people in the pickup bed were laying down, but they still got bounced about a bit. One of the tires got punctured by a zom's broken rib, but Uncle Danny kept on trucking.

Coming to a stop right behind the other pickup—which Uncle Danny had used the day before—he killed the engine. Opening the side door, the Big Mexican began to climb out of the cab to reach the bed.

Snatching out, a zom tried to grab his coat.

Instantly, a sniper's bullet went through its head, and it collapsed. Swiftly, Danny crawled into the bed as two more zoms, who had been trying to paw at him, went down.

"Look!" cried Giselle excitedly.

A stocky Asian man repelled down the side of the Old Armory on a rope and saw the Big Mexican.

"You're still here," grinned Sergeant Wu.

"I had friends," said Uncle Danny, and he pointed to a nearby building.

Wu turned, and saw Liberty with her sniper rifle. Beside her, Colin was helping spot.

The sergeant gave a perfect salute and a warm smile.

Turning to Uncle Danny, Wu said, a little uncertainly. "I almost had your niece come up to the roof. But then, I thought if you're leaving right away..."

"Oh!" replied Uncle Danny, and he nodded slowly. "I guess that would be..." But his voice trailed off.

"I felt it was almost a mean prank," continued Wu rapidly. His face scrunched up. "As is when I told her your message, she...well, cried a bit. A bunch. So, after that, I thought...Sorry."

After a moment, Uncle Danny straightened his shoulders and took a deep breath.

"I think you're right," said the Big Mexican, and the policeman's chest loosened. "But, please take care of her."

Wu met his gaze, which is not an easy feat.

"I promise," swore the sergeant.

A big smile grew on Uncle Danny's face. "*¡Muchas gracias!*"

"*De nada wey.* Just doing my job," said Wu, and he immediately looked away. He always felt uncomfortable when he was complemented. Instead, he turned quickly to the rest of the refugees. "Hello. My name is Sergeant Wu of the LAPD. Let's get you inside safely."

***

The moment that Uncle Danny managed to slip through the horde of zoms, he took off running. Any real pursuit was dissuaded by a bullet to the head, courtesy of the Librarian.

Soon, they were walking together on the street, dodging around knots of zoms.

"Well, that was bracing," chuckled Uncle Danny. He still looked like he had the flu, but nevertheless, he was in good spirits. "She's okay."

"Who's...," started Liberty but then said. "Oh! Your niece!" She made a sad noise. "They're really good people. They'll take really great care of her."

Uncle Danny nodded. *"Mi Abuela* would say, 'We can't choose what happens, just how we react to it'."

"Like helping us," nodded Liberty. She didn't want to say this next part, but she felt that she had to. "You know, you don't have to go with us?"

Uncle Danny looked at her quickly.

"You don't want me to go?" he asked, almost worried, and Colin looked up at her too. "Are you worried I'm going to turn?"

"No, no! Not that. Actually, I'm *really* happy for the help," said Liberty quickly. "It's just, I don't want you to feel...I don't know. Obligated, or something."

Uncle Danny gave a little chuckle and said genuinely. *"¡Orale!* I understand, and I appreciate that. *Gracias,* but I probably don't have much time, so I'd best use it well." He paused for a moment. "But, if I get too sick. I may need you to..."

The Librarian cut in. "Let's cross that bridge when we come to it."

"No, no," said Uncle Danny in a flat voice. "I don't...I don't want to be a danger to anyone. The idea of me biting someone and killing them...well, I don't want to hurt someone, even after I'm gone."

"I can see that," said Liberty sadly and thought, only out here was a conversation like this almost normal.

"But I can't do it myself," said Uncle Danny.

"Why not?" asked Colin. "My uncle did it. He..." The boy looked forward; his eyes widened.

Liberty put out a hand and gripped the boy's left

shoulder comfortingly. Then she noticed Uncle Danny had done the same on the other side. They saw this and both chuckled.

"No," said Uncle Danny, a little loudly to pull the boy's attention from the horrors behind his eyes. When Colin looked up, he continued. "I was raised Catholic, and even though I'm not a great one, they don't take kindly to offing yourself. I mean, it's a Mortal Sin."

"Wouldn't God understand that you were doing it to protect others?" asked Colin.

Uncle Danny smiled down to the boy. "Probably, but I don't want to chance it. Besides, I'm not worried about him."

Liberty and Colin both looked at him in confusion.

"*Mi Abuela* is…," started Uncle Danny.

"Your what?" asked Liberty.

"His grandmother," supplied Colin.

"Yes," nodded Uncle Danny. "My grandmother is up there too. And she…well, She *Really* Might Not Understand Me Breaking God's Laws."

"Oh!" said Liberty. "That's understandable. Okay, I'll help, however I can." But then she paused for a moment. "But, if I can confine you and leave you in a place you won't hurt anyone, I might just do that."

Uncle Danny gave a big smile.

"Actually, if I start getting really sick, I want to be locked in a nice car, seatbelt on," he said. "You know, like a nice Lexus, or a Jaguar."

"Corvette?" asked Colin. "My Dad always talked about

45

the one he had. He really loved it."

Uncle Danny made a face. "I guess...if we have to." Suddenly, he turned to them seriously. "But no Kia cars."

Liberty looked at him with amusement.

"Why not?" she asked.

Uncle Danny an aggrieved noise. "When I was helping my brother in his garage, we'd always listen to the radio. And there was this really, really, *really* annoying KIA ad. *¡Porque no!* And it played alllllllllllllllllllllllllll the time!"

"Got it," said Liberty with mock seriousness. "Snazzy vehicle, hold the Kia." She looked at him. "I'd go for an SUV myself. More room to flail about."

Uncle Danny looked pleasantly thoughtful. "Maybe." But then, his face turned serious. "I just don't want to put you two in danger."

"I'll get Colin clear," promised Liberty.

Uncle nodded solemnly at that.

"And don't forget to leave me a few magazines to read," smiled Uncle Danny.

"Deal," replied Liberty. "But...that's not till later."

"Actually," said Uncle Danny. He slowed and took a moment to get his breath.

"You gonna be okay?" asked Colin with a sharp concern.

Uncle Danny straightened and squared his big shoulders. "I'm okay. Getting to be an old man too."

"If you need to rest," added Liberty helpfully.

"Let's just get to A.U.," insisted Uncle Danny. "Hard to sleep out here, but...Oh! Your buddy did give me this."

Danny offered Liberty a backpack. She had noticed it but planned to ask later. The pack was stocked full with energy bars and other portable foods.

"Sweet," said Colin.

"Oh! He shouldn't have," said Liberty, feeling almost guilty. But then, she did have someone to feed now. She pushed the bag towards Colin.

"What?" asked the boy as he took it reluctantly.

"We're on guard duty," said Liberty. "So, you get food duty."

"What? Really?" whined Colin.

"Really," said Liberty with finality, and then she turned to Uncle Danny.

"Okay, enough melancholy," declared the Librarian loudly.

"Melon—what?" asked Colin.

"Melancholy is like sadness," explained Liberty. "Now, let's vote. Do we want to find this science building, or look for a better place?"

"Me too?" asked Uncle Danny with a happy surprise.

"Yes!" said Liberty with mock seriousness. "You're not getting out of this *that* easily mister!"

"Ooooooh," taunted Colin jovially. "She called you 'mister'. You're in trouble!"

Uncle Danny grinned. "I'm for the science building. I mean, we don't have anything else to do today."

"It's a start," nodded Colin.

"Okay," said Liberty and they started to move towards

47

City of Angels U.

Uncle Danny glanced down at Colin.

"Come on, lil guinea pig," he said.

"Hey!" cried the boy indignantly, but there was a hint of a smile there too.

Danny straightened. "You're right, I shouldn't use that word." He paused a second. "*Cobayo*, that's a better word."

Just as Colin was about to ask, his eyes widened with concern. He whipped around to look at the Librarian. "Are...are they going to poke me a lot?"

"They are probably going to have to draw some blood to examine it," nodded Liberty.

"We'll make sure they don't take too much," said Uncle Danny with a gruff assurance. "Make sure they leave one or two pints left."

After a moment, the boy asked. "Do you really think they can help us?"

"Maybe," said Liberty. "A science building would be a good start for a vaccine."

## Chapter Three

"**THAT'S A LOT** of zoms," commented Uncle Danny dryly.

The Big Mexican—who was feeling his age— crouched on the roof, to take a breather. He knew that if he sat on his butt, he'd have trouble getting back up again.

They were all so weary now.

"So... we're boned?" asked Colin tentatively.

Liberty glanced side-eyed at the boy. She debated if she should comment on the use of the word 'boned'. But then again, she wasn't certain if it even was a swear word. Or, if it was, was it even a bad one?

So, the Librarian looked back towards the university lawn, which was covered in zoms. In fact, the poor creatures were almost shoulder to shoulder, and there— sticking up out of the middle—was the Dyson science building at the City of Angels University.

Uncle Danny had commented when they had first seen it. "It looks like a giant wedding cake, but upside-down."

Currently, they were on top of a nearby building, trying to find a way in. Liberty definitely didn't have that many bullets. Maybe if she had that lightsaber. A green one, she thought, and suddenly recognized her own fatigue. She pulled her attention back to the problem at hand.

Liberty said, almost to herself. "When we talked to them, they said that the building was apparently designed with a situation like this in mind. Which means, they might have a way in, you know, off the ground."

"What about that?" asked Colin. The boy walked across the roof they were on. He leaned over the edge towards another roof, which was only a small gap away.

They quickly saw a covered walkway, which was attached to the next building. It stretched all the way to the science building.

Uncle Danny chuckled. "A bridge to safety?" He turned to Colin, proudly. "Good eye *Cobayo!*"

The boy straightened with happiness at the compliment.

The next building was pretty close, so Liberty and Uncle Danny could easily step over the gap. However, the tall people decided that poor Colin had to be carried, which he was quite resentful about.

"What...I'm not a baby," grumbled Colin.

"I know," replied Liberty without an ounce of remorse. "But I can't have you hurt."

"It's just a short gap," said Colin. "I could've easily

jumped it."

"I know," agreed Liberty.

While the Librarian and the Boy debated the boundaries of 'overprotectiveness vs prudence' concerning children, Uncle Danny looked over the edge of the roof and down onto the covered walkway. The drop was less than six feet.

Liberty suddenly noticed him climbing—a little awkwardly—onto the edge of the roof.

"Do you want me to go first?" she asked quickly.

"Naw," replied Uncle Danny, and a smile played across his etched face. "If we're wrong—and this thing collapses —what're they going to do? Bite me?"

Liberty ran over to spot him anyhow. A little ungracefully, Uncle Danny dropped onto the covered walkway below.

While the Big Mexican waited to see if it would collapse, he lamented getting old. He fancied that, back in the day, he could've easily jumped down, even done a somersault in mid-air. But he pulled himself up short on that last one. Still, there was a time he could've jumped down easily.

But the covered walkway was rock solid. Just in case though, he bounced up and down on it, to Liberty's chagrin.

Finally, he looked up at her.

"Solid. Now, if you'll give me the guinea pig...," began Uncle Danny.

"Hey!" came an indigent voice from above.

"Sorry, I mean Cobayo," said Uncle Danny rapidly with mock contrition.

"You think you're so funny," grumbled Colin. "You know, one day, I'm gonna look that word up."

"Going to," said Liberty. "Not 'gonna'."

"Everyone's picking on me," whined Colin.

Once they were all on the walkway, Uncle Danny took point with Liberty at the rear. The flat awning not only had a solid top, but it also had metal pillars at regular intervals for support. Still, Uncle Danny tested each new section to make sure that it was indeed secure.

Almost halfway across, Colin wandered away from the middle to look over the edge. Below them, a mob of zoms reached up, but the awning was too high for them.

A hand snagged the back of his shirt and pulled the boy backwards.

"Hey," protested Colin mildly.

"Stay in the middle," ordered Liberty.

"It's not like I'm going to catch the virus," huffed Colin.

"Would still hurt if they bit you," suggested Uncle Danny.

Colin was about to make a snarky comment, but then he paused to look at the zoms. One of them chomped crusty, greenish teeth at him. Wisely, he did not press the issue.

Following the curve of the walkway, they reached a door, which was slightly ajar.

"¡Aquas!" whispered Uncle Danny. While Liberty did not know what that meant, she understood his signal to wait. She pulled back with Colin and Uncle Danny opened the door carefully. But when nothing jumped out, he swung it open.

Stepping out of the sun, the three found themselves on a short landing. Before them was a set of stone steps that reached up and down. While Uncle Danny looked up, Liberty looked down, but the staircase was empty.

"*¡Fíjate!* There's this really serious-looking door up here," reported Uncle Danny. "Closed."

"I got another one down here," replied Liberty. "Also closed."

"There's someone," called out Colin from between them.

Past the stairs was another small landing, and then a glass wall.

Suddenly, a man with a gigantic grin appeared at the other side of the glass.

"Welcome to *Casa de* Dyson Experimental Science Facility," declared the man joyfully with a French accent.

"Wha…?" began Uncle Danny.

"Oh, you poor kids," chirped the thin man, who was dressed all in black. "I am Renoir, like the artist, but much, much better!" He paused for a second. "Okay! At least with hair. And I am…" This time he gave a dramatic pause. "The Welcome Wagon."

Liberty tried to say something, but she could not think of anything.

"It's okay," said the razor-thin man. "You are tired, and hungry. We have food and clean water. Even showers."

"What? Really?" asked Liberty with wonder.

"Yes, apparently this building was testing a… well, something…," said Renoir with an exaggerated shrug. "*Je pense que j'ai compris l'idée, mais pas tout les mots.* You'll have to ask Dr. McTaggert when he arrives."

"Are you...a scientist?" asked Liberty.

"Only of hair," said Renoir. "No, I was most fortunate to have found refuge here."

"Wait? You're not Renoir of Renoir's Masterpieces of Hair, are you?" asked Liberty with surprise.

"Ah! You have heard of me," grinned Renoir, but then his brow knitted. "But wait! Am I such a fiend, that I have forgotten a patron of my humble *petite* shop?"

"Oh...um...no," replied Liberty quickly with a bashful smile. "It was always...a little out of my price range."

"Well, you're in luck!" said Renoir. "I have a chair open." He leaned towards the glass conspiratorially. "Actually, everyone's hair is now perfect, I've already planned a Luah—complete with paper leis— for Friday, and now, here I stand. Just earning my daily bread, as they say."

Colin looked the man up and down, taking in Renoir's skinny jeans to his extremely tight t-shirt.

"You're a hairdresser?" asked Colin.

"*Oui*, that means 'yes'," said Renoir.

"I know," said the boy thoughtfully. "My Dad said that all male hairdressers were gay."

Liberty stiffened, but before she could say anything, Uncle Danny jumped in.

"*¡Neta!* Hey *Cobayo*, not cool," he said urgently.

Colin squinted up at him. "But...why?"

However, Renoir laughed with a bright joy. "It's okay!!

54

Really! Actually, my Papa—back in France—he asked the same thing, and you know what I told him?"

Colin looked at the man, curiously. "What?"

"I said to my Papa that, 'You—Papa—are a magnificent barber, one of the best ever! And—all day long—you see only old men in your chair'," said Renoir. "'But I! I will cut hair all day long too, but in my chair, there will be beautiful women'. *And* he could not argue with that one. I must say though, poor Dr. Hauser was disappointed, but Dr. Milton —on other hand—she is thrilled!"

"Um, can we talk to the scientists, or the head scientist?" asked Liberty, because she was not sure where that conversation was going.

"Take me to your leader!" said Renoir happily. "Of course, I babble. Dr. Milton always chides me for the babbling. "Actually, Dr. McTaggert should be here any…"

The metal door above made a sound like a pressure vessel unsealing. It swung ponderously open and revealed a figure.

Uncle Danny muttered in shock. "Well, there's something you don't see every day."

"Coooooool!" said Colin in awe. The boy started forward, but Uncle Danny snagged the back of his shirt, and held him firmly in place.

"Hey!" grumbled the boy in protest, but he stayed put.

"Is that…?" began Liberty.

At the top of the stairs was a man in a complete suit of medieval armor. His helm even had a full visor. The suit began to carefully maneuver down the stairs. One

55

handheld the metal handrail with a death grip.

On the other side of the glass, Renoir laughed until tears fell down his cheeks.

Shortly, the suit of armor reached them, stepping carefully onto the landing. He turned towards Renoir.

A cavernous voice from the armor grumbled. "You didn't tell them, did you?"

"How could I, Monsieur Doctor?" asked Renoir. "I have so little left to entertain me."

The suit of armor sighed, without any heat. "It's okay. And I'm not a doctor."

Renoir sniffed. "Welllllll...not officially. But it is such a trifle."

The suit of armor turned and lifted up their visor. Inside was a rather handsome man in his mid-twenties.

Liberty suddenly wished that she had been in Renoir's chair before meeting him. Or, at least had a shower. Distracted, she desperately wondered when the last time was she had had a proper shower; not just stood in the rain with an ancient bar of soap.

"Sorry about that," said the man. "My name is Miles McTaggert. But you can call me Tagg."

"Who should be a doctor," insisted Renoir.

With warm amusement, Tagg rolled his eyes.

"I was waiting to do my PhD defense, when all this happened," he explained.

"Which Fred said you had would easily complete," murmured Renoir.

"Well...," said Tagg, looking at the ground.

Now that Liberty had had time to find her breath, she could rescue Tagg.

"And the suit of armor?" she asked.

"Oh! Someone walked in wearing this," explained Tagg. "The only person to make it through the doors at ground level...well, at least after all those poor infected people arrived."

"Wish I had a suit of armor," chuckled Uncle Danny.

"I don't know," said Tagg uncertainly. "Ted—who arrived in this armor—can't look at it now without having a full-blown panic attack. I really wish we'd managed to save at least some of the Psychiatry department...you know, before all this went down. Maybe they could've helped him."

"I hear you," said Liberty. "We just had a tattoo artist."

Tagg made eye contact for only a second, but then bashfully looked away. "I can see that." He did nod his chin at her full sleeve tattoos. "Um, are the designs Japanese?"

Liberty lifted her left forearm, so that he could see the name 'Mr. Jamie' almost hidden within the ink.

"We wanted both form and function. Mostly, I didn't want anyone important to be forgotten," said Liberty solemnly. However, she did not want to fall down that rabbit hole, so she quickly asked. "Anyway, how'd you end up a walking tin can?"

Colin snickered. "Tin can!"

Tagg gave a big shrug. "Um. It seems that I'm one of

the few people who could fit into this. Well, and still move around."

"You need Iron Man armor," said Colin seriously.

"Right!" chuckled Tagg as he smiled down at the boy. "We've spent more than one night discussing that very thing!"

"And you have electricity in here?" asked Liberty.

"There are solar panels on the roof, which gives us a modicum of power," said Tagg, but then his voice grew heavy. "But really, I do need to assess who's been bitten."

Wearily, Uncle Danny asked. "And if they have?"

"They go to the first floor," said Tagg. "We've outfitted a room there with all the essentials, so they'll be comfortable until...well, they'll have food, water and a clean bed, or at least pretty clean."

"Do you kill them after they change?" asked Liberty with concern.

"Oh no!" replied Tagg quickly. "That'd be too dangerous anyhow. We used to have to push them outside in this suit—which wasn't fun—but now we just set off the fire alarm."

Uncle Danny blinked. "What?"

"We have a video monitor down there and found, during an accidental fire alarm..."

"My fault," interjected Renoir meekly.

Tagg looked at HairArtiste kindly and insisted. "It's okay! No one was hurt." Then he turned back to his audience. "And, actually it was fortuitous, because we saw that all the people, who had succumbed to the infection, crowded by the door leading out," said Tagg. "And, since we can open that door remotely......well, we opened the door."

"And none came in?" asked Uncle Danny with interest.

"They appear to hear the alarm as well and back off," shrugged Tagg. "Fred thinks that it's because it's so ingrained to flee a fire alarm; that they get scared off." He suddenly looked crestfallen. "But really, I do need to establish who's been bitten."

"Well, that's a bit complicated," said Liberty.

Tagg shook his head sadly. "Once the virus is in the bloodstream, it's only a matter of time."

"Well actually, this boy might be the key to it," said Liberty. "You see..."

And Liberty told Tagg the whole story, starting with first seeing the UFO, to rescuing Colin, to where she stood right now.

Tagg interrupted only once because the whole building had been buzzing about the UFO.

"So, you think the boy might be the key to a vaccine?" whispered Tagg thoughtfully as he looked professionally at the bite on Colin's arm, which had mostly healed. "Okay, let's go downstairs."

"But don't we need to go upstairs, where the scientists are," said Uncle Danny.

Tagg shook his head. "We can't break quarantine now. But I'm going to help." He turned towards Renoir. "Could you ask Fred to video link with me?"

"Of course, *mon ami*," said Renoir, and he sprinted off.

The suit of armor turned to Liberty.

"Please, let me go down first," said Tagg, a little sheepishly. "I haven't fallen in this thing yet. But.... there's always a first time."

Amused, Liberty gave a little bow and—with a flourish—waved one hand towards the stairs. "Then by all means, after you."

Tagg grinned at her in response, and her belly shook with nervous delight.

Carefully, the Scientist clanked down the stairs, and moved towards the bottom door. Just as he reached it, the door opened.

Without turning back, Tagg explained with warm mirth. "Ted is watching us on camera, so that only looked like magic."

Nodding approvingly, Uncle Danny glanced down at Colin. "It was still cool."

Ushering everyone into a large, rectangular room, Tagg closed the door behind them. Opposite them, at the other end of the room, was another door. And, between those two doors, were five beds and two card tables.

One of the tables held canned food and a large glass cylinder of water. On the opposite table was a lone laptop.

Tagg, playing the genial host, said. "Oh, the water's free of contaminants."

"You got a really good Brita?" chuckled Uncle Danny.

The Scientist smiled broadly and explained without explaining. "Actually, this building was testing a water filtration system for JPL."

"J. P. what?" asked Colin.

And Liberty was happy that he had asked because she did not know who that was.

"JPL is NASA's Jet Propulsion Laboratory," explained Tagg to the boy. "You're familiar with NASA...?"

Colin shrugged. "Sure, spaceships,"

Tagg smiled. "Exactly! And they were hoping—if the water filtration system worked out—that a ship to Mars would have sustainable water." He sighed. "I just wish I could tell them what a success it's been." He looked at them. "Anyhow, has everyone here been bitten?"

Uncle Danny immediately nodded at Liberty and said. "Not her."

"But I'm still staying right here," said Liberty with cold iron in her voice.

Tagg looked at her in surprise, but then he looked nervously away towards Uncle Danny.

"Ah...and you've been bitten? How long ago?" asked Tagg.

Uncle Danny shrugged. "Couple of days now."

Dr. McTaggert blinked. "Really? But...it's interesting that you haven't changed."

"I feel like shit," suggested Uncle Danny with a helpful smile.

Liberty cleared her throat. The Big Mexican glanced at her, and she looked pointedly down at Colin.

"*Mierda*?" asked Uncle Danny, mischievously.

"That's just *that word* in Spanish, right?" asked Liberty

icily.

"Oh, come on," whined the boy. "It's not like I don't know all the words."

"Still," sniffed Liberty. She turned with a sigh to look at Uncle Danny, but then stopped. After a second, she leaned closer to look at him.

"¿*Mande?*" asked Uncle Danny,

"Now that he mentions it, you don't look any sicker," said Liberty with quiet surprise.

"As long as I 'm still pretty," sniffed Uncle Danny with an airy voice.

"He should be wanting brains by now," nodded the Colin sagely. And then the boy added. "Braaaaaaaaaaaains."

Liberty squinted at him.

"Colin," she said repressively. "That's not very nice."

"But it's true," grumbled Colin with a whiny reply.

"Nevertheless," said Liberty. "When someone's sick, a little kindness goes a long way."

"Okay," huffed Colin.

Liberty put her arm around his shoulders and pulled him into a side hug.

"Did I say I wanted a hug?" asked Colin icily, but he did not move away.

Uncle Danny looked at Tagg.

"So, how's this going to work?" asked the Big Mexican.

"How's what?" asked the Scientist.

"How're you going to make a vaccine?" asked Uncle Danny. "Do you need to take samples?"

Tagg said. "Um, before anything else, we need to tell Fred. He's the unofficial leader around here."

The Scientist sat before the laptop, opposite the food. Stripping off his gauntlets, Tagg opened a window, which shortly soon showed an older man.

"Hello Tagg," gumbled Fred. "Renoir pulled me out of a nap."

"I figured," winced Tagg. "But these people saw the UFO up close."

Abruptly awake, Fred leaned closer to the camera. "What?"

Once they had told their story, Fred leaned back.

"You're shitting me," said the older man.

"Please don't swear in front of the boy," said Liberty repressively.

"Sorry," replied Fred, sincerely. "It's just...I don't know."

"I saw that ship close up," said Uncle Danny. "It wasn't any Hollywood trick."

"And it has a heat beam?" asked Fred.

"Hot enough to turn asphalt into liquid like this," said Liberty, and she snapped her fingers.

"My Lord," said Fred. "I wonder at what temperature that happens."

"Actually, it's not that much," said Uncle Danny. "About 120. My friend Pepe tried to start a paving business at one point."

"Wait? 120 degrees Fahrenheit?" asked Tagg in surprise.

"Huh?" started Uncle Danny. "Oh, no it's 250 Fahrenheit."

"Really?" asked Tagg. "I mean, not that I don't believe you, but that explains why asphalt gets sticky on a hot day."

"And while 250 doesn't sound like much, I wouldn't want to get hit by that," continued Fred.

"I don't think they saw us come in here," said Liberty.

"We've been careful," added Uncle Danny.

"Still," said Tagg thoughtfully. "We might not want to stay long anyhow."

Liberty's heart leapt with excitement.

Forcing her voice to be calm, she asked. "Us?"

Fred forward leaned towards his camera. "What're you thinking Tagg?"

"Is the Fleet still off the coast?" asked Tagg.

"Last I heard," nodded Fred.

Liberty chimed in. "The Fleet?"

"Yeah," explained Tagg. "A group of ships, naval and civilian, that were out to sea when the outbreak hit. And more sailed out to escape the mainland."

"Oh No! I mean, we've heard of the Fleet, but...," started Liberty.

"Oh! Sorry," said Tagg quickly. "I thought you hadn't heard about it."

"¡Neta! We had, but in the vein as you hear Bigfoot or *La Llorona*. You know, all bullsh...um, just bull," said Uncle

Danny, recovering quickly.

"Oh, it's real," said Tagg. "There's even an aircraft carrier...it's the ...well, it's named after one of the Roosevelts. Don't remember which one."

The Unofficial Leader, Fred, cut in. "At the very least. We need to tell them that the virus is a bioweapon."

"Um, we might want to keep the whole 'made by alien's thing quiet," suggested Tagg.

"Yeah," said Fred with a little chuckle. "We don't want them to hang up on us."

Liberty shook her head. "No. We need to tell them. If all else fails, just tell them that some crazy woman came in claiming that she saw 'aliens and flying saucers in what looked like geometric shapes'."

"And that they made the virus?" finished Tagg worriedly.

"Exactly," said Liberty with assurance.

"But are you sure you're okay with that?" asked Tagg, worriedly.

Liberty grew thoughtful, and Uncle Danny spoke up.

"Actually," he said. "If people think it's just the mad ravings of some *loca Niña* ..." He looked at the Librarian. "No offense."

Liberty just waved his concern away.

Emboldened, Uncle Danny continued. "If they think it's crazy talk, it might spread to more of the Fleet."

"True." She looked at Tagg. "But, what's really so important about this Fleet?" asked Liberty.

"Um. The last time we checked, they had a fully stocked medical ship, the Jonas Salk," explained Tagg. "If the boy has the ability to create a vaccine to this virus, then that's probably the best place to start working on it."

"First, we should see if that med ship is still there," said Fred.

"I'm coming up," announced Tagg.

"But...we just got here," said Colin in a soft voice.

The Scientist turned to address the boy.

"I'm sorry," said Tagg sincerely. "If I thought I could even make a vaccine here, then I would, but...I just don't have the equipment."

"*You're* going to make the vaccine?" asked Liberty in surprise.

"Well, not me alone, if I can find some help," admitted Tagg.

From his screen, Fred proudly said. "Tagg here is not only a medical doctor, but a virologist."

"Vir...what?" asked Colin.

Looking at the boy, he kindly explained. "I study diseases, viruses like rabies. Which is also why I meet everyone coming in, because it's my area of expertise as both a doctor and a specialist."

"That's why he was one of the first people to hole up here," said Fred. "He practically dragged me in here." The unofficial leader gave a sad, little chuckle.

Uncle Danny looked at Tagg and said thoughtfully. "I don't know how fast you'll go in that suit of armor,"

"Oh this? I'm going to have to leave this here," said Tagg and he patted his chest with a metallic noise. "Raj's been losing weight—what with food rationing—so he'll have to take over."

"He's not going to be happy about that," said Fred.

Tagg smirked at the screen.

"Glad I'm not the boss," he said.

Fred sighed. "Dammit."

"Tell him...," began Tagg thoughtfully, but then excitedly he added. "Yes! Tell'em that—as an eminent medical doctor—he's the most qualified."

Fred's mouth opened in surprise. "Actually, that might just work."

"Before we leave though, Colin's going to need a good night's rest, and food!" insisted Liberty.

"Yes Food!" seconded Colin.

"Of course. We should be safe enough for tonight," smiled Tagg, and he dared to meet Liberty's eyes for almost three seconds. His heart was racing for so many different reasons. "Besides, we might not get through to the Fleet right away."

***

"Soooo," said Colin slowly. He looked down at his can of Hormel Chili. "It's mean to think someone is gay because of their job."

"Well, best not to assume," nodded Uncle Danny as he

patted the boy on the shoulder.

The door upstairs suddenly unlocked remotely. Down the stairs came Tagg, clanking in his armor.

"Um, hey," he said, a little apologetically. "Sorry. I forgot something."

Liberty saw the concerned look on Tagg's face and stood up immediately, while the guys followed.

"What's wrong?" she asked urgently.

"Oh! Nothing bad," he said quickly, raising his hands in supplication. "It's just...I am going to need a blood sample." He stopped and looked directly at the boy.

"Aw man," moaned Colin, who still held his can of chili protectively.

"Sorry, but before I go calling everyone, I do need to examine your blood," explained Tagg sheepishly.

"That makes sense," nodded Uncle Danny.

Colin looked at him. "Are you sure it does?"

"*Si*. We came in talking a lot of crazy, *Cobayo*," said Uncle Danny. "We can't blame him for wanting to make sure that we can back up our claim."

Liberty looked at Tagg. "Are you going to take the sample?"

"Oh no, no, no," smiled Tagg quickly. "Wouldn't have any idea how to do that. I brought Dakarai, he's a nurse."

An African man looked cautiously through the door.

"You sure about this Tagg?" he whispered.

"It's okay man," said Tagg. "They're not going to attack."

Dakarai looked at Uncle Danny especially, whose etched face would be scary, even on Christmas morning. "What about him?"

The Big Mexican saw that the man was looking nervously at something, so Danny looked down. His hand was at the handle to the cleaver on his belt. Slowly, he took his hand away.

"I can stand back," said Uncle Danny diplomatically. "As long as one of us stays with the boy." And he looked at Liberty. "Can you...?"

"Absolutely," she nodded.

Looking down at Colin, she guided him towards the stairs as Uncle Danny took a few steps back and tried—vainly—to look non-threatening.

"Is this going to hurt?" asked Colin who still held his chili.

Dakarai put on a disarming smile. "It's going to be okay. I've done this a million times."

"Okay," agreed Colin wearily. "As long as I don't have to look."

"I never look when they give me a shot," called out Uncle Danny, and he gave a theatrical shudder, which made the boy smile.

While she stood protectively near Colin, she found herself distracted. She snuck a glance at Tagg and caught him looking at her. Liberty was able to suppress a smile, but not the faint blush.

Dakarai, for his part, was very efficient, and soon it was done.

"That didn't hurt much," said Colin in surprise.

"Sorry I don't have a cookie, or something," apologized Dakarai to the boy.

"He should eat some more real food anyhow," sniffed Liberty.

Tagg took the proffered vial of blood from Dakarai.

"Thank you," he said to Colin. "You were tough as nails dude."

The boy straightened happily at the compliment.

## Chapter Four

**THE FIRE ALARM** went off, jolting Liberty awake.

She raised her rifle and swept the room. It took a moment for her to remember where they were, in that science building.

Liberty jumped out of her uncomfortable plastic chair. Her back howled in protest, but it wasn't barking loud enough to slow her down.

Colin sat bolt upright in his bed. "What's that?"

"Fire alarm, I think," said Liberty. "Come on, get on your shoes."

Slinging her rifle behind, Liberty took out her Glock 22, because it was better in cramped conditions. However, she kept it by her leg. Her eyes swept the room again, but it was definitely clear of trouble.

"Is it a fire?" asked Colin nervously.

"Shoes first," said Liberty, without looking at the boy.

As Colin put on his shoes, she went over to Uncle Danny. The big Mexican was already standing.

"*¡Hijole!* I had only gotten to sleep," yawned Uncle Danny.

"I remember sleep...and showers too," said Liberty a little wistfully, and she patted his shoulder sympathetically. "Mind you, that was a long time ago."

The door to the stairs unlocked and swung open.

"Oh, my poor babies," cried a French accent. Moving as fast as he could, Renoir appeared on the stairs, burdened by a giant backpack. "Sorry! The fire alarm accidently went off. Please! Follow me!"

Turning a little awkwardly, Renoir began to climb back up the stairs.

Uncle Danny and Colin looked at Liberty in confusion.

The Librarian shrugged. "I guess we follow, for now."

"Hurry," panted Renoir from above. The HairArtiste climbed up to where they had first met him and Dr. Tagg. Stepping onto the landing there, he leaned against the wall, taking some deep breaths. "Really I need to take up jogging."

"What's going on?" asked Liberty when she and the guys reached HairArtiste.

Before Renoir could answer, the door up above opened.

Tagg trotted swiftly down the stairs. He had traded it in his armor for a turtleneck and jeans. Curiously, he was carrying a box with four tubes sticking out one end.

"Sorry! Sorry! I somehow triggered the fire alarm," cried Tagg as he reached them. He turned to Renoir. "Here, let me take that."

Tagg easily took the giant backpack but had to juggle it and the box with tubes for a moment.

"Sorry it's a little heavy," said Tagg to the HairArtiste.

Renoir smiled gamely. "Just a few compressed vertebrae. Dr. Milton, she will sort it out later. But are you sure you'll be able to carry all that?"

"Going to need to," said Tagg with a shrug of his big shoulders. He looked at Renoir in concern. "Sorry I'm going to miss your Luah."

"Just stay safe *mon ami*," said Renoir earnestly.

Liberty—who had been momentarily stunned by Tagg's barrel chest—found her voice.

Using her You-Cheesed-Off-The-Librarian voice, she asked. "What. Is. Going. On?"

Tagg actually gave a little jump.

"Oh, sorry," he said with surprise and chagrin. "Um, that UFO is back. We gotta go."

"Wait, what?" asked Liberty.

But Tagg was already at the outer door. He started to open it, but immediately slammed it shut.

Under the door—in that tiny space—a blue light played across the gap. Then it was gone.

Tagg glanced out the door.

"Okay, let's go," he said and went out onto the walkway

roof.

"Do we have to?" asked Colin with a small, sad voice.

Renoir knelt before the boy. "Have courage *mon ami*." He handed the boy a small plastic bag that read 'Higgly-Piggly Grocer'. "Open this later." He shot to his feet. "Now! May we meet again, in happier times!"

Uncle Danny and Colin looked at Liberty, but she holstered her handgun and unslung her rifle.

"If we stay here, we're endangering everyone," said Liberty, and she went through the door.

Uncle Danny sighed. "Come on *Cobayo*. We got you."

Once outside, they found Tagg putting down the box-with-tubes on top of the walkway. He moved it as if he were aiming it.

"Keep going," said Tagg quickly when they reached him. "I'm just making sure...damn!"

The UFO, shaped like an octahedron, swung around the side of the Dyson building and headed towards them.

Liberty took Colin's arm and started to run across the walkway. Uncle Danny followed close behind.

Desperately, the Librarian wanted to look back. Her chest clenched, worried for Tagg. But another part of her, chided her for being so silly. They had only just met.

Nevertheless, she really, really, really wanted to look back.

Reaching the building that they had started from, Liberty let go of Colin and hopped up on to the brick. Like a spider-monkey, she swung her legs up and over the top. Turning, she reached down.

Uncle Danny arrived right behind Colin and scooped up the boy.

"HEY!" cried the boy with fiery indignation.

Liberty took him and deposited Colin atop the roof. Then she reached down for Uncle Danny, who was already climbing up.

"I need to start doing pull-ups," grumbled Danny. Struggling to lift himself, he immediately locked eyes with her. "You gotta promise to make me do more pull-ups."

"Um," started Liberty.

"No!" insisted Danny as he tried to pull himself up. "You gotta promise."

The Librarian nodded. "I promise."

Satisfied, the Big Mexican worked to haul himself up. Liberty reached down to help, but as she did, she tried to casually glance at Tagg.

The Scientist was still where they had left him. He was trying to do something to the box.

As a lighter sparked fitfully in the darkness, the Octahedron was getting closer.

At the box, a small flame sprang to life, and a fuse caught.

Hopping up, Tagg ran across the walkway. Now that Uncle Danny was up, he and Liberty watched, curious.

The box-with-tubes suddenly erupted as fireworks shot out. Four rockets soared through the air, with piercing whistles, and they hit the UFO. The Octahedron lurched backwards for a moment, almost surprised.

"What was that?" asked Liberty when the Scientist reached them.

"Just a little distraction I cooked up," said Tagg. He tried to climb up, but he was unable to.

"Take off your pack," said Uncle Danny urgently.

"Oh yeah! Well *duh*, why didn't I think of that," grumbled Tagg to himself.

Whipping off his backpack, he handed it up to Uncle Danny, who grunted a little at the weight.

Freed of that, Tagg tried to climb again, and Liberty could not help but notice that underneath the Scientist's turtleneck was solid muscle. Still, it was a little hard for him.

Liberty and Uncle Danny helped him onto the roof. Once Dr. Tagg was on top, he admonished himself again, looking down in embarrassment.

"Sorry. I'll skip pudding tonight," he huffed, out of breath.

"It's oka...," began Liberty kindly.

Out of the bottom of the octahedron, a red light shot down. Zoms burst into flames as the ship sailed above the ground. Liberty watched in horror as the creatures made horrible, screeching noises.

"That's hotter than 250 degrees," whispered Uncle Danny in horror.

And Liberty saw Tagg move subtly between Colin and the terrible sight, before the boy noticed.

The UFO went right over the walkway with the now empty box. The metal awning began to warp and soon collapsed, leaving a wide gap.

"Hurry," hissed Liberty, and she tugged on the guys. She herded them, and the boy, towards the fire escape. "Hurry! Down!"

They hit the fire escape just as the Octahedron turned back. The beam turned blue, hunting them.

At the bottom of the fire escape, Liberty saw that there was a large, wide-open alley.

Unexpectedly, she screeched to a halt on the metal platform

Liberty called out. "Wait!"

Swiftly, she swung the stock of her rifle and punched out the window of an apartment. In a moment, she had knocked out all of the glass into the dark apartment. Uncle Danny—who had been ahead—returned and, flicking on a flashlight, went through first. Satisfied that it was clear, he took the boy, and then the backpack with a grunt.

"What're you carrying in here?" grumbled Uncle Danny about the backpack. "This is heavier than *Cobayo*."

Once Tagg was through, Liberty nearly dove through the window, just as the blue light lit up the alley. Her momentum was too much and, as her beret fell off, she was about to tumble right onto the glass.

Arms enveloped her and kept her above the glass. Tagg lifted her easily, just enough to make sure she could get her footing.

Liberty looked up into his blue eyes.

"Th... thanks," she murmured.

"Oh! Um...," stammered Tagg with a stunned smile.

Too nervous and shy to hold eye contact, he looked down and realized that he was still holding her. He let her go. "Oh! Sorry."

Stepping away from her, Tagg easily picked up his backpack.

Colin appeared at Liberty's side with her beret.

"Thank you," she smiled at the boy. Almost unconsciously, she kept making furtive glances at Tagg.

"Let's go you two," smirked Uncle Danny.

As Liberty walked past the Big Mexican, she gave him a dirty look. "You! Be quiet."

Feigning mock innocence, Uncle Danny asked. "*¿Mande?* What did I say?"

\*\*\*

Later that day, Liberty saw Colin's heavy footfalls and spoke up. "I think we need to rest."

Shortly, they were happily sitting on a fire escape above an alley. Even the unforgiving metal grate under them felt restful.

"Feels good to rest," said Uncle Danny with a weary smile.

"Can we find some food next?" asked Colin with a hopeful whine.

"Yes," said Liberty. "Of course. We do need to find something. Not sure where. I never spent that much time in this part of town."

"If we were in Guadalajara...," started Uncle Danny with a wistful sadness. "Oh, the food. We could get such great food." But then he gave a little shrug. "But I am just a tourist here."

"Wait! You're on vacation? During all this...? That's terrible," cried Tagg with sympathetic horror.

"Well. Yes...and no," said Uncle Danny thoughtfully. "If I wasn't here...I don't think that my niece would have gotten to safety. Actually, considering her Papa's bad back..." And he trailed off.

"Your good deed," smiled Tagg.

"I hope," said Uncle Danny with a melancholy uncertainty..

Liberty reached out and bumped her fist against the Big Mexican's arm. "I'm glad."

Danny straightened up, shaking off the bad feelings, and he turned to the boy. "Anyhow! Did that hairdresser guy give you something?"

"Oh yeah! I forgot," said Colin in surprise, and he fished the grocery bag out of his pocket. He quickly opened it and across his face a grin exploded.

"What is it?" asked Uncle Danny curiously.

Colin did not answer, but instead held up a Hershey's chocolate bar and a pack of Reese's Peanut Butter Cups.

Uncle Danny nodded approvingly. "Well played hairdresser."

"You should save those for dessert," said Tagg seriously.

"Dessert?" asked Colin hopefully. "As in, there's food before this?"

Tagg opened the top of his pack, and then he dropped something in front of the boy.

"As long as you don't have a nut allergy," he said absently. "This is better for you."

Colin looked from the protein bar to the Scientist.

"Well...somewhat," admitted Tagg, who had misread the boy's look.

"Really?" asked the boy, as if he couldn't believe it.

"Dig in," insisted Tagg with a smile, and then he began to hand out bars to everyone.

"Is that what you've been hiding in your pack," smirked Uncle Danny. Famished, he tore open the wrapper.

"Not hiding," said Tagg, a little defensively, who had not caught the joking tone. He busied himself handing out small plastic water bottles as well. "I packed some food and water before I went to sleep, just in case."

Liberty opened up her water and held it up in toast. "Well, here's to 'Just in Case'."

Surprised, Tagg grinned as he hastily lifted up his water bottle as well.

Colin looked in confusion at Uncle Danny, who explained. "She's raising her bottle to say, 'thank you'." And then the Big Mexican added pointedly. "Which, we should do too!"

Danny lifted his water bottle. "Here's to the Army and Navy, and the battles they have won."

"Hear, hear," grinned Liberty.

Danny turned to Tagg and purposefully thanked him for

the food. Then he looked at the boy with pointed expectancy.

"Oh!" said Colin swiftly. Under Uncle Danny's watchful eye, the boy immediately turned to the Scientist. "Yes! Thank you!

"No problem," replied Tagg bashfully as he looked down. "While I was ransacking my makeshift room— which used to be a classroom—I thought of it."

With a *faux* airy tone, Liberty smiled. "I prefer to be light of purse and baggage."

"Well, I also needed my laptop and books on virology," said Tagg with a little smile. He was working hard at not staring at her.

"If, this isn't just a wild goose chase," said Uncle Danny with a bemused shrug.

"It isn't," said Tagg without hesitation. His voice was rocksteady, all traces of nervousness were gone.

Everyone looked up at him in surprise, but he happened to be looking down at his water bottle.

Tagg started. "Last night—before we called the Fleet—I checked...," However, he suddenly stopped and gestured at the boy. "I'm Sorry! I'm really bad with names."

"Colin," supplied the boy, unbothered.

"Thank you. Colin," said Tagg. "I checked Colin's blood against a recent sample of infected blood."

"What happened?" asked Liberty with fascination.

"Nothing," replied Tagg quietly. "Colin's blood would not get infected. In fact, it looked like his blood was trying to interact with the infected blood. But I didn't get a chance to look any further."

"Shit," muttered Uncle Danny, but then he immediately looked at Liberty. "Sorry. That one slipped out."

"It's okay," said Liberty. "And... I totally agree."

"Shit," piped up Colin.

However, Liberty gave him a stern look. "I didn't say that you could use that word."

This produced a general chuckle from the adults, much to Colin's displeasure.

"Sure, laugh at me," grumbled Colin.

"Okay," grinned Uncle Danny.

And the boy made a face at him.

"Come on," said Liberty as she stood. "Looks like we need to move quicker than we thought."

\*\*\*

The Librarian led the way down Santa Monica Pier, towards the ocean.

"I wish we had time to stay," said Colin wistfully as he looked at the Ferris wheel. "I mean, Ferris Wheels are kinda lame...but still..."

"Me too," said Liberty with a gentle smile. "Unfortunately..."

"I know, I know," cut in Colin quickly. He was not mad, just disappointed.

Suddenly, Danny whipped around to look behind them.

82

Just as Liberty noticed, the Big Mexican called out.

"I need to swear again!" called out Uncle Danny. "It's coming this way!"

Behind them, closing on the pier, was the Octahedron. It stalked them slowly, but surely.

"Fast!" cried Liberty. She grabbed Colin's hand and towed him down the pier as the guys followed.

They quickly reached the end and looked below, but there was no boat in sight.

"Um," started Tagg.

"It was the Santa Monica Pier, right?" asked Liberty. She tried to keep her voice from sounding too sharp.

"YeahYeahYeah!" said Tagg, quickly and breathlessly. "I talked to the Fleet, an' tol' them what I'd found. And they said they'd send a boat out right away. So that when we got to the pier, we'd be able to leave." He paused. "Right away!"

"Maybe they're late," suggested Uncle Danny reasonably.

"They repeated it...twice, and even made me say it back," kept on Tagg with a rising panic.

Liberty saw a torrential consternation bubbling up swiftly and reached out. She touched his arm for a moment, and he flinched.

"It's okay," she said softly. He looked at her, and so she repeated herself. "It's okay."

Letting out a ragged breath, he relaxed a little. Liberty turned, scanning the ocean. But it was dusk, and she could not see out that far.

Suddenly, there was a loud noise behind them.

Jumping around, they saw that the UFO was firing down at the beginning of the pier. The red beam immediately drilled right through, and the superheated ray began to set the wooden planks on fire.

Then the Octahedron began to move towards them, as if it was enjoying this.

"We could jump into the water," suggested Uncle Danny.

"Not a good option!" said Liberty quickly.

"Why? Because that beam would boil us like lobsters?" asked Uncle Danny.

"Lobsters?" squeaked Colin.

"Oh no!" said Liberty. "It's mostly because the water around the Santa Monica Pier is really dirty."

"Actually, I heard that too," confirmed Tagg.

"So, we stand our ground?" asked Uncle Danny.

Liberty nodded. "Unfortunately."

The Big Mexican nodded stoically.

"Can I get a gun?" asked Tagg.

The Librarian looked at him in surprise. "H... have you ever used one?"

"No," admitted Tagg. "But...now seems like a good time to try."

With a slow nod, Liberty said. "Okay." She took out her Glock. "You stand forward a little bit."

"Sure," agreed Tagg, and he took two steps forward.

She handed him the gun.

"Safety's off, so hold it with both hands and point it that way," said Liberty and she pointed towards the approaching ship.

"It's heavier than I thought," murmured Tagg, but he held it in a steady grip.

And for a second, a memory flashed up. Liberty's prudish Mom was stepping into the next room when her grandmother leaned over to chuckle, 'they say big hands means a big….'.

The Librarian stopped herself. They were about to die. She didn't need to get distracted.

But she did allow herself two seconds to grieve. Grieve for the boy, for Uncle Danny, for Tagg and herself.

But then she straightened up and shouldered her rifle.

"Okay, everyone get ready," she ordered with a rock-solid voice.

"Can I get a gun?" asked Colin.

"No!" said all three adults at once.

"That's not fair," complained Colin, but he looked scared.

Uncle Danny shifted to hold his shotgun in his right hand as he said a quiet prayer. Hopefully, his *Abuela* will be okay with him leaving Tessy at the Old Armory. Hopefully!

With his other hand, Danny pulled Colin to his side. The boy didn't even protest.

"Fire on my word," ordered Liberty. She stepped onto the other side of Tagg, so that he and Colin were between her and Uncle Danny. She aimed her rifle.

The Octahedron was drawing closer, picking up speed, and behind it the pier was consumed in flames.

Something shot over their heads and hit the UFO like a sledgehammer.

The alien ship began to wobble. Part of the ship had been torn off. The red beam cut out. With a dip to the right, the UFO only just missed getting hit by another shot.

The ship veered away from the pier, and then drifted to limp away over the town.

"Um," said Tagg, but he still held the Glock, pointed forward.

Liberty reached past him and took the handgun. Holstering it, she turned back to the ocean.

"Is that...?" she asked.

"I think that's worthy of a swear word too," grinned Uncle Danny.

Out of the dusk came an old submarine, across the water.

"I'll allow it," said Liberty.

"Shit yeah!" cried Uncle Danny with joy.

Colin started to open his mouth, but then he caught Liberty's eye. The boy decided not to risk it.

Regardless, the Librarian patted his shoulder with genuine affection.

With the pier burning behind them, they did have to jump into the dodgy water after all. However, the submarine quickly fished them out.

"Sorry it took us so long to help," said a broad African American man. "We weren't even sure if the old gun'd work." He gestured at a large weapon, which was set into the main deck of the boat.

"We're just happy it did," replied Liberty enthusiastically. "Thank you!"

"We were in the neighborhood," shrugged the man with a smile. "By the way, I'm Captain Otowa."

"How old is this sub?" asked Tagg curiously.

"World War 2," said Captain Otowa proudly. "She was decommissioned, until things got bad. Cut off, we had to commandeer it from its museum."

"And Thank God," said Uncle Danny.

"Come on," said Captain Otowa. "Let's get you someplace safe."

"We'd appreciate it," said Liberty.

"But...," hesitated Captain Otowa.

"What?" asked Liberty with concern.

"If the boy and man have been bitten, I do need to restrain them, while they're on my boat," said Captain Otowa.

"But we're not dangerous!" snapped Colin hotly.

However, Uncle Danny put a comforting hand on the boy's shoulder.

"It's okay *Cobayo*," said the Big Mexican. "As long as Liberty is there to protect us."

Captain Otowa nodded. "Of course. Besides, if what we hear is true, I'll be happy to apologize at a later date."

"Can we go underwater?" asked Colin, excitedly.

"That's possible," said Captain Otowa. "But first, we need to…"

"Um! I think we might need to," called out Liberty. She pointed back towards the City of Angels.

A half dozen more Octahedrons rose above the town.

"That's okay. As long as they can't swim," chuckled Captain Otowa.

"How does that saying go?" asked Tagg. "Run Silent."

Liberty caught his eye. "Yeah! And run deep." And—in that tiny moment—she saw a spark of interest there. But then everyone started rushing about.

***

By the time the Octahedrons arrived, the waves had smoothed over, leaving not a trace.

**Volume Two**
*Chapter Five*

*Now*

Liberty looked through the scope of her sniper rifle. Malibu beach was right where she had left it.

She was leaning over the bow of a small boat, which rocked gently on the water. To her left was Malibu Pier. That cheesed-off alien ship had done a number on it, but some of it was still standing. And on the sand, only a few zoms milled about.

Turning, Liberty looked back at Uncle Danny.

"Looks quiet," she reported.

"That's good," said the Big Mexican slowly. But he looked pensive.

"Or...do we need to abort?" asked Liberty.

The other two men in the boat, Smalls and Bordeaux, looked over at her with surprise, but she ignored them.

However, Uncle Danny just shook his head. "No. This needs to be done."

"It'll help people," she agreed with soft assurance.

Taking a deep breath, Uncle Danny gave a wry grin. "Okay, we go."

When Liberty was convinced that he was truly okay, she turned to the soldier manning the outboard motor. "Can you take us in?"

"Yes ma'am," replied the young Army soldier, Rex Bordeaux.

Liberty's eyes went back to the beach as they closed in on the shore.

***

### *12 hours earlier aboard the Salk Medical Ship*

*"There's a guy in a really cool-looking uniform looking for you!" said Colin excitedly. The boy immediately looked back out into the hallway. "Hey! She's over here!"*

*Stepping up to the door, but not inside it, a man who was indeed in a really snappy Naval uniform. He held his white hat in one hand.*

*"Ms. Liberty Schonhauer?" asked the Naval man, though he seemed reasonably certain that it was her. Admittedly, Liberty did not think that there were many beret-wearing Librarians with full sleeve tattoos running about.*

*Liberty stood. "I am. Are you the Admiral?"*

*"Actually, Rear Admiral Antony Cirilo," replied the Naval man.*

*This made Colin snicker. "**Rear** Admiral?"*

*Not knowing what kind of man Cirilo was, Liberty immediately squinted past the man at the 11-year-old boy.*

*"Colin?" she said dangerously. "Don't you have some homework to do?"*

*"But I wanna hear what the **REAR** admiral has to say," said Colin, which set him off to full-blown giggles.*

*"It's not funny," insisted Liberty.*

*"It's kinda funny," insisted Colin between laughs.*

*Liberty saw Cirilo turning to the boy and her stomach dropped. This was the man who ran the whole show. Before the Rear Admiral could say anything, Liberty jumped in.*

*"Colin! Homework! Now!"*

*The boy made an unhappy noise. "But I don't wanna read today."*

*"Tough," replied Liberty. She pointed towards the room that she shared with the boy. "You need to have that book done by Friday, and next week, Uncle Danny is going to start you on Spanish as well."*

*"Can I at least go up onto the deck to read?" pleaded the boy.*

*"You can," allowed Liberty. "But hold on to that book carefully. It can get windy up there. And I have more than one copy of 'To Kill a Mockingbird' you know."*

*With a melodramatic sigh, Colin stomped to get the book. He quickly returned to sulk past them.*

*As the boy was passing, the Rear Admiral piped up. "It's actually a really good book."*

*Colin opened his mouth to say something biting and sarcastic, but then he saw Liberty. Her Look promised a world of trouble if he said **anything** biting and sarcastic.*

*"Okay," said Colin, and then he zipped out the door.*

*"And don't bother the sailors!" called out Liberty.*

*"Yeah, yeah, yeah," came a distant and dismissive reply.*

*Resisting the temptation to throw the boy overboard, Liberty reminded herself that he was a kid in weird circumstances. She turned to the Rear Admiral. "Sorry about that. He's a really good kid."*

*"It's okay," smiled the Naval man quickly. "I raised a few kids myself." And for a moment, a dark shadow crept over his face. However, it quickly disappeared.*

*At the Old Armory, people often talked about what they were feeling. Grandma Rollins didn't like feelings bottled up. But the social etiquette in the Fleet was not to pry. If someone wants to talk, they will bring it up. Though, she wasn't sure how healthy an idea that was, long-term.*

*And seeing that pain, her perturbed feeling went away. Colin was okay and safe, and that made her breathe easier.*

*Instead, she asked. "Can I help you?"*

*"I hope so," replied Rear Admiral Cirilo, calm and genial once again. "News of your dramatic escape has been running through the Fleet."*

*In truth, the vast flotilla of ships only had a handful of U.S. Navy vessels—including the Medical Ship that they were on, and the aircraft carrier USS Theodore Roosevelt. The rest of the* floatilla consisted of a mishmash of ships that people generally referred to as 'the Fleet'.

"And, I have to admit," said the Rear Admiral. "I... did have trouble believing 'aliens' at first."

"Me too," smiled Liberty gently.

Nodding, he continued. "We need your help."

"How so?" asked Liberty wearily.

"After I took command of the fleet, I repurposed almost all the soldiers at my command to serve as peace officers," said the Rear Admiral. "It was chaos at first, with no real authority, so I had to take control."

"So, we're under military rule," stated Liberty carefully.

"For the moment," nodded the Rear Admiral. "But we really need to change that—create a more democratic process—but...but we're getting off-topic. I need soldiers."

"Am I being drafted?" asked Liberty, even more wearily.

The Rear Admiral shook his head.

"Nothing that dramatic," he said. "I understand that you were able to navigate through the City of Angels pretty handily."

"Well, more or less," said Liberty. "And I had help."

"Uncle Danny, correct?" asked the Rear Admiral. "Is he your uncle?"

Liberty chuckled. "Oh no! He's uncle to a little girl that I helped save, but not to any of us. However, we somehow took to calling him that, and it stuck."

"Ah! That makes sense. Well, is he around?" asked the Rear Admiral.

"Dr. Tagg is trying to keep his zombie virus at bay," said

*Liberty.*

*"So, he really does have it," said the Rear Admiral.*

*"Yes. But he's held it off so far. But why do you need to see him?" asked Liberty protectively.*

*"I was hoping that the two of you could help us," said the Rear Admiral.*

### Now - Malibu Beach

The moment the boat hit the sand, Liberty was up and over the bow. She dropped down, rifle up. But there were still only a few zoms on the beach.

Uncle Danny, Bordeaux and Smalls climbed out after her.

Smalls spotted a nearby zom—in the dress of a surfer dude—and it looked from the waves to him. He swiftly brought up his M4 Carbine rifle, ready to shoot, but Liberty pushed down his barrel.

"Wait," said the sniper softly.

### 4 Hours ago - The Aircraft Carrier

*A drop of sweat wandered down Liberty's back, tickling as it went. She tried not to look nervous, despite being utterly terrified.*

*"...so, that's our mission," she said to the assembled team.*

*Liberty was at the front of a meeting room, having to speak in public. She had had nightmares about this. And it didn't even help that this was a small group. This is why she had liked being a librarian, she decoded. Books didn't need speeches.*

But there was Uncle Danny smiling encouragingly, which made her feel a little better.

"Any questions?" she asked, and she was proud-- Thrilled! -- that her voice did not quake.

"So, you came outta The City of Angels," said the soldier, Rex Bordeaux eagerly. "Didja have to shoot your way out?"

"Actually...," started Liberty thoughtfully, and her brow furrowed. "I'm not sure we had to shoot anyone."

The Librarian looked at Uncle Danny, who shrugged in agreement.

The Big Mexican continued in his gravelly voice. "Zoms ain't that fast. ¡Gracias a Dios!"

"But aren't there a lot of them out there?" asked Brent Smalls, the Navy mechanic, nervously.

"A city full," nodded Liberty. "However, the real danger is getting boxed in. As long as we keep moving, we're relatively safe."

"But what if they get too close?" asked Smalls.

"Don't engage, unless we have no other choice," said Liberty.

"Believe me," chuckled Uncle Danny darkly. "We don't have enough bullets for them all."

"I've seen people who've tried that," added Liberty.

"What happened?" asked Bordeaux with excitement.

"Zombie food," replied Liberty simply.


**Now**

"It's okay," said Liberty to Smalls.

She led her team up Malibu beach, and away from the zoms.

"Just feels...wrong to leave'em like that," said Smalls as he hefted his bag of tools. "I mean, are they in pain?"

Liberty's eyebrows furrowed and she looked to the Big Mexican for his opinion.

Uncle Danny shrugged. "They don't seem to feel, well really, anything. Hot, cold, sunburn, rain..."

"Until you wound them," added Liberty.

"That does tend to cheese'em off," finished Danny with a chuckle.

"I guess that makes sense," nodded Smalls. "I'd be upset too."

"But that's probably more of a reflex thing than actual thought," said Uncle Danny.

"Like a knee jerk reaction?" mused Smalls.

Once they reached the highway, they turned left and began to weave in and amongst the knots of zombies.

Bordeaux suddenly snapped. "Damnit!"

Liberty twisted around to see what the young soldier was looking at. But she only saw an abandoned burger joint.

"What's wrong?" she asked in concern. Uncle Danny was now at her side, ready for action.

Bordeaux spoke in a hollow voice. "It's...really gone, isn't it?"

"What?" asked Uncle Danny, getting annoyed.

"Jack in the Box," wailed Bordeaux, and there were tears

in his eyes. "I'm never going to get a burger like that again."

Uncle Danny looked like he was about to explode, and Liberty was not amused.

"Dude!" cried out Smalls, who was eyeing the oncoming zoms. "Is this funeral over yet? 'Cause the wildlife is getting restless."

Bordeaux wiped the tears on his sleeve. "Oh! Oh yeah, sure. Sorry. It's just..."

And Liberty's annoyance melted away. She patted Bordeaux on the shoulder and egged all the guys along.

"It's okay," she said gently.

Uncle Danny's face was still clouded over with anger.

Liberty spoke softly, but not to any of them in particular. "The end of life as we knew...."

Danny looked thoughtful and nodded. *"Todo va a estar bien.* It hits everyone at different times, and in different ways."

"So!" asked Smalls, incredulously. "We're just going to wander until we find one? Is that the plan?"

"No Google," replied Liberty.

"Now, if we *Do* see a phone book...," suggested Uncle Danny.

"But...I mean, do they even make'em anymore?" asked Smalls. "I mean, not 'now' of course. But before everything fell?"

"Over there!" called out Bordeaux.

"What this time," grumbled Uncle Danny.

97

"No, really!" insisted Bordeaux.

Liberty turned around and saw the young soldier pointing at a UFO descending less than a mile away.

"Hey, that's an octahedron," said Smalls.

"What?" asked Liberty.

"Oh! That's the geometric shape," explained Smalls.

"Really! Thank you!" said Liberty sincerely. "I had a feeling that it wasn't just random, but Geometry was a little while ago."

"That's our UFO too," said Uncle Danny.

And Liberty spotted the scar in the upper right where the submarine had hit it. The damage gave it a cockeyed, angry look.

"Wish we could see what it was doing," said Liberty.

The Octahedron was stationary for a moment. But then it rose quickly into the air and moved away from them.

"Was it picking up, or dropping off," wondered Uncle Danny.

Liberty made a noncommittal noise and said. "Well, let's not find out."

They kept on moving but did not have to travel far when they reached their target: TrueAid Pharmacy.


### 11 Hours Ago

*"We're not thieves," exclaimed Uncle Danny, hotly.*

*Rear Admiral Antony Cirilo reared back in surprise. His dark eyebrows furrowed.*

"But is this stealing?" he asked, and then he swiftly added. "I mean that question sincerely. Of course, if the owner is there, manning her store, then that's one thing..."

Liberty looked at Uncle Danny and spoke to mollify him.

"And we're going to **specifically** target pharmacies that have been abandoned," she insisted earnestly.

"I really doubt that anyone at the TrueAid corporate headquarters-- wherever that is-- is in a position to object," said the Rear Admiral. "**And** we are—really quickly—going to run out of medicine in the Fleet."

Wearily, Uncle Danny asked. "What do we need?"

"Um, everything really," said the Rear Admiral quickly. "Blood Pressure medicine, Tamiflu, and... well, anything we can get our hands on."

"Why us?" asked Uncle Danny.

"Because you made it through," said the Rear Admiral.

"We're victims of our own success," moaned Liberty melodramatically.

And Uncle Danny looked down in thought.

Liberty turned to the Rear Admiral.

"Can you give us a moment?" she asked.

The Rear Admiral obligingly slid out of the glorified closet where Uncle Danny roomed with Tagg. The door shut quietly, and Liberty looked at Uncle Danny. He still looked under the weather, despite Dr. McTaggart's efforts.

"Do I look any better?" he asked.

"You look like you have a bad cold," admitted Liberty.

Uncle Danny touched the bite on his arm, which was healing

*well.*

*"Tagg's been experimenting with the boy's blood, to see if he can stop the zombie virus completely," said Uncle Danny. Liberty knew this but gave him time to talk. He let out a little laugh. "I mean, I teased Colin about being the guinea pig, el cobayo. But now I'm the one getting poked all the time."*

*"If that means we get to keep you...," smiled Liberty warmly.*

*"Like a bad penny?" asked Uncle Danny.*

*"I don't know about that," said Liberty, who did not get the reference. "At least there're not armed guards following you, anymore."*

*Uncle Danny shrugged. "They were actually pretty nice to Cobayo."*

*"**Please!**" chuckled Liberty. "If they'd been mean to Colin, you'd have torn their ears off. And I would've held them down for you."*

*Despite himself, Danny let out a little laugh. "I guess...that's true."*

*In all seriousness, Liberty leaned forward. "**But** if you don't want to go, I completely understand."*

*Uncle Danny chuckled warmly. "Hah! You're not getting rid of me that easily."*

*And the knot in Liberty's chest loosened.*

### Now

Despite being unlocked, the front doors of the pharmacy did not want to open at first. But Uncle Danny and Bordeaux still managed to pry them apart. Liberty slid in

100

with her handgun, now affixed with a silencer, courtesy of someone on the aircraft carrier. She didn't know who, but the Rear Admiral had brought it to her just before they left.

The second set of doors opened easily, as Smalls tugged on them. She slid past him and saw a zom in a TrueAid vest behind the register. The silencer helped mask the noise. Then, there was only the sound of a zom hitting the floor.

"Best new toy," she whispered with a grin.

Closing the front doors on a zom, Uncle Danny asked Bordeaux and Smalls to wait in the small foyer.

"We need to make sure that it's safe," said Danny in a hushed voice.

Smalls nodded quickly, holding his bag of tools in front of him, protectively. "Okay."

"Sure, you don't want any help?" asked the soldier eagerly.

Uncle Danny nodded at Smalls. "Make sure he's alive when we get back."

"Yes sir," said Bordeaux with a resigned voice.

With his shotgun in his left hand, Uncle Danny drew out the old Chinese cleaver at his right hip.

"What're you going to do with that? Cut their heads off?" asked Bordeaux with a mixture of wonder and horror.

"¡Nunca! No, it's nice and dull," said Uncle Danny. "The best weapon actually."

"What?" asked Bordeaux.

"Anything sharp can get stuck. In a wooden doorway, or

101

a skull. And even if it's just stuck for a few seconds, that can get you dead," explained Uncle Danny with a languid smile. "But this...this'll break bones."

Turning, Uncle Danny plunged into the store after Liberty.

"Thank God he's on our side," whispered Smalls.

The Librarian moved to the left side of the store with her gun ready. So that nothing could get behind her, she went first to the outer wall. On the sales floor, 7-foot shelves stood in rows, perpendicular to the wall. However, there was an aisle between the edge and the shelves.

The Librarian neared Aisle 1, which reached out into the store.

A zom suddenly lurched out, hands grasping for her.

A dull cleaver descended on the zom's left arm, breaking it instantly. This caused it to stumble. And Uncle Danny knocked the zom to the ground.

Before the zom had bounced twice on the floor, Liberty put a double tap in its head.

Uncle Danny and the Librarian looked up immediately to scan the area, just in case any other zoms got nosy.

"Thanks," whispered Liberty.

"You'd have had them," shrugged Uncle Danny. "But I needed to get warmed up, being an old man and all."

With amusement, Liberty shook her head at that.

They moved deeper into the store with her in front and Uncle Danny watching the rear. A zom shopper appeared and Liberty easily dropped it.

Another zom tried to charge them from behind, but Uncle Danny slammed his cleaver against its knee. It smacked to the ground hard. Before it had a chance, Uncle Danny hit it square in the back of the neck. He flinched at the sound of the neck breaking.

"¡*Mierda!* I hate that noise," grumbled Uncle Danny softly.

"You and me both," replied Liberty sympathetically.

They reached the back of the store, however there were twelve more zoms waiting in front of the pharmacy window. Liberty and Uncle Danny backed up, out of sight.

"Almost as if they're waiting for a pharmacist, hoping to get better," whispered Liberty sadly.

"Let me take the lead," said Uncle Danny.

Suspiciously, Liberty squinted at him.

"Tagg?" she asked with a dark and dangerous voice.


### 6 hours ago, after agreeing to the mission.

*"Stay still, or I'll take your ear off," ordered Liberty. She planted a hand firmly on top of Colin's head to hold him still. "And we don't want that, do we."*

*They were in the bedroom that she shared with the boy. Liberty had almost been sent to one of the refugee ships. But, Tagg had managed to wrangle two rooms aboard the Jonas Salk Medical Ship because he needed to examine Colin and Uncle Danny. And he explained to the captain of the Salk that Liberty would be ample guard, just in case.*

*In reality, she wasn't going to leave the boy.*

103

*"You're cutting it too short,"* complained the boy, which pulled her back to her present challenge.

*"It'll grow back,"* replied Liberty, without an ounce of pity. *"And after you were rude to the Admiral..."*

*"Rear Admiral,"* corrected Colin with a smirk.

*Liberty just leaned around the boy and fell—unknowingly—into her You-Cheesed-Off-The-Librarian voice. "You're already going to clean our room, and then help Tagg in his lab. You want more?"*

*Colin tried to meet her gaze, but his eyes soon dropped. "No."*

*The Librarian moved back behind him. "Now, if that nice Mr. Renoir were here, we'd ask him to take care of it." She thought of her hair, which had already grown past her shoulders. She had been due for a haircut before things went bad. Her thoughts went to Tagg and continued fervently. "Both of us! But for now..."*

*A man with a barrel chest walked into the open door and suddenly screeched to a halt.*

*"Oh!" he said in surprise. "I... I can just come back..."*

*Whipping around, Tagg practically shot out the door, leaving behind a mildly puzzled Liberty.*

*Shrugging, she looked down at Colin, turning back on the electric clippers that she had borrowed. She was in the middle of shearing the boy when Tagg flitted past the door.*

*Liberty switched off her clippers.*

*Outside the room, Tagg leaned against the wall, anxiety pouring off of him.*

*"What's wrong?" asked a voice, and Tagg jumped.*

*"What?" asked the Scientist in surprise.*

Liberty leaned against the door frame. "You're acting suspicious."

"I am?" replied Tagg. "I mean, I wasn't...I just..."

"You heard about the mission, didn't you?" said Liberty softly. "I guess I should have told you earlier. "

"Oh No," said Tagg, swiftly. "It's not that. You don't have to report to me..." He raised his voice. "And I heard some short person was rude."

"Hey!" cried Colin, unseen from the room.

"Uncle Danny said that you'd put him to work after we left," said Liberty. Her brow furrowed. "I hate to do that..."

Quickly, Tagg said to her, in a normal speaking voice. "It's okay." She looked up at him. He managed to hold eye contact for longer this time. He smiled warmly and then continued loudly. "He's better than that type of behavior."

"It was just a joke!" came the boy's voice within the room.

Liberty did not take her eyes away from the Scientist but smiled as well and said loudly as well. "I agree." But then her smile faded, and voice became soft. "But I can't help wondering why you're visiting." She immediately added, worriedly. "Not That I Mind."

"It's not that I don't trust you. **I Do!** " he said quickly in a normal voice.

"But...?"

"I....," started Tagg, however he deflated. Screwing up his courage and said quickly. "I Like You, and I'm worried. But I can't tell you not to go."

"That is true," she agreed gently, but firmly. "However, I'll be careful. I promise."

*"Promise?" asked Tagg. "Wait! You can't promise that. Sorry."*

*"It's okay. Besides—here in the Fleet—there's little for me to do. There's a library on the carrier, but they already have four librarians. So, unless I want to be some kind of cop...," said Liberty, and her face scrunched up.*

*"Not a good fit for you?" asked Tagg curiously.*

*"Zoms, and the occasional alien, are one thing," finished Liberty.*

*Colin called out from inside the room. "Are you two smooching?"*

*Liberty's back went rigid and she swung around to glare back into the room.*

*"Where'd you get that word?" she asked with a frosty voice.*

*"Uncle Danny said that you guys need to smooch," replied Colin defiantly.*

*Tagg blushed and stepped away from the wall. "Oh! Um, maybe I should go."*

*But Liberty skipped towards him and planted a soft kiss on his cheek. He smelled of soap.*

*"I like you too," she whispered.*

*With a hop back, Liberty's eyes shone with delight, and she gave a big smile. After a few goodbyes, she reluctantly turned to go back into her room.*

*Once inside though, her face grew serious.*

*"You—Young Man! —need to keep your nose out of other people's business," said Liberty.*

*"You get in mine all the time," complained Colin.*

*Liberty sniffed. "That's my job."*

**Now**

In the pharmacy, Uncle Danny gave a cheery grin. "Tagg did visit, but he didn't ask me to take care of you."

"He didn't?" asked Liberty, a little hurt.

"*¡Neta!* Tagg knew he didn't have to ask me to do that," said Uncle Danny as he sheathed his cleaver.

And Liberty's stomach gave a joyful little dance.

Uncle Danny said. "No, I wanna go first, and then while I'm reloading…" He left that thought there.

With a soft chuckle, Liberty made a flourish gesture with her hand. "Age before beauty."

Uncle Danny gave her a look of mock pain, but he stepped forward and cocked his shotgun loudly.

That, the zoms heard.

The closest one looked up quickly, just as a deer slug hit its head. As it fell, the Big Mexican put another shell into the chamber and fired.

The zoms lurched towards them and Uncle Danny fired as quickly as he could. A deer slug went wide and missed.

"Shit," he growled.

The zoms drew closer, and the Big Mexican fired again, but this time, he didn't miss.

"I'm out," cried Uncle Danny and he stepped aside, reaching for a cartridge belt of deer slugs around his waist.

Into that space came Liberty, her silenced weapon rising to face the creatures. Soon, the most prominent sound in the store was that of the now truly dead, collapsing upon the floor.

Reloaded, Uncle Danny called out. "Okay! I'm ready to…" But then he saw that the rest of the zoms were now dead. "*¡Hijole!*" He gave her a look of mock annoyance. "See! *This* is why I went first."

# Chapter Six

LIBERTY AND UNCLE Danny scouted the interior of the abandoned drug store, including the back room. But there was no more trouble.

Without any pleasure, Uncle Danny hit all the fallen zoms on the back of the neck with his cleaver, just in case. Now satisfied, the two headed back up to the front.

However, the abandoned drugstore was getting to Liberty.

"It's like, eerie-quiet in here," she said, feeling like she had to whisper. "Right now, I'd even appreciate some elevator music. Like the 'Girl from Ipanema' or even Christmas music.

Uncle Danny glanced at her with *faux* seriousness. "You know—sometimes—I really worry about you *Mija*."

"Is it safe?" called out the Navy engineer, Smalls, as he stepped into the store.

"We're good," assured Liberty. "Still, I'm going to lead us to the back, and…" She nodded at Uncle Danny. "…he'll cover our *derrière*."

Liberty led them to the other side of the store and down the aisle, which was free of zombies. They quickly reached the door to the pharmacy.

Smalls looked in horror at the zoms on the ground. "Oh God. Couldn't…was all this really necessary?"

"You mean having to shoot them?" asked Liberty, trying to understand.

"There's nothing left," said Uncle Danny softly, and he tapped a finger against his own temple.

"But…," muttered Smalls. This was the first time he had seen this.

"It's not like they're even shootin' rabid dogs," said Bordeaux. "Actually wait! It's exactly like a rabid dog. Fido ain't coming back."

Uncle Danny nodded towards the pharmacy door.

"Roe sham boe?" he asked eagerly as he readied to do rock, paper, scissors.

"It's okay," said Liberty with a little smile. "You can check it out."

Uncle Danny grinned as he raised his shotgun.

Shortly enough came a gruff voice. "Nothin'".

Liberty walked in and stopped by the dispensing window. There were several zoms outside, looking confused.

"I'm kinda glad it was empty," she said.

"Boring you mean," he grumbled.

"I like boring," she retorted playfully.

"You're boring," grouched Uncle Danny with mock annoyance.

"Hey!" said Liberty, slowing her pace. "Just because I'm a librar..."

Suddenly, she stopped and whipped towards the window. Her Glock up and ready.

Immediately, Uncle Danny was there, ready to rock. His eyes roamed the scene. Directly past the window was a knot of zoms, with a brick wall farther back behind them.

"What've you got?" asked Uncle Danny softly.

"Not sure," admitted Liberty.

"Animal, vegetable or alien?" smirked Uncle Danny.

"Animal? Gray-ish. Feathers?" said Liberty. "Moving close to the ground."

"Bigger than a dog?" asked Uncle Danny.

"Much," said Liberty.

"Maybe it escaped from the zoo?" suggested Uncle Danny. "A *avestruz*...but I don't know it in English. Lays really big eggs."

"Ostrich?" asked Liberty.

"Could be," said shrugged Uncle Danny. "Maybe. So, should we be worried?"

Liberty lowered her handgun, and he mirrored the

movement.

"Maybe nothing," shrugged Liberty.

Uncle Danny shook his head. "Maybe. But still, we'd better be careful when we leave. Just in case."

"Just in case," nodded Liberty fervently. Taking a deep breath, she companionly bumped her arm against his, and then turned back to the other men.

"Is...is everything all right?" asked Smalls.

Liberty tried for a confident smile. "Depends on your definition." But then her face grew more serious. "So, as to what we're doing here. We need to get every piece of medication off these shelves and back onto the boat."

Smalls looked uncertainly at the shelves. "I'm not sure we can carry that much."

Looking from the men, she scanned over the rows of medicine.

"Huh. It is a lot," she admitted. "Okay, why doesn't everyone look around for something to carry the medicine in?"

Annoyed, Bordeaux, said. "Maybe we shoulda thought of that before we left the Fleet."

"On the Coast, we think on our feet," replied Liberty without heat. "Besides, I didn't see anything back at the Fleet that would help us. Or at least anything that we could cart about in our little boat."

"Cart...," said Uncle Danny thoughtfully.

Liberty looked at him curiously.

"When you said 'carting'," murmured the Big Mexican.

"I think that's exactly what we need."

"Shopping carts?" asked Liberty, and her face lit up.

Uncle Danny continued. "We could get a lot of medicine in four shopping carts. Then, it's just a matter of pushing'em back to the boat."

"But...carts on a sandy beach?" asked Smalls skeptically.

"Let's see if we can get the shopping carts first," suggested Liberty gently.

"Well, we didn't see a market on the way in, so why don't we look West first," suggested Uncle Danny.

"And if that doesn't work, we go North," finished Liberty. She turned to Smalls. "Can you stay here while the rest of us go get some carts?"

"And not go back out there?" asked Smalls. "Absolutely!"

"Okay," replied Liberty with amusement. "But I don't think we're going to be back right away."

"True, we're on foot," said Uncle Danny. "Unless we find a vehicle."

Smalls looked around the pharmacy. "That's okay. That'll give me time to get into the safe with all the controlled medication."

Satisfied that Smalls would be okay, Liberty led the guys out of the store. They pushed a few zoms out of the way and then moved West. The Soldier eyed the former people as they weaved around them.

"It feels kinda weird to be running around these...," began Bordeaux, but then he stopped.

"I usually just go with 'zoms'," said Liberty helpfully. "Easy. One syllable."

"And luckily, they lurch pretty slow," said Uncle Danny.

"But don't get cocky," warned Liberty swiftly, with genuine concern. "All it takes is one bite, and that's it."

However, Bordeaux looked at Uncle Danny.

"But he has it, doesn't he?" asked the soldier.

"Probably not the best example," said Liberty.

Uncle Danny grinned. "I'm special."

"Actually, he is, kind of," said Liberty. "Dr. Tagg isn't sure why he doesn't want to...well..."

"Eat brains?" asked Uncle Danny with a chuckle.

Liberty shrugged. "Wellllll, I wouldn't put it so crudely..."

"That's because you're not a jerk," nodded Uncle Danny proudly.

Tongue-tied by the compliment, Liberty turned to Bordeaux. "I don't know about you—but I'm not going to chance it."

"Hey!" said Uncle Danny as he pointed down the street. "Tell me that that doesn't look like a grocery store."

They picked up the pace.

Which unfortunately caught the eye of something nearby.

However, with all the zoms lurching about, this masked that they were now being followed, hunted.

Kramden's Grocery Store had a scattered array of cars in

the parking lot as they walked through it.

"I don't see any carts in the lot," observed Uncle Danny.

"The cart boy was on point that day," said Liberty unhappily. "We'll probably have to break in."

Their path led them by some cars, but not so close that any ankle-biters could grab them from underneath.

Liberty looked at the front of the store. It was a wall of glass with automatic double doors in the center. But she doubted that they were working.

"Wait here," she said. While the guys waited, she went up to a window and peered in. "There're carts in there."

"Zoms?" asked Uncle Danny.

"At least a few," said Liberty. She tried the automatic door, but it was locked.

Suddenly, a bestial shriek came from behind the guys.

Bordeaux glanced back and was dumbfounded.

It could've been a light grey bird, but it's head reached up almost to his shoulder. The bird was almost upon him, and it unfurled its wings, which then shook wildly. The underside was a vibrant kaleidoscope of colored feathers. Bordeaux tried to make sense of it, but he did not have time.

The bird slammed one of its powerful legs down upon Bordeaux's left leg, breaking the femur instantly. As the soldier began to tip back, the creature's curved beak slashed at the side of Bordeaux's neck, cutting it wide open.

Uncle Danny turned and fired, but his deer slug went wide.

115

*"Klas du ren!"* cried the bird-thing.

It kicked out at the Big Mexican, who jerked aside.

The creature missed Danny's leg by an inch. And it's foot—with its curved talons—punched right through the side of a car. However, when it tried to pull out, the talons stuck.

Its attention was pulled to Liberty, who was pulling Bordeaux away. So, when the first deer slug hit it square in the chest, the bird-thing looked up at Uncle Danny in surprise. He fired again.

The bird-thing gave a piercing cry. *"Tasssss!"*

In stages, it slumped to the ground, holding on until its last breath.

Liberty had dragged Bordeaux a little ways away, but he was trailing a lot of blood. She stopped and took a deep breath, but then tried to pull him again.

However, he was dead weight now.

Uncle Danny walked over and laid a hand gently on her shoulder.

Instantly, she growled. *"No!"*

Despite herself, Liberty looked down. Bordeaux's eyes—still with a look of surprise—stared up at nothing.

"He's gone *Mija,*" whispered Uncle Danny. "And we need to…"

*"Ranns!"* cried a voice nearby.

"Was that…?" asked Liberty.

*"¡Ya te cargó el payaso!"* hissed Uncle Danny, but then he turned to her. *"¡Aquas!* The bastard brought friends."

Liberty snarled as she let Bordeaux down gently.

Uncle Danny looked at the grocery store. "Tell me that the front door is open."

Pivoting around, Liberty pulled her handgun and put a bullet through the glass by the door. As the window shattered, a generous hole was left for them.

"That works too," muttered the Big Mexican dryly.

The Librarian led Uncle Danny through the broken window, entering near the front registers. A zombie bag boy turned towards them.

Uncle Danny hit it in the head with his cleaver, but he looked unhappy.

"Just a kid," he moaned.

The two went across the front of the store when Uncle Danny let out in a harsh whisper.

"¡Fíjate! Window!"

The Librarian turned and saw more of the bird-things entering the parking lot.

Appearing behind them, a zom slid between the two registers. It grabbed Liberty's shoulders and snapped at her, but it only got air. Overbalanced though, Liberty started to tumble, but she turned it into a roll.

Losing its grip, the zom fell down, not far from her knees.

Before Liberty could pull away, the zom bit down her knee, hard.

Uncle Danny's stomach lurched.

Out of Liberty came an involuntary noise as she yanked

her leg away.

With her clear, Uncle Danny came in swinging, rage in his eyes. He swung the cleaver low and with a crack, hit the zom upside the head.

As the one creature collapsed, another zom came towards them. Uncle Danny positioned himself over Liberty to cover her, just as she would have done for him. He was more than happy to take out his fear and anger on this creature.

"*¡Estoy que echo chispas!*" growled Danny.

What he didn't want to do was to look down. What he did not want to do is see blood. So, he cracked the zom in the head several times more than was probably necessary.

Below him, a litany rose up from his friend.

"Oh No, No, No, No," hissed Liberty as she patted the jeans covering her knee.

Mustering every ounce of courage, Uncle Danny looked down at his friend.

His heart jumped.

There was no blood. However, he did not dare relax yet. He knelt to take a closer look.

Finally, he said with relief. "*¡Gracias a Dios!* You're good."

However, Liberty continued to pull at her jeans, inspecting them minutely.

The Big Mexican put a hand on her shoulder, and she flinched, hard. Then the Librarian looked up at him.

Uncle Danny spoke softly. "You're okay *Mija*." He

smiled. "No blood. This is why we can't wear those jeans with the knees worn out, like all those fashion models."

Despite her panic, Liberty let out a chuckle. "I am SO not a fashion model."

"I think Tagg likes you the way you are," smirked Uncle Danny.

The Big Mexican's patter was already helping to bring her back, but then she realized what he had said about Tagg. She looked at him in surprise.

Playing it cool, Uncle Danny was already standing to face a zom.

"*¡Orale!* You want some too?" asked the Big Mexican of the creature with a joyous laugh.

The zom went down, but with only enough violence to get the job done.

Satisfied that they were safe for a moment, his attention wandered out into the parking lot. The bird-things were fanning out to search.

"We gotta go," he whispered urgently.

Liberty nodded a little shakily. However, by the time she had collected her Glock, the Librarian stood, rock-steady and ready. She pointed towards the back of the store. "We can go back."

"Right," agreed Danny. "That'll give us some breathing room. You ready?"

Liberty squared her shoulders and brought up her silenced handgun with a smirk. "What're we standing around for? An engraved invitation?"

Uncle Danny returned the grin, feeling almost giddy

after that scare.

They went to the side of the store, so they'd have a wall at their backs.

Moving down the formally frozen aisle, the two scooted around a couple zoms that were milling about. Inexplicably, one even had a shopping basket with cold medicine in the crook of their arm. Behind a glass door, ice cream had broken free of its containers to congeal at the bottom of the fridge in a moldy mess.

"This place must have been hell when all this food went rotten," murmured Liberty.

Speeding up, they reached the door to the back stockroom.

Just as they did, a voice came from the front of the store.

"*Guk fowe,*" said a bird-thing.

Liberty and Danny pushed through the swinging doors and let them shut behind them. There was only one zom in there, in an apron.

"Got it," said Uncle Danny and he went towards the zom, lest it creep up behind them.

Though grimy little windows, set into the door, Liberty was able to peer down the frozen aisle. The two zoms, that were still in the aisle, began to slow down.

A voice, right beside Liberty, asked. "What've we got?"

The Librarian jumped a little.

"Sorry," winced Uncle Danny.

"It's okay. Not your fault," said Liberty quickly.

Uncle Danny looked out the window. "Huh. Zoms

already getting bored?"

"You know, I never really took time to watch them before. It always made me remember...well, bad things," whispered Liberty.

"¡*Neta!* I can understand that" said Danny with a heavy voice.

"But regardless...," said Liberty with a smile. She focused on the zoms once again. "You know, they could need eye contact to chase."

"Maybe what's left of their brain can't keep up the hunt?" suggested Uncle Danny.

"That's plausible," nodded Liberty. "Uh-oh,"

One of the bird-things stepped into the aisle and looked down the length of it. The zoms were lurching, but the bird-thing just shook its feathers in annoyance and turned away.

"Didja see that?" asked Liberty in a whisper.

"What?" asked Uncle Danny.

"There was something sticking out of the back of its head," said Liberty.

"¡*No manches!* Like what? A horn or something?"

"No. It actually looked like some type of mechanical device," said Liberty.

"Weird," muttered Uncle Danny.

"The aliens I saw were covered in tentacles, but there's bound to be more than one type out there," said Liberty.

"Maybe our alien ship was dropping off their *amigos*," he said.

"Maybe," replied Liberty, thoughtfully. She stepped back from the door and looked down at the knee that had been bitten. She moved the jeans in the light to reassure herself that the zom's bite had not gone through.

"You're going to be okay," said Uncle Danny gently.

"I know," said Liberty. "It just...scared me, that's all. I saw someone get bit like that, and the teeth only went in a little bit, but...that was it. Took a little longer, but..."

"Well, take a moment if you need it," said Uncle Danny. He looked around the stockroom and settled on a door out. "I say we do what we normally do. Sneak out the back and live to fight another day."

Liberty looked up with a smile. "Agreed. I don't want to take those things on, until we know more."

"At least we know they bleed," said Uncle Danny.

"That's a start," nodded Liberty. "But...we still have to come back for Bordeaux, and the carts later."

"Absolutely!" replied the Big Mexican.

\*\*\*

Not long after, Liberty glanced up from her scope.

"Six of those bird-things just left the store," she said to Danny. Then she looked back through her scope at the front of the grocery store.

Having ducked out the back door, they were now on top of a nearby building, hoping to make sense of what had just happened.

"I need to get some binoculars," mumbled Uncle Danny off-handedly.

Liberty lifted her rifle. "Want to use this?"

Carefully, Uncle Danny took the rifle with unfamiliar hands. Mostly, he didn't want to drop her beloved rifle. Squinting through the scope, he quickly got the hang of it.

"Why aren't they attacking the zoms?" wondered Uncle Danny.

Liberty opened her mouth to comment but stopped. She had not realized it until now, however that had been bothering her too. Taking back her rifle, she watched the bird-things some more.

They're moving right past the zoms, but they attacked us," said Liberty thoughtfully. "But why? What were we doing different?"

"We were just walking to the grocery store," said Uncle Danny. "Nothing special."

"Was it the direction we were headed?" asked Liberty rhetorically. "Or our heat signature?"

Uncle Danny scratched his chin. "I might have a thought."

***

Liberty was extremely unamused.

While she had stayed on her rooftop, Uncle Danny had snuck over to a building beside the grocery store and now Big Mexican now lay on the roof. He was right near the lip

123

of the roof, to provide a little more cover.

While the Librarian hated this plan, what really rankled her was that she did not have a better one. And that didn't help her mood, not one stinking bit.

Shouldering her Steyr rifle, she watched her friend lift up one of several wooden boxes that he had brought from the alley. However, she stopped to look at her to first give her a thumbs up, and then a finger crossed.

Uncle Danny pitched the box. It arced into the parking lot and smashed into the windshield of a Beemer.

Two of the bird-things immediately ran over to investigate, making angry noises.

Hefting a second box, he threw that one as well.

From Liberty's vantage, the bird-things immediately spotted the box arcing through the air. But, they did not wait for it to hit.

Snapping open their large wings, the birds shot up into the air. Within seconds, they had dropped onto the roof, just a little ways from Uncle Danny. His finger was on the trigger of the shotgun, however he waited—not even breathing—for them to descend upon him. He did not even dare to breathe.

Liberty aimed her rifle at the nearest bird-thing. As it scanned the rooftop, she noted that it had a tuft of red feathers atop its head.

But it did not pounce on Uncle Danny.

In fact, it puffed out its feathers in what looked like a gesture of annoyance. After an eternity, from Uncle Danny's standpoint, both of the bird-things jumped off the roof and disappeared.

A small, relieved chuckle escaped Liberty's lips.

Uncle Danny raised one hand and gave the thumbs up. With the roof clear, he moved to the edge and peeked over. There were still several birds there.

"Come back," whispered Liberty, even though he could not hear her. "Enough testing for one day. Come Back! Let's go back to the pharmacy."

Almost as if he had heard her, Uncle Danny lifted up a finger to ask for more time.

"Oh no no," said Liberty. "What're you doin'?"

The Librarian lifted up her rifle as Uncle Danny chambered a round into his shotgun.

"Oh no, no, no," chanted Liberty under her breath.

Slowly, Uncle Danny stood fully upright. He stepped forward at a snail's pace and went right to the edge of the roof. The bird-things looked around and the Red Tufted bird even glanced in Uncle Danny's direction.

But then its eyes kept roaming.

"What the...," she muttered.

Stepping up onto the lip of the roof, Uncle Danny began to slowly stroll back and forth, but the bird-things just ignored him. Finally, Uncle Danny slowly stepped back from the edge.

Turning to Liberty, he gave a huge grin and a sedate thumbs up. She responded with the one-finger salute, which made him silently laugh.

Carefully going to the back of his building, Uncle Danny

125

climbed down, but he did not return.

"Oh, this keeps getting worse and worse," muttered Liberty, miserably.

The Big Mexican moved to the edge of the building and appeared to take a deep breath.

Liberty squeezed her eyes shut and squeaked. "I can't look."

But immediately, she peeked to watch.

Uncle Danny moved into the parking lot at a zom's pace. Leaning over the edge of her roof, Liberty watched him through her scope, and then she glanced at the nearby bird-things.

With careful, deliberate steps. Uncle Danny moved between the abandoned cars and towards Bordeaux.

"*Rux too?*" called out one of the bird-things near Uncle Danny, and the Big Mexican froze.

"*Het,*" replied another bird-thing.

The nearest alien to Uncle Danny hopped up onto a car by him.

Liberty zeroed in on its red tuft, ready to take the shot.

Uncle Danny froze. He tried to keep his breathing steady and hoped to God that those things couldn't smell sweat.

The bird-thing walked across the car, until it was almost on top of Uncle Danny.

Liberty put her finger on the trigger, ready to squeeze.

## Chapter Seven

**STEELING HIMSELF, UNCLE** Danny stepped away from the alien and towards the front of the grocery store. After a moment, the bird-thing turned and stalked in another direction.

Atop a nearby roof, Liberty suddenly realized that she had been holding her breath. She let it out slowly and dropped her head on top of her rifle.

"I'm gonna kill him," she moaned softly.

However, she immediately looked back up to cover her friend. Even if she did think that he was a bit of an idiot right now.

Below, Uncle Danny watched the zoms nearby. He saw that they were moving faster towards him. Resisting the urge to run, he put on just a little more speed. The bird-things did not seem to notice.

There was still a big hole in the front of the store, so he stepped inside and looked around. The front was clear of zoms. However, he drew his cleaver, just in case.

The shopping carts were corralled to the right, so he went over. Drawing out a full-size shopping cart, he set the cleaver in the child seat and slowly spun around.

The bird-thing with the red tuft was standing right in the broken window. Uncle Danny froze, and a sweat broke out on his forehead. He was scared, but not for his own life.

If Liberty decided to shoot it, then the other bird-things would race directly towards her. He wished he could tell her that he was okay. They really needed walkie-talkies.

"*Garak du somme,*" snapped the bird-thing in irritation.

Then it went back out the hole.

Once it was clear, Uncle Danny went back out at a zom's pace.

There was a zombie closing in on him, but he was able to head in the opposite direction. He did not dare attack it with those bird-things nearby, and he couldn't just run away. So, he set a pace just ahead of it.

The rattling cart did not seem to attract the notice of the bird-things. Reaching the edge of the parking lot, Uncle Danny lifted the cart up onto the grass, but he did have to drag it to the next parking lot. Luckily, the zom that was following stumbled over a curb.

Above, Liberty backed slowly away from the edge of the roof and climbed off her building. Uncle Danny came around the corner with his cart and the zom following.

"One moment," he said, once they were out of sight.

Taking his cleaver from the child seat, he swung it, aiming low. The blunted blade slammed into the side of the zom's knee, and it dropped quickly. However, the zom did not give any indication of any pain.

Returning to the cart, the Big Mexican smiled at Liberty, and she punched him in the upper arm.

"Ow," he said softly with a smile.     "You got bony knuckles *Mija*."

"You deserve it," hissed Liberty fiercely.

"¡*Neta!* I won't argue that point," nodded Uncle Danny.

"And I would've had to tell Colin what happened," said Liberty. She meant it as a growl, but it came out as a whine.

Danny's face fell.  "And Tessy is out there too."  He sighed.  "I'm sorry.  I just couldn't go back empty-handed. And we needed to figure out how to move around with those things."

Liberty gave a sigh herself.  The crawling zom had just about reached Uncle Danny.  The Big Mexican moved and put a boot on the zom's shoulder, pressing down.  It flailed somewhat, but it was good and pinned.

"If we were out here being tourists, that would be one thing," said Uncle Danny.

Liberty nodded in agreement.

"Now," she said.  "If we both go back, we can get two more carts, and Bordeaux."

"Agreed," nodded Uncle Danny.  "We can't leave him."

"We have to be careful," said Liberty.     "Colin's not getting orphaned again this year. Nor Tessy!"

"They won't," said Danny earnestly.

Grabbing the cart, Uncle Danny hopped off the zom and the two headed back towards the highway. There, they left the cart by the side of the road and then headed—at a zom's pace—back towards the grocery store.

"I wonder if we should moan more," smirked Uncle Danny.

"Let's just get out of this in one piece," said Liberty repressively.

"*¡No Pos Wow!* Hey, you already punched me," insisted Uncle Danny. "With boney knuckles no less! So, you're not allowed to still be angry with me anymore."

Liberty rolled her eyes good-naturedly and gave a little smile. "That's true, I guess I can't."

At the grocery store parking lot, they left room between them and the bird-things. However, they still had to avoid the regular ol' garden-variety zoms as well.

"*¡Fíjate!* You got a secret admirer," teased Uncle Danny.

A zom in Gucci stumbled towards them and was soon joined by another in flannel.

"This way," whispered Liberty. "I didn't see anyone under the cars, but..."

"I'll keep my eyes open for ankle biters," nodded Uncle Danny.

To get to the store, they had to move through a row of parked cars. However, as they slid between two vehicles, one of the bird-things came to a stop right before them, blocking their exit.

"Shoot," hissed Liberty with barely a sound.

Behind them, Gucci, and Flannel Zoms were closing.

Uncle Danny then nodded towards the car on his right.

"Over?" he suggested. As slowly as he could, the Big Mexican climbed up onto the car on his right.

Taking his lead, Liberty climbed up onto the car on her left. A quick glance showed that Uncle Danny had already climbed over his car and was clear. However, there were more zoms on the other side of her car.

With trouble on both sides, Liberty placed her feet carefully and started to climb up onto the roof.

Gucci Zom snagged her boot, and it began to tug insistently. Liberty almost tumbled into the zoms, but she did just manage—barely! —to keep her grip on the roof. Leaning forward, she slid as slowly as she could towards the back.

The bird-thing with a magenta tuft was still in front, looking around.

Now, the zoms on the other side of her car were coming straight towards her. Gucci zom was still holding onto her boot and following.

She'd be snack food in a second.

Her top half reached the edge of the trunk.

With the bird at the opposite end, Liberty took a chance and let herself fall forward off the trunk. That pulled her boot out of Gucci's' grip.

She heard a bird noise, which sounded like curiosity, and the car shook as the alien jumped on top of it.

Quickly sliding underneath the car, she disappeared just as the bird-thing looked over the edge of the trunk.

131

Immediately, Liberty heard a soft moan close to her. Her stomach dropped. An ankle biter zom was crawling underneath her car. It was almost upon her. In the confined space under the car, she could not draw a weapon.

Bringing up two fingers, she poked the zom in the eyes.

"Uh! Uh!" grunted the zom, as it shook its head blindly.

The car shook again and the Magenta bird-thing moved away.

A moment later, a hand gripped her shoulder.

"Shit!" hissed Liberty.

"It's okay *Mija*," said Uncle Danny urgently. He helped her out and away from the zoms.

"Okay, that was waaaaay too close," whispered Liberty with a relieved, and terrified, chuckle.

"I wanted to run over," said Uncle Danny, earnestly. "But I couldn't, not with that thing watching."

"It's okay," said Liberty, patting his shoulder, and it was. "Let's just go get those carts."

They moved at a zoms' pace towards the front of the store, but Liberty faltered as they grew near. Uncle Danny looked at her questioningly, but then he realized what she was looking at.

With a consoling voice, Uncle Danny said. "We could keep him safe from the zoms, but who could've guessed alien-birds?" And he said it as much for himself, as for her.

Liberty sighed and slowly turned away from the young soldier's body.

"We've got to get the carts first, and put him in one," she

said.

In the store, the front was still empty. So, they grabbed the carts as quickly as they dared and returned to Bordeaux.

"Feels kinda wrong, stuffing him in a cart," said Uncle Danny sadly.

"I know," agreed Liberty.

A zom was getting close, so she gently pushed at it with her cart. It lost its balance and tipped over. The movement caught the eye of a bird-thing, but it quickly lost interest.

As it went off in another direction, Liberty took a deep breath and moved over to Uncle Danny.

"Let's just get out of here quickly," she said. "Our luck isn't going to last forever."

"Agreed," replied the Big Mexican with feeling.

Gently, they picked up Bordeaux.

"Ugh, he's heavy," hissed Liberty.

"What was he carrying?" grunted Uncle Danny. The broken leg was also flopping around. But they managed to get him into the cart. However, he ended up face first, with his butt in the air.

Uncle Danny made an unhappy sound. "¡*Huy!* He looks so uncomfortable. I know it's stupid, but..."

"No. No. It does feel wrong, disrespectful," said Liberty. "*But* we need to go. When we're safe, we can rearrange him."

Resigned, they headed out with their carts and Bordeaux. Because the bird-things had fanned out to search, it was easy to slip between them. They added the other cart to Liberty's and kept going.

"I hope he's being good," muttered Liberty.

Uncle Danny blinked and then looked at her questioningly.

"Oh! I mean Colin," said Liberty.

Danny grinned. "Ha! I thought you meant Smalls."

"Oh No!" said Liberty with quiet laughter. "No, I feel like we had to sort of dump Colin on Tagg. I just hope they're getting along."

"I know," said Danny. "But we'll be home soon, or at least back to the guys soon."

"Not soon enough," said Liberty. She thought of Colin's happy little grin, which made her smile.

Weaving around the knots of zoms, they moved as fast as they dared and finally reached the TrueAid. Uncle Danny looked around, but he did not see any of the bird-things. Pulling open the front doors, they pushed in the carts and closed the doors behind. Several zoms bumped up against the window, but they could not get in. The creatures moaned sadly.

"Is it stupid that I feel bad for teasing the zoms?" asked Liberty.

"¡Si!" said Uncle Danny seriously.

Liberty looked at him in surprise. But then a big grin grew across his face, to show that he was kidding, and she returned it with relief.

"Hello?" came a tenuous voice from inside the store.

134

Turning, they saw Smalls hefting his M4 Carbine rifle. A great big smile leapt across his face.

"You're safe!" cried Smalls. "You're all safe!"

But a darkness washed across Liberty and Uncle Danny.

"What?" asked Smalls.

***

A short time later, back in the pharmacy, Smalls spoke, softly, sadly. "So, that's what I've been up to." His shoulders drooped. "I hope he gets his In and Out."

Uncle Danny blinked. "*¿Mande?* I mean, 'what'?"

"Bordeaux," said Smalls. "I hope..." And he pointed towards the roof. "I hope that he gets his In and Out burger Up There."

Liberty smiled. "What would heaven be without an In and Out?" Though, she had never eaten there because no Sushi.

"Well, we should probably fill up our carts and go," said Uncle Danny.

Smalls glanced in concern at the shelves. "What if we can't get it all?"

"We get what we can, and worry about the rest later," said Liberty. She rolled a cart into the pharmacy.

Smalls looked at the pharmacy shelves. "I don't know what any of this stuff does. I mean, I can barely remember what I used to take."

Liberty's eyes lit up. Sprinting out of the pharmacy, only

135

to return a moment later.

"A book about pills!" she said excitedly. "That'll help anyone cataloging all this."

"Especially if we get stuck with that," chuckled Uncle Danny.

"Oh! Exactly," said Liberty with concern. "I hope that doesn't happen."

"¡Sin duda!" said Uncle Danny earnestly, and he looked over the shelves. "Should we look for certain things?"

"Let's see how much the carts will hold first," suggested Liberty.

Clearing the shelves turned out to be very easy. Uncle Danny parked the cart under the first set of shelves and—with one big arm—shoved all the pills into it. With two shelves down, Liberty nodded towards the store.

"I'm going to get some over-the-counter stuff," she said. "There might be something handy there."

Liberty moved out of the pharmacy as the guys secured the medication.

But people needed other stuff as well, thought Liberty. Tylenol for one.

Picking up a shopping basket near the pharmacy, she stepped carefully around the ex-zoms, because she felt that that would be rude to step on them.

After collecting all the aspirin, Tylenol, Motrin, and Aleve she could, she glanced up and her heart skipped a beat. It was the same skip as when she had first read "To Kill A Mockingbird".

Shortly, she returned to the pharmacy and poured her

basket into the cart.

Turning, Liberty did a perfect pirouette and remembered wistfully. Her Mom had loved ballet almost as much as Liberty hated it, even though she was really good at it.

At the door, she realized that Uncle Danny was speaking.

"Dora the Explorer?" repeated the Navy Engineer with amusement.

Liberty looked over her shoulder at the top of her new backpack.

"Just picked up a little something," she said briskly.

"It looks pretty full," smiled Uncle Danny.

"It won't slow me down," said Liberty, though she was not sure why she was being so defensive. "I gotta go."

In less than an hour, they had filled two shopping carts to the brim.

Uncle Danny experimentally moved a cart around, and then tipped it a little. Several bottles spilled over the edge of the cart.

"That's not good," he muttered and immediately disappeared into the store.

"Can we grab some food too?" asked Smalls carefully. "And more importantly, drinks."

Liberty's stomach rumbled with assent. "Actually, we should grab something for the road!"

They took a moment to get some food and drink. Smalls appeared with a 2 liter of Mountain Dew in each hand.

The Navy Engineer looked at her defensively. "Don't

judge me."

Trying not to smile, Liberty held up her hands in supplication. "It's all good!"

Uncle Danny reappeared with several boxes of saran wrap.

They quickly wrapped the two shopping carts so that the medicine didn't fall out all over the place.

"Great idea!" grinned Liberty.

"Of course," sniffed Uncle Danny haughtily. But as he looked at the medicine, his face grew thoughtful. When he spoke, his voice was so soft. "Maybe we're pirates now."

"Pirates...?" started Liberty, which set her mind racing. He looked so sad. Then she straightened with excitement. "Yes! Actually, that works! Did you know that some pirates worked for the British Crown, and harried enemy ships? Maybe that's what we're doing? But, instead of the Spanish, we're pirating from the zoms, and—really! —they don't care."

Uncle Danny blinked. "Pirates for the Fleet? That does sound better than common thieves."

Liberty smiled warmly at her friend. "You are many things, but never 'common'. And definitely not a thief."

Uncle Danny grinned with relief. "And this medicine *will* help a lot of people who need it."

They moved the carts towards the front of the store when she realized Uncle Danny was wearing something.

"Are...are you wearing an Avengers backpack?" asked Liberty.

"I don't know what you're talking about," replied Uncle

Danny airily.

Liberty glanced over and saw that the rack of paperback books was now practically empty. She hadn't been able to take as many books as she wanted, because she had needed some lady-stuff too. The Librarian looked back at him with surprise and delight.

"Every library has to start somewhere," he shrugged, not looking at her.

"Thank you!" grinned Liberty and she gave a happy little bounce.

At the front door though, there was no sign of the bird-things.

Smalls suddenly spoke with a searing heat in his voice. "You left him like that?"

As they turned, he gestured at Bordeaux's butt in the air.

"¡*Por Dios!* Sorry!" said Uncle Danny earnestly. "Thank you for reminding us,"

Terribly embarrassed, both he and Liberty took a moment to readjust Bordeaux's body.

"He still looks uncomfortable, but at least he looks a little more dignified now," muttered Uncle Danny.

Smalls suddenly spoke up, nervously. "Hey guys? How are we going to get all this in the boat?"

Liberty and Uncle Danny looked at the contents of their carts, including Bordeaux.

"We're going to need a bigger boat," said Smalls.

Uncle Danny chuckled.

The Engineer blinked. "What?"

"Seriously? You just quoted *Jaws*," said Uncle Danny.

Smalls—and Liberty too—shrugged.

"Tsk," moaned Uncle Danny with mock despair. "I'm surrounded by heathens."

With no bird-things in sight, Liberty and Uncle Danny barreled out of the TrueAid as quickly as they could, knocking a few zoms aside.

Having made a path, Smalls followed, pushing Bordeaux. In no time, they found a way through the slow moving zoms, and Liberty immediately motioned for them to slow down.

"We have to make sure that we only walk a little faster than the zoms, or we'll get noticed," explained Liberty to the Navy Engineer. They started walking back towards Malibu pier.

"So, what do these things look like again?" asked Smalls.

"Just, big birds," said Uncle Danny.

"Um...is it crazy that I want to see one?" asked Smalls tentatively.

"Yes," said Liberty and Uncle Danny in almost perfect unison.

"Still," muttered Smalls with a tiny voice.

Liberty shrugged apologetically. "I guess it's different, once you've seen them in action." Unconsciously, she glanced at Bordeaux with sadness.

"¡Neta! I don't want to go toe to toe with even one of 'em," said Uncle Danny seriously. "They're like *cats*, all sharp points."

Past the In and Out, they made their way towards the beach.

However, when they arrived, there was still a decent stretch of sand between them and their boat.

"You know, if we pull the shopping carts, we should be able to get them across the sand," suggested Uncle Danny.

Pulling his cart onto the sand, he tugged the cart behind him with both hands. The cart was wobbly and resisted, but it did go.

"Better than carrying it," shrugged Liberty.

With varying degrees of success, they got their carts close to the beached boat. However, ten feet from the shore, poor Bordeaux's cart fell over, which stopped their advance. Now, he wasn't just dead, but sandy as well. They quickly picked him up and tried to brush him off.

Winded, they left the carts with Uncle Danny while Liberty and Smalls walked over to their boat. The vessel looked really tiny now.

"It's definitely not going to fit us, and Bordeaux, and all the medicine, is it?" said Liberty slowly, thoughtfully.

"Maybe someone has a bigger boat back at the Fleet?" suggested Smalls.

"Apparently, the problem is lack of fuel," said Liberty thoughtfully. "The submarine that picked us up is now just a floater, at least until we find more fuel." She started to walk back towards the carts.

"Maybe we could..."

"Above!" cried Uncle Danny. He grabbed Liberty and pushed the Librarian towards the boat.

141

One of the bird-things landed in a spray of sand near the road. It gave a shrill cry and shot towards them.

But Uncle grabbed one of the carts full of meds. At the last moment, he shoved it in front of the bird-thing. The alien immediately crashed into it and fell over hard.

"Boat!" cried out Smalls. "Get in the boat!"

Uncle Danny and Liberty ran towards the boat. Smalls shoved it into the water and hopped in. He climbed over the rails towards the outboard motor. Liberty grabbed the boat.

"In!" she ordered of Uncle Danny. He didn't bother to argue and awkwardly climbed in. He dropped his shotgun into the boat because he needed both hands, but he was soon inside.

Liberty dove into the boat and they started to drift away from the shore. After several unsuccessful attempts, the outboard motor started. Smalls aimed them away from the shore, where the medicine and the fallen Bordeaux remained.

"Dammit!" growled Uncle Danny, a fire in his eyes.

## Chapter Eight

**GLANCING BACK TOWARDS** the shore, Uncle Danny suddenly reached down into the boat.

"What...?" started Liberty. She twisted around.

On the beach, the bird-thing had gotten upright. It suddenly jumped into the air, big wings spreading and flew directly towards them.

"Faster!" cried Liberty. A distant part of her heard the panic and chided herself. But another part thought that this was completely reasonable, considering a freaking dinosaur was flying straight towards her.

"It can't go any faster!" replied Smalls, who purposely did not look back.

Almost on top of them, the bird-thing screeched. *"HAJAT!"*

Uncle Danny raised his shotgun. The noise was thunderous. The deer slug slammed into the bird-thing's chest. It instantly dipped to one side. Plowing into the water, the bird slid right under.

"Is it...?" asked Smalls.

The bird-thing surfaced, sputtering, and glared at them for a moment. But then it sank back under, eyes growing unfocused.

Smalls kept going, just in case.

*"Rit Rit Rit!"* cried a voice from the shore.

Back on the sand, two more bird-things, one with a red tuft on its head, was shaking its feathers in frustration. Both looked like they were ready to take flight.

"Veer right!" ordered Liberty.

"What?" asked Smalls.

"Right!"

They turned starboard.

Liberty lifted her rifle and leaned over the edge of the boat. Firing twice at the shore, the bullets kicked up sand between the two birds. Both of the aliens jumped away and immediately retreated.

"That'll make them think twice," laughed Smalls.

Uncle Danny grinned at her in admiration. "Good shooting Tex!"

"Tsk," grumbled Liberty with disappointment. "I was aiming for them."

"But it got the job done," said Uncle Danny encouragingly.

Liberty vacillated for a moment, but then she nodded, a little grudgingly. "True."

Once the boat was safely away, Smalls turned around to get a better look at the shore. The birds were starting to move back towards the shopping carts.

"But...we can't just leave Bordeaux there," hissed Smalls.

Liberty aimed her rifle.

The bird with the red tuft briefly glanced over the ex-Bordeaux, but then the alien stepped away to look at the other carts.

"Looks like we'll have to fight our way back," said Uncle Danny.

"And we still have to get all the medicine in here," said Smalls, worriedly.

Liberty's eyes widened.

"Oh!" she chirped excitedly and immediately began to dig around in the tiny boat.

"What're you looking for?" asked Uncle Danny, curiously.

However, the Librarian did not answer at first. She found a waterproof map and straightened up. The Big Mexican leaned over as she opened it.

"I think Smalls is right," said Liberty at last.

"I am?" asked the Navy Engineer, cautiously. "About what?"

"You said 'we need a bigger boat'," explained Liberty.

Uncle Danny suddenly understood. "*¡Orale!* And Malibu harbor is super close to here!"

145

"To get a new boat?" asked Smalls with growing excitement.

"That's the plan," replied Liberty.

"Okay. Which way is it?" asked Smalls.

"We just need to follow the shore that way," said Liberty, and she pointed away from Malibu pier.

Following the shoreline, they soon reached the harbor, but it was not the answer to their problems.

"Call me crazy," said Smalls. "But shouldn't a marina have like—you know! —boats in it?"

The few boats which had been left, didn't look like they would make it out of the marina, much less back to the pier.

Liberty looked around thoughtfully.

"Well, that's okay," said Uncle Danny encouragingly. "We'll just have to find another way to get that medicine back to the Fleet."

The Librarian suddenly leaned over and pointed her sniper rifle out to sea.

"Mija?" asked Uncle Danny, curiously.

"Not...sure," said Liberty. She looked back at Smalls. "Hey, how're we doing on gas?"

Smalls tapped the spare can, which sounded full.

"You want to check something out?" asked Uncle Danny.

"I'm not in any hurry," admitted Smalls, almost guiltily. "I mean, I've pretty much been below deck since the outbreak. Soooo, it's really kind of nice to see the sun for more than 5 minutes."

"Well," said Liberty with mock seriousness. "We better

not rush back." She looked at Uncle Danny.

"*¡Orale!* That would be terrible of us," said Uncle Danny with the same tone.

The Engineer grinned.

Smalls turned the boat, and they went further out to sea. Shortly, they were at their destination.

"Well...," said Liberty. A smile grew across her face. "Do you think that'll hold all the medicine?"

Uncle Danny pretended to give a mock scowl. "*Pequeñito.* I mean, I've had dogs bigger than that."

They stopped at the rear of a large, anchored yacht.

Liberty turned to Smalls. "We should check the ship. Can you stay here?"

"Just in case we need to leave...," explained Uncle Danny.

"...At top speed," finished Liberty.

After a quick game of roshambo—with rock breaking scissors—Uncle Danny smugly climbed out.

Immediately, he scanned the area—shotgun ready—but all was quiet. Without looking back, he made a quick gesture behind his back.

Liberty climbed onboard and stopped next to Uncle Danny.

"It'll take longer," she said. "But we need to stay together."

"Said no white girl ever," piped up Smalls from behind them.

Liberty's eyes widened with surprise, and she looked

147

back to the tiny boat.

"Quiet you!" smiled Liberty.

Grinning, Smalls ducked his head. "Sorry, couldn't resist."

Liberty switched from her rifle to her silenced Glock 22, in case of close encounters. Moving forward, the two of them started going room to room.

"Man, this is boring," grumbled Uncle Danny as they moved through the deck.

"I like boring!" chirped Liberty.

"You're boring!" grumbled Danny.

"Hey! Just because I'm a librarian...," began Liberty, and they both smiled.

They reached the bedrooms.

"*¡Fíjate!* I got blood over here," hissed Uncle Danny. He moved over to one of the VIP staterooms. But there was no body. However, there was a large pile of stuffed animals on a small bed.

"Well, that's not spooky at all," said Liberty softly, sadly.

"Or heartbreaking," added Uncle Danny. "My niece had a big collection of stuffed animals, but we were never able to get home."

"But at least she's safe now," reminded Liberty.

"*¡Gracias a Dios!*" whispered Uncle Danny.

After a thorough search, they headed above deck.

"I got someone!" hissed Liberty. They went to the port side of the ship.

There—facing away—was a man standing in a long blue robe and a captain's hat.

"Hello? We mean no harm," she said, lowering her Glock a bit. "We didn't know that there were any people onboard."

Slowly, the captain turned around with a low moan.

Uncle Danny sighed. "And no person is."

The zombie, wearing a captain's hat, regarded them for a moment. But it didn't charge. Instead, it just opened its hand, and something clattered onto the deck.

It suddenly lurched towards the edge of the boat, legs smacking into the rail.

The zombie captain pitched forward and tumbled off the edge of the boat.

As it hit the water, Liberty and Uncle Danny ran forward. While she leaned over carefully, the Big Mexican scanned the area, in case of trouble.

Below, the zom sank slowly out of sight.

"Is it weird that I wanted to help him?" asked Liberty.

Quickly, Uncle Danny glanced at the water. The captain's hat bobbed on the surface.

"Yeah," he whispered sadly. "But, then I'm weird too."

Liberty glanced down and gave a start.

"We got keys," she said.

"What? Is that what he was holding?" asked Danny in surprise.

Liberty picked up the ship's keys attached to an orange floaty.

149

"Okay, this is just weird all over," said Liberty. But she shook it off and looked at the Big Mexican. "These are going in a zippered pocket for now, but I say we go over the ship, one more time."

"Agreed," replied Uncle Danny with feeling.

\*\*\*

Smalls came on board, and they guided him to the Pilot House.

"And you're sure it's safe?" asked Smalls again.

Liberty saw Uncle Danny gritting his teeth, so she jumped in quickly.

"We're safe," she said. "Really!"

Smalls stopped. "I know. It's just...it just sounds almost too good to be true. I mean...this is a luxury yacht. Like, the kind Warren Buffett would buy."

"We've checked the ship from top to bottom," assured Liberty.

"But neither of us have driven a boat before," continued Uncle Danny. "So, we were hoping that you could help."

"Oh Yeah! Absolutely," said Smalls with delight.

The Navy Engineer quickly figured out how to make the ship go.

"GPS is still working!" cried Smalls excitedly.

"Really! I wondered if those satellites were still up there," said Liberty, and she looked skyward. "Okay, let's head back and hope that the drugs are still there."

***

Anchored near Malibu Pier, Liberty now lay on the deck of their newly acquired boat. Through her sniper scope, she scanned the shoreline.

"Anything?" asked Uncle Danny. He was standing at the rail, trying to see through the power of squinting.

"Bordeaux's still there, and he looks intact," said Liberty.

"Well, that's something," breathed Uncle Danny with relief. "Poor guy is missing out on a perfect Saturday at the beach. Or whatever day it is."

"Yeah, who knows what day...," chuckled Liberty, but then she started with a fresh horror. "Wait! What day is it? What month?"

With growing concern for his friend, Uncle Danny looked back at her. "*¿Mija?* What's wrong?"

"Did we miss Christmas?" asked Liberty with rising panic. "This would be the first Christmas we celebrate with Colin. If we missed it...if...."

"No," said Uncle Danny firmly. "When we were at that science facility, it was almost November. So, we're probably coming up on Thanksgiving."

Liberty sighed loudly. "Oh. Thank God! That...would've been terrible. We would have been such bad...well, whatever we are to Colin."

With amusement, Danny huffed. "I'm a Fake Uncle. Being an uncle is a lot more fun than being a..." But now he froze with horror.

151

Liberty saw a stricken look on Uncle Danny's face and asked worriedly. "What's wrong?"

"Tessy!" said the Big Mexican with alarm. "She's still at the Armory. We can't just leave her there. Thanksgiving is one thing, but *la Navidad?*"

Liberty blinked. "Damn." She looked down in thought for a moment and then back up at him. "But it's not Christmas yet! We still have time."

"Time to do what?" snapped Uncle Danny. But then he realized how he sounded. "*Perdóname por favor.* I mean, sorry. I just..."

Liberty stood up and faced him. "We still don't have a safe way to get her, or really anyone else out, but...we can always visit her. On or around Christmas Day."

Uncle Danny looked up with interest. "That...that would be nice. And I can bring her a present."

"Maybe we could play Santa for the whole Armory," suggested Liberty.

Suddenly, The Big Mexican stood tall. "I'm not playing Santa."

The Librarian blinked for a moment. "That's okay. I wasn't even thinking that, but...we can say that Santa dropped the presents off with us, to deliver to the kids."

"That...," said Uncle Danny admiringly. "That is really sneaky."

"Thank You," smiled Liberty.

"And if we at least visit her," said Uncle Danny. "I wouldn't be such a rotten uncle then."

Liberty suddenly rounded on him so fast, and so fiercely,

that he almost took a step back.

"Hey!" she growled. "You're not a rotten uncle. You thought you were dying!"

"I know, but…," mumbled Uncle Danny, but he looked away.

Liberty punched his arm.

"Ow!" he said, more in surprise. "Bony knuckles."

*"You are the 'Good Uncle',"* said Liberty fiercely. "To both Tessy and Colin. Now me, on the other hand, in relation to Colin. I'm a… well, I'm definitely a… 'Something' to him."

The Librarian started to lay down again, but bounced back up, and Danny envied her young knees. The Librarian twisted to look at him with a serious expression.

"But!" she said. "We do need to start planning for Christmas. Even if it's just something craftsy for Colin and Tessy. Like…. I don't know…even macaroni art!"

"We will," nodded Uncle Danny.

Satisfied, Liberty lay back down and looked through her scope at the beach.

"I say we just go," she suggested.

"Can you shoot something from here?" asked Uncle Danny curiously.

"Range is good. Little wind," said Liberty thoughtfully. "What're you thinking?"

"Let me and Smalls go in with the tiny boat," said Uncle Danny.

"Dangerous," commented Liberty.

"That tiny boat's too small for Bordeaux, the drugs, *and*

all of us," said Uncle Danny. "So, if me and Smalls go in, you can cover us."

"I... I don't know," said Liberty uncertainly. "I did miss earlier."

"Then you miss," said Uncle Danny firmly. "If me, or Smalls, stay on board, then we'd be just sitting here, twiddling our thumbs."

"True," admitted Liberty reluctantly.

"You'll be fine *Mija*," said Uncle Danny warmly.

***

The moment the tiny boat hit shore, Uncle Danny jumped out and grabbed it. It was not that big, so he was able to tug it partly onto the sand. He held it steady while Smalls climbed out and lifted his M4 Carbine.

The carts were still 10 feet from the water.

Bordeaux sat in his cart, knees to chest. He looked ready to go to some ancient burial mound.

Saran wrap covered the carts with the prescription meds, though one was still knocked over.

Shouldering his shotgun, Uncle Danny began to move forward. After a moment, Smalls followed.

"Hey," whispered Uncle Danny to Smalls. "Can you get that cart upright?"

Moving forward, the Navy Engineer lifted the cart. Once done, he looked around and noticed something.

"Looks like Liberty scared the feathers off one of 'em,"

he chuckled.

Uncle Danny looked at the discarded feathers and saw that—near them—the sand was slightly mounded.

"*Ya te cargó el payaso*," he hissed.

The sand exploded in a half circle around the carts. Uncle Danny involuntarily closed his eyes as he was pelted with sand.

"Get back!" cried Uncle Danny as he tried to move away.

His mind raced. They had been waiting in the sand. And if even two of those things are here...I'm sorry Tessy.

The sand died down and he opened his eyes, steeling himself for a razor-sharp beak.

But there was nothing.

A quick glance showed that Smalls had fallen back, but he was still trying to blink the sand out of his eyes.

Looking around quickly, Uncle Danny did not see any aliens that were ready to pounce.

Regardless, the Big Mexican moved over to Smalls and stood guard. Turning towards the sea, he did give a quick thumbs up to Liberty, because he knew she was probably worried. Then he went back to guarding.

Shortly, the Engineer croaked. "I'm good."

With a glance, Danny saw that, despite red eyes, Smalls was indeed good.

Turning out towards Liberty, he held up one finger, and idly hoped that she didn't shoot him out of annoyance.

To Smalls, he ordered. "Wait here!"

The Big Mexican had been watching from a distance, but

now he needed a closer look. He moved over to the carts.

Just past the nearest cart, he saw a bird-thing, partly buried. Their head and wings had been just under the dry sand, which is how they had created that impromptu sandstorm. But, from the chest down, they were stuck in wet sand, effectively trapped.

"What's going on?" asked Smalls.

Now, the birds were trying to pull themselves out. Leveling his shotgun, he aimed at the closest one. The bird-thing saw and struggled harder to get out of the wet sand.

"Are they trapped?" cried Smalls. "Shoot'em! They killed Bordeaux!"

The Big Mexican made a quick movement and pulled the trigger.

The bird-thing looked surprised. The deer slug had kicked up sand between the first two aliens.

Swiftly, Uncle Danny pointed the shotgun back at the alien.

Without taking its eyes off Uncle Danny, the bird stilled.

Stepping back, Uncle Danny lowered his weapon.

Another of the alien birds began to struggle against the wet sand.

The Big Mexican was there in an instant, pointing his weapon right at the alien. It froze. After a moment, Danny stepped back again and pointed the shotgun downward, once again.

"Smalls?" hissed Uncle Danny.

"Wait? What just happened?" asked the Navy Engineer.

"I think...that I just bought us some time," said Uncle Danny. "I need you to get Bordeaux back to the boat and onto the ship. Then, come back with Liberty."

"Wha...What're you going to do?" asked Smalls.

"I dunno. Hang out. Have a couple fruity drinks with umbrellas in them," chuckled the Big Mexican. He was almost drunk on the idea that he was not dead. That he did not fail Tessy, or Colin. "Maybe the guys here and I'll play a little beach volleyball."

Despite wanting to ask a lot more questions, Smalls quickly left with Bordeaux's body, and Uncle Danny found himself standing guard over four the bird-things. The sun wasn't pounding on the Big Mexican, so that was good. He looked at the bird-thing on the left, which had a red ruft coming out of its head.

"You guys don't speak English, do you?" asked Uncle Danny hopefully.

The bird-thing with the Red Tuft looked at him without responding.

"*¿Hablas español?*" asked Uncle Danny. "No?"

Red Tuft said. "*Tass V Da.*"

Uncle Danny sighed. "I wish I could understand your language."

So, the Big Mexican just stood and waited. He figured that it'd take at least a few minutes for Liberty and Smalls to come back.

But, if he could stand as an altar boy through a whole Catholic mass, he could do this. However, it was starting to get hot. Moving over to the nearest cart, he found a bag full

157

of bottled water on top. He opened one and started to drink.

The bird with the Red Tuft watched him intently. Unconsciously, its purple tongue began to stick out.

Uncle Danny stopped.

All the other aliens were watching him too.

"Do you guys drink water? Aqua?" asked Uncle Danny. He glanced back at the yacht, but their small boat had only just reached it. By the time they got back and took all the medicine offshore, it was going to be another hour or two. Then the aliens would have to lever their way out. He looked up at the sun and felt its warmth, which was mostly pleasant. But that was right now, and he wasn't trapped.

Uncle Danny shrugged and took a new bottle.

"Well, there's nothing else for it," he said to no one in particular. Because he knew what his *Abuela* expected of him.

Stepping towards the bird with the Red Tuft, he saw it stiffen. Squatting, a little way away, Uncle Danny poured a little water out, to show what it was, and then he offered the bottle to the alien.

Hesitantly, the bird-thing stuck out a very long tongue. It then made a little gully in the middle, which reached right down to its mouth. Carefully, Uncle Danny began to pour the water. But when Red Tuft looked like it needed more, the Big Mexican tipped the bottle higher. Once the bottle was empty, he leaned back.

"It's okay, right? It's not poisonous, is it?" asked Uncle Danny.

Red Tuft made a little hoot, which sounded like a good noise.

"*Ung lak?*" asked the bird-thing with the magenta tuft. And Green Tuft made a similar noise.

Uncle Danny got the bag of water bottles and opened one in front of Magenta Tuft. The alien made a similar gully in its purple tongue.

After Danny had given each a bottle of water, he found himself back in front of Red Tuft. He held up the bottle in front of him.

"Water," said Uncle Danny. "We call it water." Then he pointed to himself. "I am Danny. Danny..." And then he pointed to Red Tuft, who watched him cautiously. Finally, Danny smiled genially and looked back towards the yacht. "That's okay. Never mind."

"Rakduson," came a voice.

Danny looked at her in surprise.

Red Tuft spoke again. "Rakduson." And she pointed her beak down to her feathered chest.

Uncle Danny grinned. "Rakduson? *¡Chido!* Pleased to meet you. Well..."

Behind him, the Big Mexican heard the sound of an outboard motor. He stood and felt oddly guilty, but he swatted that idea away. He moved a little to the side. Here, he could watch the aliens and the incoming boat.

Before they were even close, Liberty called out. "Sorry!"

The moment the boat hit sand, she jumped out with her sniper rifle. She was ready to rumble. The alien-birds stiffened.

159

"Sorry it took so long," she said breathlessly.

Uncle Danny smiled. "*¡No manches!* We're all good."

The Librarian came to a halt. She looked between him to the alien birds, trapped in the sand. "We are?"

"*Si.* If you want to start loading the boat, I'm good," said Uncle Danny genially. "Really! I promise."

"O... okay," said the Librarian slowly. As she backed away, slinging her rifle behind her.

Taking one of the carts of medicine, Liberty pulled it towards the water. Smalls was watching the birds in confusion, but she nudged him, and they started dumping the drugs into the small boat.

In the end, she and Smalls had to make two runs to the ship, before they could come back for Danny and the last few meds.

"We're all set," she called from the water.

Danny began to back away. The aliens had settled down into the wet sand pretty good. And instantly, he knew what he needed to do. Turning, he ran back to the boat, but didn't climb in.

"What...?" asked Liberty with concern.

"I just...," started Uncle Danny, but he couldn't find the words. Placing his shotgun in the small boat, he looked at Liberty. "I'll be right back."

"What're you doing?" asked Liberty, confused.

"Got...I've got to do something," said Uncle Danny and he jogged back towards the aliens.

"Is he crazy?" asked Smalls.

"Jury's still out on that one," murmured Liberty.

## Chapter Nine

UNCLE DANNY SPRINTED back towards the alien-birds. But he did stop within a few feet of the red tufted alien, Rakduson, who was still trapped from the chest down in wet sand.

The Big Mexican held up his hands to show that they were now empty. Slowly, he moved around the alien and knelt down behind her.

Immediately, the alien-bird's head whipped around— 180 degrees—on her flexible neck. Danny froze. All his attention was on Rakduson's razor-sharp beak, hovering just in front of him.

Carefully, Uncle Danny leaned down and began to move the wet sand aside. Then, when the alien did not do anything, he started to work more quickly.

Under the bird's weary eye, Danny began to dig out her

torso. At one point, he dug a little too close to her and caught some feathers, giving them a slight yank.

Rak made an aggravated noise.

"Oops. *¡Disculpe! ¡Disculpe!*" muttered Danny swiftly, and he tried to be more careful around the torso.

The alien-bird shifted hard to the left and came out a little. But one of Rak's wings swung wildly and accidentally whapped Magenta Tuft.

"*Yi!*" cried Magenta Tuft indignantly. The two birds began to snap at each other.

Uncle Danny jumped back. However, he soon realized that this was more like old friends bickering, rather than fighting. Brushing the sand off his pants, Danny was about to speak when the device in the back of Rakduson's head emitted a high-pitched noise.

The alien-birds shook violently, as if they were having a seizure.

Danny was about to take a step forward.

Suddenly, the birds began to go crazy.

They thrashed around madly against the wet sand, desperate to get out.

The Magenta Tuft bird whipped her head around and spied Uncle Danny.

She shrieked bloody murder.

Rak turned and saw Uncle Danny as well.

"*Klas du ren!*" shrieked Rakduson with madness in her eyes.

Enraged, Rak started struggling hard against the sand.

162

Pushing down with her wings, the alien-bird began to lever herself out.

In stunned horror, Uncle Danny just stood there frozen.

A gunshot tore through the air. He jumped in surprise and reached for his shotgun. But, with an icy chill, he realized that he did not have it.

The shotgun was in the boat, where Liberty was holstering her sidearm.

"RUN!" cried Liberty—once again! —now that she had gotten his attention.

The Big Mexican sprinted towards the water. From behind, he heard more screaming.

"*HAJAT!*" screeched Rak.

Reaching the boat, which was still partly on the sand, Uncle Danny leaned down. He slammed his shoulder into the bow and pushed the boat into the water.

Liberty had to grab the side of the boat or be pitched face-first into the fiberglass.

Afloat, Uncle Danny hoisted himself partway inside the boat. Liberty reached over and grabbed the back of his belt. She leaned heavily to port to haul him in.

The moment the Big Mexican tumbled into the bottom of the boat; Smalls started the outboard motor. The Navy Engineer turned the boat around and raced back towards their ship.

"What happened?" asked Liberty, confused, and worried.

But Danny did not answer. Utterly perplexed, he just shrugged his shoulders. So quietly, Liberty just crouched

163

by him. Facing the beach, she held her sniper rifle ready.

Most of the alien-birds on the shore were still too busy getting out of the wet sand. But Rakduson was now free. She shook her feathers fiercely.

Seeing the small boat racing away, Rak gave chase. Uttering a high-pitched scream, she ran towards the shore.

Hearing that, Uncle Danny's head whipped around.

"No, no, no, no," he muttered, almost as if in prayer. He glanced at his shotgun, still on the bottom of the boat, but he hesitated.

Liberty noticed but turned her focus back to the alien-bird, just in case it managed to get airborne.

Rak was flapping her wings hard. But even from the small boat, Uncle Danny could see chunks of wet sand falling off. Instead of going up, Rakduson plowed right into the water. Enraged to a point of almost madness, the alien-bird began to attack the waves.

"We're almost there," called out Smalls.

While Uncle Danny watched the aliens on shore, Liberty turned to Smalls.

"When we reach the big ship, can you head straight to the pilot's house?" asked Liberty. "I'll take care of this boat if you can get us going. Annnnnd, can you please take your rifle?"

"I was watching the big boat as well," said Smalls quickly. "I didn't see anything flying around it."

Liberty started to open her mouth.

He hastily added. "But I'll bring my rifle, just in case."

The Librarian smiled gently. "Thank you. I just..." But her voice trailed off.

"It's okay," said Smalls, and it was. They had lost one of their own on this trip, so he understood a little over-protectiveness.

Inwardly, the Navy Engineer suddenly froze. He was including himself with Liberty and Danny. So, he soberly reminded himself that he was just helping today. A temp. Tomorrow, he'd be back on the carrier, away from the sun. But, he decided, it was good while it lasted. And he gave a little smile.

The moment they reached the yacht, Liberty jumped aboard and tied off their little boat. She helped Smalls off. The moment the Engineer was on board, he shouldered his M4 Carbine and headed straight for the pilot's house.

Liberty emptied the boat of the last remaining meds, which she literally dumped with the others.

The ship's engine started, and she raced back to the small boat.

"Uncle Danny?" called out Liberty. "I need you to come on board."

The Big Mexican blinked and looked up at her with a furrowed brow.

"*¿Mande?*" he asked.

Unsure of what he said, Liberty gestured towards the big ship. "I need you to come up here. I don't quite trust that rope that's holding that little boat on. And I *can't* leave you behind!" She smiled and added with a little manic nervousness. "Colin'd never forgive me, and rightly so!"

"What?" he asked softly. He did not move at first, but then he nodded more attentively. "Oh. Okay. Sorry."

Liberty helped Uncle Danny onto the ship. Instantly, she jumped back into the boat for his shotgun, which he had left behind. The moment that she was in the little boat, the big ship started to move and the rope between it and her little boat went taut.

The Librarian nearly tumbled face-first into the fiberglass, but she caught herself at the last second. A quick glance showed that the rope was stretched almost to its breaking point.

But it held.

Letting out a breath of relief, Liberty saw that there was only a small gap between the boat and ship.

Uncle Danny was standing a little way off, staring off into the distance. She did not want to bother him, so she began to climb carefully forward.

"*Mija!?!*"

Suddenly, the Big Mexican was at the little boat. He reached out and helped get her safely onboard.

"Thanks," said Liberty. She glanced back and was satisfied the small boat would be good.

However, when she turned back around, she saw that her friend was back to staring at the shore. His lined face set into a deep frown.

Cradling Uncle Danny's shotgun in the crook of her arm, the Librarian looked back herself. Luckily, the alien-birds were not following. On the sand and looking sopped to the bone, Rak shook her feathers in annoyance, but she was

166

now facing away from them at least.

Still, Liberty went over to Uncle Danny and waited until the shore disappeared. Once the beach was gone from sight, the Big Mexican slowly turned and gave a start.

"¡*Újule!* What're you doing here?" asked Uncle Danny in confusion. His brow furrowed. "Wait? Were you guarding me?"

Liberty sniffed dismissively. "As if 'The Uncle Danny' needs guarding." She absently handed him his shotgun. "Now, let's get out of the sun. We don't want to get heat stroke."

After a moment's hesitation, Uncle Danny followed her. They walked to the closest room, and he found its floor was nearly carpeted with prescription meds. To his surprise, he found himself chuckling.

"No wonder it took you so long," said Uncle Danny.

"A few escaped to sea," said Liberty apologetically. "But, not as many as I thought would."

"We're winging it *Mija*," reassured Uncle Danny, who had noticed her tone. "This *chamba*...I think we did the best we could, under the circumstances."

"I guess," muttered the Librarian.

"And it was the first day trying this," said Uncle Danny. "First days are often hard. You should've me and Pepe the first day his restaurant opened. *¡Que horror!* What a mess!"

Liberty looked at him and gave a little chuckle, feeling better. It had been a long day and losing some of the medicine had really frustrated her.

"Maybe garbage bags next time," suggested Uncle

Danny helpfully.

"Or. maybe a tight net bag that won't break so easily," said Liberty.

"True," nodded Uncle Danny with a chuckle. "We don't want to have a plastic bag split in the middle of the street."

"We'll have to ask," said Liberty. "Maybe the carrier— Or one of the fishing boats! —has something that we can use for our hauls."

"Well, if we're pirates, wouldn't that be plunder?" asked Uncle Danny.

"Arrr, that's true matey," said Liberty in her best pirate impression, and the Big Mexican gave a bark of laughter, which seemed to surprise him. She sighed in mock pain. "Whhhhaaaaat? I'm just trying to get into the spirit of things?"

Uncle Danny nodded with mock diplomacy. "That's true. I shouldn't laugh. Arrr, that was a fine bit of pirating."

"Arrr," grinned Liberty, but then her face turned thoughtful. "Okay, that's pretty much it for my pirate vocabulary."

"We'll have to learn more," said Uncle Danny with mock seriousness. "So that we can do our job properly."

"Pirates for the Fleet," grinned Liberty.

Uncle Danny looked across the carpet of medicine and spotted Bordereaux's body in the corner. Liberty followed his gaze, and her smile drifted away.

"We should wrap him in something," said Liberty. "And maybe also see if we got some bags on board, to put these drugs in. Want to join me in the search?" She waited a moment, but he did not reply.

Trying not to step on any medications, the Librarian moved closer and lightly touched her friend's arm. Uncle Danny gave a start, whipping around.

"What?" he asked in concern.

"When you're ready to talk, I'll be ready," said Liberty softly. "In the meantime, we need to get some bags for the meds. And something for..." She did not finish, but just nodded at Bordeaux.

"Oh. Okay," he nodded.

They were part way through their search when Uncle Danny slowed to a stop and gave a very long sigh.

"Something happened on the beach," he said.

Liberty turned and waited patiently for Danny to finish collecting his thoughts.

"They're not dumb," he said at last.

"What? Oh, the bird-things?" asked Liberty.

"I... I don't know that I could call them 'things' anymore," admitted Uncle Danny. "They're definitely intelligent."

"How intelligent?" asked Liberty. "Like ant, bunny, gorilla or human?"

Uncle Danny looked at her with a curious surprise. "Bunnies are intelligent?"

"Sure, to a degree," said Liberty. "My bunny Princess— who I had when I was a little —got two biscuit-treats every night. She'd wait by her door, but sometimes when she got the second one, she'd run away, in case I tried to pick her up. Which was a very valid concern because she was very fluffy."

"So, you think...," he started.

"No. I know," said Liberty. "She could count to two."

"Okay then," replied Uncle Danny with surprise.

"So, how intelligent are these aliens?" asked Liberty.

The Big Mexican replied immediately. "Human."

Liberty's eyes widened. "Really?"

"Did you notice the one with the red ruft on their head? I identified myself as Danny, and when I pointed at them, they said 'Rakduson'."

"So... they have names," muttered Liberty slowly.

"And they can say their names," said Danny. "Until...well, until whatever it was that happened...I thought they might be very intelligent."

"But then they...," started Liberty. However, she didn't know how to soften it. "...um, went a little...crazy."

"I just...," began Uncle Danny, but he stopped.

Liberty gave a warm smile. "It's going to be okay."

The Big Mexican returned the smile and nodded. "Okay, *Mija*."

*** 

Rear Admiral Antony Cirilo stood at the bow of the yacht with an expression of shock and wonder.

170

Uncle Danny however was distracted by the fact that the Naval officer's uniform always looked cleaned and pressed. He was wondering if the Rear Admiral did that himself when Cirilo finally spoke.

"I mean...," started the Rear Admiral. "...I know when you radioed that you had found a yacht, but..."

"That we were just exaggerating?" asked Liberty, with amusement. She had never seen the Rear Admiral at a loss for words. Not that she had known him that long, but she had the feeling that this didn't happen often.

"But *this* is a real, honest-to-goodness yacht," said Cirilo. "So, what're your plans for it?"

"We're not turning it over," said Liberty firmly.

The Rear Admiral chuckled. "I wouldn't."

"And we also figured that you might need us to do more work," added Uncle Danny.

"True," agreed Cirilo with a nod. He was about to say more, but several sailors appeared carrying Bordeaux's body.

A shadow fell over Liberty's face.

"We didn't even know about those aliens until Bordeaux was...," said Liberty urgently, her voice rife with guilt. And she could not finish.

The Rear Admiral nodded sympathetically and said swiftly. "I understand. It can happen like that. A new player shows up, and suddenly someone is..." He stopped. "Well, please know that if he has any family in the Fleet, I'll make sure that they know that he went trying to help us all. And we'll make sure that he gets a proper burial."

"We'd like to be there," said Liberty immediately. "When you...well, probably bury him at sea."

The Rear Admiral nodded solemnly. "I'll make sure it happens."

Liberty looked at Uncle Danny and Smalls.

"It's only right," she said, almost defensively.

"Absolutely," agreed Uncle Danny quickly.

Smalls nodded heartily. "Oh Yeah! For sure."

"Okay," said Liberty slowly. Then she turned back to Cirilo. "Did you just imply that you might have more work for us?"

"Yes," replied the Rear Admiral. "One of our fishing trawlers spotted a tanker adrift. She might be carrying oil, diesel or gas."

"Really?" asked Smalls in surprise. "Intact?"

"Looks like it," said the Rear Admiral to the Navy engineer.

"And you need us to check it out," nodded Liberty.

Smalls looked at Liberty and said excitedly. "We're going to need more fuel for the yacht." But then he froze, and a burning embarrassment rushed up to his face. "I mean...you're going to need more fuel to get wherever you're going."

"We can provide the fuel," interjected Rear Admiral. "And the GPS coordinates."

"But the tanker might have drifted," said Smalls to Liberty. "You may have to go in a circle until you spot it. But it's big, so you should be good."

172

Liberty glanced at Uncle Danny and then back to the Rear Admiral.

"Can we have a moment?" she asked of Cirilo.

The Librarian and the Big Mexican stepped a little way away from the Navy men. Smalls almost followed. But luckily, he remembered his place. However, embarrassment still coursed through him. He turned, a little awkwardly, to the Rear Admiral and tried to think of something to say.

"So…," murmured Smalls. "At least the weather is nice. We could be up near Alaska."

"True," agreed Cirilo absently, but he was—without looking directly at them—keeping an eye on Liberty and Uncle Danny. The two were in a quiet conference, a little way away.

"Anything interesting happening on the carrier?" asked Smalls.

But the Rear Admiral did not respond.

In desperation, Smalls started whistling. However, he couldn't think of any songs, so he started whistling absently. Suddenly, he started wondering if his whistling was bothering the Rear Admiral, so he stopped, just in case.

After a moment, Liberty and Uncle Danny came back.

"Is everything okay?" asked the Rear Admiral of the two. There was a trace of concern in his voice.

"There's one more thing," said Liberty.

Smalls looked out to sea.

"First, to take this tanker, we'll have a better chance if Mr. Smalls is with us," said Liberty. "If he'd like to help us

173

more."

The Navy Engineer looked back in surprise.

Uncle Danny added. "Really, it'll be better if he drives this ship. We wouldn't want to run it aground somewhere."

"I mean, we could do it if we had to," shrugged Liberty, uncertainly.

"But we don't want to mess it up," said Uncle Danny.

"That'd just be embarrassing," finished Liberty.

"Wait? What?" asked Smalls in surprise.

"Done," said the Rear Admiral.

Smalls looked at Cirilo in shock. "Wait? What?"

The Rear Admiral looked at him. "You're on temporary assignment to the..." He stopped and looked at Liberty. "What's this ship called?"

"Actually, she doesn't have a name," supplied Smalls with keenness. "Maybe she was so new that they didn't even name her yet?"

"Okay," said the Rear Admiral, and he turned to the Navy Engineer. "You're assigned to this ship—whatever-it's-called—for the time being. But *Remember This*, you are still a member of the United States Navy, and I expect you to conduct yourself as such."

"Yes sir," said Smalls. He saluted smartly and tried not to grin like an idiot.

The salute had not been necessary, but the Real Admiral gave one back indulgently and said to the Engineer. "I'll get you the GPS coordinates, though the tanker has probably drifted since then, as you said."

"And could I get any weather maps for that area over the past few days Sir?" asked Smalls.

"Done," said Cirilo.

"I'll find her," said Smalls, and he saluted once more out of happiness.

The Rear Admiral nodded with a hint of a smile, and then turned to Liberty.

"And how many men do you need?" asked Cirilo.

"Men?" asked Liberty in confusion.

"He's trying to set you up on a date, I think," whispered Uncle Danny with mock seriousness.

Liberty gently punched the Big Mexican's arm.

"Bony," he muttered with an unrepentant smile.

"No, I mean soldiers," said the Rear Admiral quickly, a little off-guard. "To take the tanker."

In surprise, Liberty looked at Uncle Danny.

Her face contorted, and he nodded in agreement. She turned back.

"No one," said Liberty.

Cirilo's brow knitted. "What?"

"I don't want to risk any more people," explained Liberty.

"*¡Orale!*" nodded Uncle Danny fervently.

"I mean, if we can't handle it, we'll come back," said Liberty. "But..."

"We're going to be okay," said Uncle Danny to Cirilo.

175

"We won't bite off more than we can chew."

"You've certainly proved yourself," nodded the Rear Admiral with a little smile. "I'll have your fuel and GPS coordinates before nightfall. Can you leave tomorrow?"

"Should be," shrugged Liberty.

For a few more minutes, they made some small talk with the Rear Admiral, but he soon had to return to the Fleet.

Smalls turned to Liberty and Uncle Danny.

"Thank you," he said.

Liberty blinked. "For what?"

"Well, for one thing," chuckled the Navy Engineer. "Not saying 'You're killing me Smalls' at any point."

Uncle Danny blinked. "What?"

Liberty looked at the Big Mexican. "It's from a movie called 'The Sandlot', which we should show to Colin, because I love it." Then she turned to Smalls. "I figured you'd heard it already."

"Still, thank you," smiled Smalls.

"Okay," said Liberty with a clap of her hands. "Now that we know that the Admiral isn't going to fight us for this ship, I do want to check in on Colin and Tagg."

"Yeah! They're going to go crazy over this," grinned Uncle Danny.

"We can have a sleepover!" said Liberty with delight, but then her face fell.

"What?" asked Uncle Danny worriedly.

"Oh No! We should've grabbed some junk food," said Liberty and she sighed. "Wish we could hit a 7-Eleven."

"We have Mountain Dew," said Smalls excitedly.

"But...that's your personal stash," said Liberty earnestly.

"I'm happy to share," said Smalls, and then he added earnestly. "Really!"

"And *Cobayo* probably shouldn't have that much of that anyways," said Uncle Danny. "He's liable to swim back and forth to the Coast a couple of times, if he drinks too much Mountain Dew."

"Then he can get Doritos while he's there," suggested Smalls

Liberty laughed out loud, and it felt good.

"So then," she said with a soft, warm smile. "Let's go get the boys and... Oh! Then we really should go over the rest of the ship and see what we have."

"Like an inventory?" asked Uncle Danny unhappily, rolling his eyes.

"The previous owner's might've brought junk food in the kitchen," suggested Smalls.

"So true!" said Liberty and she beamed at the Engineer.

"Then we get to pick our rooms," smiled Liberty, and she made a point of looking at Smalls. "All of us."

"Okay," exclaimed the Navy Engineer, happily.

"Now you're talking!" grinned Uncle Danny.

"But first, the boys," said Liberty.

# 1st Epilogue for Volume Two

**COLIN CRASHED INTO** Liberty so hard, she almost fell back on her butt. However, as she began to teeter, Uncle Danny was suddenly there with a steadying hand on her back. He braced her until she got her footing.

The boy had wrapped his arms around her so tightly, she could barely breathe.

And the Librarian enjoyed every second of it.

"Hi sweetie," she said, happily.

Though she did shift a little, so his face wasn't in her boob. Then she hugged him.

With the boy's face pressed against her sternum, she soon realized that Colin was mumbling furiously. However, she couldn't make it out.

Suddenly worried, she grabbed his shoulders and pried

him back a bit, so that she could hear him.

"...thought that you were gone," he continued, still looking down. "An' you might not be coming back."

"I said that it wasn't that dangerous," said Liberty gently. Though the memory of Bordeaux's empty eyes made her stomach lurch. So, she amended it. "Me and Uncle Danny are safe. And we made a new friend."

Colin looked up with tears in his eyes.

"Honey! What's wrong?" asked Liberty swiftly and she glanced up at Tagg.

The scientist said. "He really was worried that you might not Want to come back. To us..." His eyes grew wide, but he quickly corrected himself. "I mean, him."

Liberty breath caught. "Oh no!" Panicked, he looked down at him and asked gently. "Why did you think that?"

The boy looked down, unable to meet her eyes and mumbled. "Now that you got me here, the antidote or vaccine, or whatever Dr. Tagg is making.... it's now safe. So...you didn't really have to come back."

"Bullshit," said Liberty.

And all the guys looked at her in surprise, most especially Uncle Danny.

The Librarian looked Colin dead in the eyes. "I had to come back because I missed you."

The boy's mouth opened, but no words came out.

Liberty hugged him fiercely, not caring that she had squished his face against a boob this time.

"I had to come back," she said with finality.

180

"When we were out there Colin," said Uncle Danny. "That was our biggest concern. Getting back to you."

Liberty glanced up at Tagg, who for such a big guy stood hunched over, a little way away.

"You too," she smiled softly.

And Tagg straightened with surprise and delight. He cautiously pointed to himself just in case Hugh Grant was behind him.

The Librarian grinned with all her teeth at the Scientist. "Yes, you."

Leaning back a little to look up at her, Colin asked. "What did you say?"

"Just...really, I'm just saying that I'm happy to be back here," said Liberty and she put a little kiss on top of his badly shorn head. She was going to need to figure out how to cut hair, sooner rather than later.

Colin pulled slightly away to look past her to Uncle Danny.

"D... did you really want to come back here too?" asked the boy. And he sucked in his little chest, steeling himself.

Instantly, Uncle Danny huffed like a lion and bellowed. "*¡Fíjate!* Okay, we need to make a rule!"

Everyone blinked in surprise.

Far down the metal corridor, a sailor stuck his head through a door to see what was going on.

Colin looked like he was ready to bury his head again. Without letting go of him, Liberty shifted so that she could look at Uncle Danny too.

The Big Mexican continued with a normal voice, but still with a fierce scowl on his face. "*Mi Abuela* had one important rule: No lying! Don't tell any lies, even little ones. 'Cause even little ones can lead to big ones."

"That sounds like a good rule," nodded Liberty seriously.

"Everyone who wants to adopt this rule," said Uncle Danny in his terribly serious voice. "Say '*Si*'."

All of the adults said "*Si*".

Uncle Danny looked at the boy expectantly.

Seeing the Look, the boy started. "What?"

"We need your vote," said Uncle Danny.

"Oh! Really?" said Colin excitedly. He nodded quickly. "Yes...I mean, '*Si*'."

"*Gracias*," said the Big Mexican and then he continued. "The truth is that I'm sad that I don't warrant a hug too."

"Warrant?" asked Colin in confusion.

Liberty chuckled warmly and said to the boy. "He's sad that you didn't hug him."

"Oh!" said Colin and he jolted away from the Librarian and plowed into Uncle Danny, who was not easily bowled over.

Far down the corridor, the sailor pulled his head back in his room, not wanting to see any more gooey, syrupy stuff.

Uncle Danny gave the boy a big hug and said. "We *both* wanted to come back here. Liberty and me. It was the most important thing. I just wish we could get Tessy too." He gave a sigh.

Liberty reached out and patted Danny's shoulder sympathetically.

"Tessy is your niece, right?" asked Colin. He pulled out of Uncle Danny's arms, but he didn't go far. "Why don't you two just get her, like you did with me?"

"It's not that easy," said Uncle Danny heavily.

"Why not?" asked Colin in confusion.

"With you, we didn't have a choice," said Liberty.

"Because of the aliens?" asked the boy.

"If one of the safe houses had had a gigantic gun on top...," said Uncle Danny, and he smiled, despite himself.

"That'd be fun to see," added Liberty, with a grin of her own. "Boom!"

Colin asked, his brow furrowed. "So, you had to bring me here, but not Tessy?"

Liberty looked at him. "It's not safe to travel on the Coast."

"But you two do it," said Colin, a little hotly.

"Yes, but we also lost someone on this trip," said Uncle Danny softly.

"What?" asked Tagg as he stepped forward.

"How?" asked Colin.

Liberty and Uncle Danny looked at one another and instantly came to the same conclusion.

"We're not protecting him by keeping secrets," said Liberty.

Uncle Danny nodded in agreement. "Rule one."

So, they told the two about the alien-birds and, without going into details, that Bordeaux had been killed by them.

"The concern, really...," finished Uncle Danny. "..., is getting Tessy out safely."

"Yeah," nodded Colin sadly.

"But we did find a little something when we were out there?" said Liberty.

"What?" asked the boy excitedly.

"We found a little boat for when all of us are not traveling," said Liberty.

"Us?" asked Colin and Tagg in unison.

"It's the biggest we could find," sighed Uncle Danny with mock seriousness. "I hope it's good enough."

Liberty grinned. "Follow me."

## 2nd Epilogue for Volume Two

**TAGG CALLED OUT** from the kitchen that night. "I got Tostitos!" But then he faltered. "I mean, it's not Doritos, but..."

"No! That's great!" replied Liberty from nearby.

"And there's a big bag of M&M's!" added Tagg.

"Regular, or..."

"Peanut!!!"

The Librarian cried out in ecstasy! "We got junk food!!!!!"

## Interlude One

**LIKE A GHOST,** Uncle Danny slid silently through their newly acquired yacht.

*A yacht,* he thought uncomfortably. He almost hated the word. He could hear his *Abuela* talking about wasteful spending. But then he realized that, since they didn't actually pay for it, and they certainly *did not* steal it, she might be okay with this.

Danny opened a small glass door and removed his prize. The former owner had stocked the ship with a few amenities.

Stepping lightly, he went up onto the deck and into the cool night air. He stepped towards the yacht's helipad.

Seriously, who needs a helipad, he wondered.

But then he considered that—maybe—they had earned a

little good fortune. He and Liberty had tried to save as many people as possible, since this whole zombie-virus-thing had broken out.

A deck chair, which was admittedly a little too *too fancy* for him, was now set up on the helipad. Settling down into it, Uncle Danny sighed with contentment. Okay, it was *too fancy*, and tacky, but it sure was comfy, he admitted, if only to himself.

Dr. Miles McTaggert had halted the progress of the zombie virus in Danny's system, but it had not gone away completely. Because of this, Dr. Tagg was reluctant to let Uncle Danny go on dates date, have any liquor, or even eat fried food, but this...

Savoring the moment, Uncle Danny lifted up his prize and smelled it. A hint of rum wafted up.

Danny grinned mischievously. "But you didn't say anything about cigars." Reaching into his coat pocket, he fished around for his lighter.

Suddenly, his eyes popped up.

There was something on the water.

At first, he thought it might be a whale. And wouldn't that be a great thing to watch with his cigar. But this whale was skimming over the water, directly towards them.

"*¡Joder!*" hissed Uncle Danny.

He jumped up and ran down through the great ship. Not even waiting to knock, he burst into Liberty's room.

"*Mija!*" he called out.

Liberty jerked awake. "Danny?"

"We got company," he said.

"Not friendly?" asked Liberty as she jumped out of bed and started pulling on the first thing she found, a pair of shorts.

Swiftly, Uncle Danny turned around as she did so, but he continued speaking. "I... don't know. But they're heading towards us, fast. No lights."

"Colin? Smalls?" asked Liberty.

"I'm going to tell them next," said Uncle Danny.

Leaving her, he went to Brent Small's room. The Navy Engineer had taken a VIP room in which someone had died. They had yet to pull up the blood-stained carpet. The others had been uncomfortable, but Smalls didn't believe in the supernatural.

Without knocking, Uncle Danny burst into the room. "Get up! We got trouble."

"What?" cried Smalls. While sleeping, he had gotten completely tangled in his sheets. He struggled to untie himself and fell off the bed.

Jumping forward, Uncle Danny grabbed one end of the sheet and yanked hard. It sent Smalls spinning, but he was free.

"What's going on?" asked Smalls, trying to ignore his momentary dizziness.

"Someone's coming in without any lights on."

The engineer froze. "Colin? Liberty?"

"Liberty knows. I'm heading to Colin next."

Smalls grabbed his M4 Carbine rifle and took several magazines for it. He ran past the Big Mexican and into the corridor.

189

Uncle Danny faltered, but then asked, haltingly. "Um...pants?"

Smalls, clad only in a Mudvayne T-Shirt and boxers, shook his head. "No time. Where do you need me?"

Uncle Danny hesitated for only a second, but then he moved past the Engineer.

"Can you protect Colin?" asked Danny. "I know it's not a glamorous job, but..."

Smalls held up a hand and Danny stopped.

"With my life," vowed the Engineer earnestly. "Besides, I'm not a SEAL, so I'll probably be better on defense."

"It'll make me feel better," replied Uncle Danny truthfully.

They stopped outside Colin's room. This time though, Uncle Danny knocked softly on the boy's door before opening it.

"Whatza?" asked the boy, half-asleep.

"Colin, I need you to get out of bed, and hide in one of your closets. Right now," said Uncle Danny in a calm, measured voice.

Wide-eyed, the boy sat bolt upright.

Uncle Danny continued. "Someone's coming towards us in a boat, and we don't know who they are."

"But it's the middle of the night," said Colin with alarm.

"¡Orale! That's why I want you to hide. And Mr. Smalls is going to stay in here too," said Uncle Danny.

Smalls slapped a magazine into his M4 Carbine and moved into the room. He glanced at the boy.

"You're going to hide, and I'm going to go...," started Smalls as he surveyed the room. He walked to the other side of the bed. There was a space between the wall and the mattress. "If Colin is in one of the closets, then I'm going to crouch behind the bed and shoot anyone who comes in."

"Um...," started Danny.

"Well, anyone that isn't you, or Liberty, of course," added Smalls quickly.

Uncle Danny smiled. "Good plan."

Surprised, Smalls returned the smile. "Thank you. Especially since I just came up with it."

Uncle Danny turned to the boy, who was scrambling up. "Okay Colin don't come out unless Mr. Smalls, me, or Liberty call for you," said Uncle Danny. "Can you do that?"

Colin nodded nervously.

Uncle Danny put a reassuring hand on the boy's shoulder. "It's going to be okay."

As Colin went to hide, Smalls crouched down.

Uncle Danny closed the door gently.

The second it clicked shut, he sprinted to his room. Reaching in, he grabbed his loaded shotgun, that was set above the door, to make it harder for little paws to get at.

Heading back to where Liberty waited, she pointed aft, and he nodded in agreement.

They moved quietly.

Uncle Danny went to hold his shotgun with both hands, but he found that his left hand was still full of cigar.

191

Liberty saw it and gave him a Disapproving Look.

"Dr. Tagg never said I couldn't," he whispered and even to him, it sounded pretty defensive.

Before she could comment further, they heard someone up ahead.

A voice at a normal volume suddenly said. "It's too dark."

Another person, Judah, hissed. "Keep your voice down. And don't even think about turning on a light again. You'll give us away."

"I'm just saying," grumbled the first voice, Reuben.

There was the sound of someone getting hit with a fist. Then it was quiet again.

Liberty stopped and put out her hand out to touch Uncle Danny's arm. He stilled and looked at her. Little LED lights placed near the floor gave just enough light to see each other. She pointed at him and then down a cross corridor. Then she pointed at herself to keep going straight. She brought both hands together.

*Pollas en vinagre*, he thought. It didn't help that she was right. Uncle Danny nodded in agreement. Reluctantly, he moved away from Liberty, even though it pained him.

If anything happened to her tonight, he would never forgive himself.

But this was their best chance.

Moving silently, Uncle Danny halted near the door to the movie room.

From inside, the first voice, Reuben, said in a loud whisper. "This place is so big. I wanna pick my own room."

"Will you shut up!" hissed the second voice, Judah.

Again, there was the sound of a fist hitting meat and someone fell to the floor.

Seizing the moment, Uncle Danny shot the corner, he saw three men by the pleather couches.

*"What're you doing here?"* roared Uncle Danny.

The owner of the second voice, Judah, was standing over Reuben, who was sprawled onto the floor.

With the stock of his shotgun, Uncle Danny hit Judah in the head, who went down like a sack of potatoes.

"What the...!" cried the third man, Benjamin. He started to swing around with his handgun.

Instantly, Uncle Danny dropped and landed on top of someone, knocking the wind right out of Reuben.

The third man, Benjamin, shot twice at empty air, but he was quickly getting his aim again.

The shotgun was pinned between Uncle Danny and Reuben. Before Danny could roll off, a bullet hit Benjamin in the chest. The hijacker's handgun hit the ground and Uncle Danny scooped it up.

Just as Reuben was getting his breath back, Uncle Danny punched him hard.

Scrambling to his knees, Danny brought up his shotgun in his other hand. But the three men were down. Still, he moved a little further back to cover them.

"Danny!" called out Liberty from the other side of the room.

"I'm okay," he replied loudly. "I have them."

"What happened to waiting for me?" she asked in a high, frosty voice.

"Um...I saw an opportunity," he replied, a little sheepishly.

"Turning on the lights," said Liberty, and that was all the warning she gave.

Uncle Danny flinched at the brightness. But he powered through it to keep guard on the intruders.

"Ugh, it's too bright," moaned Reuben.

Liberty came in through the other door and walked over. But she did not go over to the men. Instead, she went over to the Big Mexican and looked him over.

Satisfied that Uncle Danny was unharmed, she let out a breath of relief and rested her head against his shoulder for a second. Straightening up, she turned to look at the men on the floor.

"You recognize them?" asked Liberty.

From the floor, Reuben huffed indignantly. "Of course. They're my brothers."

Uncle Danny aimed his shotgun at the man. "She wasn't talking to you!" And then he added. *"Pendejo."* He glanced at Liberty. "I've never seen 'em before."

The one brother that Liberty had shot, Benjamin, was starting to paw at his bulletproof vest.

"Hey look!" said Liberty with relief. "He's alive!"

"Ow," whined Benjamin.

"Serves you right," sniffed Liberty. But then, she turned

to Danny. "I don't know them either. What do we do with them now?"

"Throw them overboard?" suggested Uncle Danny, half-jokingly.

"Tempting," muttered Liberty. "But first, we should call the Fleet."

"Actually, *first,* can you see if Smalls can get us some rope?" asked Uncle Danny.

***

"And what did you do then?" asked an attorney from the Army's Judge Advocate General Corps.

Uncle Danny looked up at the woman in her crisp uniform. The African American woman fixed him with radiant, intelligent eyes.

"Um, we tied them up," replied Uncle Danny, a little nervously. He had never been in a court before for a criminal case.

"Why didn't you just shoot them?" asked the JAG, Rosita Jefferson.

Uncle Danny blinked. "Um, what?"

"I'd wager that most people, if they'd caught these men sneaking aboard their boat in the middle of the night...," started Jefferson.

"Your honor," called out the Defense Attorney, Caleb Nakamura.

The JAG attorney only looked to the judge.

"I'm only trying to set the scene," explained Jefferson.

"A little less scene," replied Judge William Banks, but not unkindly.

Jefferson looked back at Uncle Danny.

"You made it a point to take the three men alive," she said.

"Um, well, yes," said Uncle Danny. "I never really thought about it. I mean, it's one thing to shoot zoms when there is danger..." His voice trailed off. "I mean—*Really!*—we got lucky."

"Why is that?" asked the JAG.

"Because they had some serious firepower," replied Uncle Danny.

"Thank you," said Jefferson with a softer tone. "No more questions."

***

Looking rode hard and put away wet, Uncle Danny plopped into a folding chair beside Liberty.

In front of them, there was a lull in the ad hoc courtroom aboard the Carrier.

"You did really good," she said encouragingly, bumping shoulders against his arm.

"Thanks," replied Uncle Danny absently. He loosened the tie that the Rear Admiral had lent him, but carefully, so that he didn't hurt it. "I can't wait to take this off."

"Don't like ties?" asked Liberty with mirth.

"It's a patterned tie on a patterned shirt," grumbled the Big Mexican. "I hate that. Either one or the other should have a patter..."

Suddenly, he stilled and then looked around.

"What?" she asked with concern.

"Colin?"

"Oh, he was having trouble with...well, everything, so Smalls said he'd show him the engine room," explained Liberty.

"The engine room?" replied Uncle Danny with interest. "Lucky kid."

"Actually, I'd like to see the bridge. That'd be really cool."

"*Maybe*, we should add that to our next deal. If we do such-and-such for the Fleet, we get a guided tour of the Carrier. Because who doesn't want to see the inside of an aircraft carrier."

The librarian grinned. "Great idea."

"*Quiet!*" hissed a harsh voice across the middle aisle.

Liberty and Danny blinked at one another.

Across the way, there was a skinny woman, who was wearing an oddly layered dress, which had seen better days. But most people in the Fleet were doing their best—Exhibit A: Danny's borrowed tie—so Liberty reined in her mean-girl judging.

"What?" asked the Librarian instead.

"Be respectful," snapped the woman. She must have been in her mid-40's and Liberty now realized that she was vibrating with anger. "Even if this is an illegal trial, show some fucking respect."

The Librarian started at the F-bomb. "We were just talking quietly."

Before the woman could say anything more, Uncle Danny touched Liberty's shoulder, and she turned back to him.

"Let it go," he whispered.

"Who is that?" whispered Liberty, almost soundlessly.

"I don't know, but...," began Uncle Danny.

"Don't you ignore me! Don't you dare ignore me!" roared the woman. She jumped to her feet and let loose a string of obscenities at them.

Liberty and Uncle Danny recoiled in surprise.

"I... I don't know what you're...," started Danny.

"You! You shut your mouth! Shut your Filthy, Goddamned mouth, right now! You've done enough," snarled the woman.

"Quiet down yourself!" boomed Judge Banks, from his table at the front of the room. "Or, I'll have you removed!"

The military police at the back of the room started to inch forward.

"Mom," pleaded one of the defendants, Reuben. "Please...?"

"Don't you 'Mom' me," snapped the Defendant's Mother. "If you'd just done what I'd told you! You wouldn't be in this situation."

"Mom!" hissed another defendant, Judah.

"No. Let her speak," said the Judge in a curious voice.

"Great," snapped the mother at the Judge. "Make up your mind."

Reuben whined desperately. "Don't yell at the judge!"

The Defendant's Mom growled at him. "I told you to move through the ship and go slow. And you lost our best guns!"

"Oh, you've lost much, much more than that," said a voice at the door with an angry purr.

Rear Admiral Cirilo was there with more military police.

The Defendant's Mom suddenly pulled a gun out of her layered dress. She began to aim it at the Rear Admiral.

Liberty was already moving, but she would not reach the woman in time. At least, not before the mom could get off a shot or two. And Liberty knew—absolutely—that everyone who had survived this long against zoms, was a really good shot.

A large book smacked into the back of the mother's head. She staggered, but thankfully did not shoot.

Liberty grabbed the mom's wrist and twisted it sharply until the woman dropped the gun.

A second later, the military police were there. They took her from Liberty and pinned her down to the ground, hard. The Defendant's Mom continued to shout, spittle flying, even as the MP's read her, her Miranda Rights.

Liberty stepped back, but she did put her foot on the fallen gun until the MP's could grab it. Her eyes went to the thick law book that'd been thrown.

Uncle Danny was at her back, fists raised, just in case

anyone else tried anything.

The Rear Admiral walked up, and nodded quickly to Liberty, but then he looked past her to the defendant's table. She turned to follow his gaze.

Standing there, one of the defendants, Reuben, had tears streaming down his face.

The defense attorney pointed to Reuben. "He threw it. To save anyone from getting hurt."

The brother, Judah, demanded. "What the hell Reub?" And he started to rise with lightning in his eyes.

With authority, Benjamin slowly turned to his brother. "Just...Shut Up, will you."

"But...," began Judah, hesitantly.

"Sit down," said Benjamin with a heavy voice. "Just...sit down."

Deflating, Judah sat heavily.

Stepping past the brouhaha with the mother, the Rear Admiral went over to the judge.

"I have another case for you to try," he said. "Once you are done with your three defendants."

"Their mother?" asked the judge.

Cirilo just nodded.

"I figured," sighed Judge Banks.

***

A week later, Liberty and Colin sat at a table, just off the kitchen, aboard their nameless ship.

"Sorry I'm late," called out Smalls breathlessly as he scrambled in.

"It's okay," said Liberty soothingly. "I just wanted to talk about what we're going to do next."

"Did the admiral give us a list?" asked Uncle Danny, curiously.

"Yeah, and I thought it best if we left," said Liberty, and then she added softly to the adults. "Soon."

"Is this about the hanging?" asked Colin curiously.

Liberty's eyes grew wide, and she turned to the boy next to her. "How'd you find out about that?"

Colin blinked. "Oh! The other day, you had me stay with Tagg aboard the medical ship, 'cause you had a thing."

Liberty wanted to correct the boy's grammar, but she figured that now was not the right time.

Uncle Danny spoke instead. "When we went to get more medicine from the coast?"

"Yeah," replied Colin. "An' I heard some people talking about it. Actually, everyone was talking about it, except for Tagg."

"Did you ask him about it?" asked Liberty.

Colin shook his head and mumbled. "Not sure I was allowed to. An' I didn't wanna get into trouble."

"You're not in trouble," said Liberty quickly and gently. "And you're allowed to ask questions."

"Really? My...my father wasn't really big on questions," replied Colin wearily. "He'd just get frustrated and remind

201

me that it was my cancer treatments that made him sell his Porsche 9-11s 1968 with 130 horsepower and leather-wrapped steering wheel." His voice became monotone as he rattled off the details of the car, as if they had been burned into his brain.

Liberty bit her tongue. She made it a point not to speak badly of Colin's dead father.

"What the hell?" asked Smalls with a growl. "But...but getting cancer wasn't your fault."

Colin looked down at the table.

"Dad said that I should thank him every day," said the boy softly. "That he gave up his dream house, for him not leaving too, after Mom left in the middle of chemo."

"*No!*" said Uncle Danny, his voice dark and dangerous. "It is *not* your fault that you got sick. Just like it wasn't my fault that I got cancer too. *WE* didn't do anything wrong."

Smalls exclaimed. "Yeah! Parents are supposed to do everything they can for their kids! Including go broke."

"And, as for your mom," said Liberty carefully. "That was a choice that *she* made. *You* can't be blamed for that."

Sniffling, Colin looked up with tears in his eyes.

"Really?" he asked tenuously. As if he could not believe it.

Uncle Danny thumped his fist firmly on the table, but not too loudly. "*Absolutely.*"

Liberty leaned over to touch her head against the boy's. "Really sweetie! You're one of us, and I always want you to know that we'll always be there for you."

Dead serious, Uncle Danny leaned forward and said. "I

swear it on *mi Abuela*."

The Librarian straightened with surprise. "Whoa! That's big." She looked at Colin. "I don't have anyone *that* important in my past. Maybe I could swear it on Judy Blume?"

Despite himself, Colin let out a chuckle. He tried to wipe his nose, but it was running heavily now.

"I got it," cried Smalls, and he jumped up to get some tissue.

After both nasal passages had been loudly cleared, Liberty turned again to the boy.

"So! I always want you to always feel comfortable asking questions," she said while giving him a quick, reassuring hug. "And I'm sure that Tagg feels that way too."

"Or you can always ask me *Cobayo*," nodded Uncle Danny.

"Or me," added Smalls happily.

Colin looked up at all of them in surprise. "Um, okay." And the dam broke. "Then, why are those people getting hanged? Isn't making them dead a little extreme? I mean, no one was hurt. And are those really the people who came onboard our ship?" The boy stopped to take a breath.

Liberty gave a little chuckle. "Okay, so you *did* have a few questions."

Colin suddenly grew cautious and said. "Um, if that's all right."

"Yes, yes, of course," replied Liberty with mock annoyance. "Don't make us swear on people again!"

"And Rule #1," reminded Uncle Danny.

"Okay, okay," laughed Colin.

"Now, as to your questions, let's start at the end. Yes, those were definitely the people who came on board our ship."

"Did their mother really send them?" asked Colin incredulously.

"That's what she said," shrugged Uncle Danny.

"But...why did they come onboard our ship?" asked Colin.

"Sometimes, people make very bad decisions," said Uncle Danny. "And sometimes, those bad decisions have very bad consequences."

Colin nodded. "I heard this one guy saying that those people were going to get hung by their neck over the edge of the carrier. And then dropped into the water with weights tied to their ankles, so that they sink right to the bottom. An' the Navy is gonna do it in front of everyone."

Smalls actually raised his hand before speaking. "Oh! That was the Rear Admiral. He's really worried about people stealing each other's boats." When Liberty and Danny looked at him in surprise, the Navy Engineer went on. "I was on the Carrier getting some parts for a little project that I'm working on here, an' I got a quick debrief about the situation."

"So, the Admiral's worried about stealing?" asked Colin.

"That's right," said Smalls to the boy. "And actually, those guys stole the boat that brought them here too. So, they really messed up."

"But...don't you guys steal from the Coast?" asked Colin. "You even say that you're pirates."

"Ah! That is different," said Liberty.

"Like how?" asked Colin, confused.

"We're not there to hurt anyone," said Uncle Danny.

Smalls cut in. "What these people were really doing was called 'hijacking'. And for a sailor like me, that's really, really bad."

"But...," started the boy.

"And they were not going to let us go." added Liberty softly.

The boy blinked and looked quickly at her. "You mean...they really would have..." But Colin stopped.

Liberty put her arm around the boy again and this time he leaned into her.

"Which is why we've started going away from the Fleet at night," explained Smalls.

"And we take turns keeping watch at night," added Uncle Danny.

"So, when you're doing 'watch', you're looking for bad people?" asked Colin.

"Yep," nodded Uncle Danny.

Liberty continued. "And we only got this ship, because it was abandoned when we found it." She decided not to delve into the odd fact that the captain had been a zom. Though he did appear to fall overboard of his own free will. She pushed that weirdness away so that she could concentrate on the boy.

205

"So…," began Colin. "You're pirates, but you only take stuff from people that're already dead."

"Exactly," replied Uncle Danny. "Because stealing from another person is wrong. *Mi Abuela* was very precise about this." Unconsciously, he gave a little wince. "But if…let's say some medicine was abandoned."

"How would you know if it was abandoned?" asked Colin quickly.

"We have to make sure that there's no one else around," explained Liberty.

Colin looked down for a moment, deep in thought. And Uncle Danny wanted to give him a hug, but he couldn't reach across the table.

"Okay," said the boy at last. And his face scrunched up. "But I really don't want to be here when they…you know!"

"Well," smiled Liberty. "As it so happens, the Admiral has quite a laundry list for us."

"We can cast off after dinner," said Smalls.

Colin looked up with bright eyes. "Hey! Can I stand watch tonight?"

"Well…," started Liberty uncertainly.

"Pleeeeeeeeease!" begged Colin.

"I wouldn't mind some company," suggested Uncle Danny to Liberty. And she smiled indulgently.

"Better than a cigar," said Liberty with a squint of mock disapproval. The Big Mexican rolled his eyes and replied with a grin. She looked back at the boy. "Okay. This time."

"Yay!" grinned Colin.

And Uncle Danny, for the first time since that night, truly relaxed.

## Interlude Two

**IT STILL HURT** Liberty that she had lost her favorite knife back in the City of Angels. It was probably still stuck in the eye of that dead zom, after all this time.

And finding a suitable replacement had been tougher than she had imagined. A good zom-killing-knife had to be long and thin, to get through the eye and into the brain. The knife-under-the-chin thing wouldn't pierce the brain unless you were using a sword.

Turning back to her current predicament, she wondered if such a knife would even be useful in this extremely delicate situation. She sheathed her new knife and went to her big ol' clodhopper boots.

However, as the Librarian leaned over, a stench arose from them.

"Gaah!!" she recoiled. "Next time I'm on the mainland, I

either need to get a new pair of boots, or a ton of that Dr. Scholl's Febreezey stuff." She considered that. "Or maybe just some napalm."

Swiftly, Liberty took out the boot knife. The blade was smaller, and actually probably better suited to the job. She returned to her private bath. As she sharpened the blade on a whetstone, the Librarian pondered how lucky they had gotten. She had been happy enough to get Colin free of the Coast.

The Librarian almost felt a little guilty, sitting on the edge of her very own bathtub. She examined the blade, which looked nice and sharp. Still, she wished she had found a pair of scissors.

Focusing all of her attention, she went about the extremely delicate work of landscaping.

\*\*\*

Liberty stepped out of her room and fought back the urge to change again. She had only managed to scrounge three dresses for tonight. And she really wanted to wear a dress. She hadn't worn one in a while, not since she had walked out of her library and had almost been eaten by a zombie police officer. Not since Mr. Jamie had saved her with his bag of library books on Russian lit.

Memories of those confounding first days started to flood in, and she looked down at the intricate tattoo sleeves on her arms. Embedded within the Japanese style were the names of those that had not made it. One name stood out, 'Mr. Jamie'.

210

Liberty immediately stopped herself and pushed back hard against those thoughts.

Out loud, she said to herself. "No, You've cried enough about losing them."

Some days, like today, that kind of talk worked, and she was thankful.

Stepping away from her room, the Librarian moved swiftly through their yacht with slippers that would have to pass for shoes today.

In one of the rec rooms, which actually had windows in the floor, Liberty reached her new favorite couch. Instantly, she screeched to a halt.

A blistering anger rose inside her.

"Where...are...my...books?" she asked in a harsh whisper, even though no one was there.

Liberty around the room, searching hard. Cabinets swung open. But her tiny collection of books—those precious few that she had scrounged from the Coast—were gone. She resisted the urge to grab her sniper rifle, but only just.

Storming out into the hallway, she nearly collided with Colin.

"Whoa!" called out the dark-skinned boy in surprise. He looked up with a grin on his face and said in mock annoyance. "Hey! Watch it Lady! I'm walk..."

Liberty looked down at him and Colin instantly froze. His eyes dropped immediately to the floor.

"Oh! Um, hey...," started the boy with a meek voice.

Liberty suddenly realized that the 11-year-old was

211

afraid. And for a second, she was worried that someone had threatened him.

Then, with a dread realization, she realized that Colin was looking away from her.

Taking a moment, Liberty closed her eyes and took a deep breath. She forced herself to relax a little. Opening her eyes, she saw Colin looking wearily up at her.

"You okay?" he asked softly, worriedly.

Liberty made herself smile. It was a little forced, but it was there. "Sorry. I just...I didn't mean to worry you."

"What happened?" asked Colin tentatively. "Can I help?"

And this time, Liberty's smile was not forced.

"Something is missing," she replied.

In a flash, she pulled him into a quick, reassuring hug.

Once freed, the boy gave an indignant whine. "Hey! What's that for?"

"Mostly for me," admitted Liberty.

"Okay," said Colin, uncertainly. "So, what's missing?"

"Those books that I brought back from the Coast," said Liberty. "You haven't seen them, have you?"

Colin blinked. "Um. They're in there." He walked past her, into the rec room. Seconds later he was back. "Hey! What happened to your books?"

"I don't know," smiled Liberty. "They were there last night."

"And why're you wearing a dress?" asked Colin, quickly shifting gears.

"I...," began Liberty. She immediately felt embarrassed for some reason. "Um, can we find my books first, then I'll tell you? I promise."

"Okay," shrugged Colin, unconcerned. He walked out into the corridor and looked around. "Where do we even start?"

Liberty looked around as well. Unfortunately—for once—this was not a small ship.

"Well, let's check the nearest rooms first," she suggested.

Five minutes later, she came out empty-handed again, from yet another room. She stopped and cocked her hip.

Out of the corner of her eye, she noticed Colin looking at something really hard. At first, she didn't understand what was so interesting, but then it hit her.

Her spine stiffened. A part of her wanted to snap, but then she quickly realized that this was not a city street. This was an eleven-year-old boy, and she needed to do this right.

"It's okay to notice, but try not to stare too hard," said Liberty with gentle reproach.

Colin jumped. "What? I... I mean...I wasn't..."

Liberty turned with a gentle smile. "It's okay. Really."

"I'm sorry. I'm sorry for staring too hard," mumbled Colin swiftly.

"You weren't," said Liberty. "But that was just extra advice. You're going to start noticing girls—unless you like boys—which is okay too, because..."

"Definitely girls," said Colin quickly. "Definitely."

"Actually though, since I am kinda your...well, guardian,

you probably shouldn't stare at me," she said Liberty. "I mean…"

"Oh!" cried out Colin as he jumped around her to continue searching. "Did I tell you that Dr. Tagg and I did an autopsy on a seagull?"

"What?" asked Liberty in surprise. She decided to let him change topics. But she did need to talk to Tagg and Uncle Danny, and really soon.

Unaware of her thoughts, Colin kept going. "Yeah. It just fell over dead on the Salk, an' a sailor was just going to throw it overboard, but Dr. Tagg stopped him."

Liberty chuckled. "I can imagine the look on the sailor's face."

"I dunno about that. But Dr. Tagg said that he was worried that it might've been infectious," said Colin, having a little trouble with the new word. "Which means it could spread a disease."

"Sounds dangerous," nodded Liberty.

"That's why Dr. Tagg made us 'suit up'," said Colin.

"Suit up?"

"He had me put on a yellow plastic suit with plastic gloves and boots, which were a little big," said Colin excitedly. "Then he taped down the hands and ankles, so that it made a complete seal."

"Wow!" said Liberty sincerely. "He was serious."

"He said that we needed to be careful, so we also put on little masks…," began Colin.

"Surgical masks?" asked Liberty.

"Yeah! That's it! Then a plastic face shield."

"He didn't want to leave anything to chance. So, did you find out why the bird died?"

"No!" cried Colin unhappily. "We looked at all the organs. There were a bunch. But Tagg said that the heart didn't look right, so he..." The boy suddenly pointed. "Are those wine bottles?"

Liberty looked further down the corridor, and she also saw wine bottles lined up against a wall.

Merlot, Pinot Noir, and more were spread out, like they were going to be paired with breadcrumbs. But only breadcrumbs derived from artisan breads, of course.

Down the hallway, at the end of the trail of wine, was a stack of books. More specifically, Liberty's books. She stopped just outside a small walk-in, with etched glass doors.

A little way behind, Colin called out tentatively. "Um, Uncle Danny! You might want to run. Like, Right Now! Fast."

With his warning given, the boy backed up a bit.

This made Uncle Danny turn around.

"*Mija?*" asked the Big Mexican with cautious surprise; he had one of her James Patterson books in his hand.

From the reaction of both guys, Liberty realized that she might be looking scary again. She tamped down her anger and took a moment before speaking.

"Hi," said Liberty, mostly-calm. "We were looking for my books."

"Ah!" said Uncle Danny. "*Disculpe*, I thought that I'd get

215

this done faster...but I kind of ran into a snag."

The peanut gallery, Colin, quickly urged. "You might even want to jump overboard, an' swim for the Fleet. Did I mention 'fast'? Just sayin'."

Liberty turned to the boy. "Yes. I was unhappy when I first saw that my books were missing, but now I see that there might be more to this."

"Unhappy?" scoffed Colin. "You were scary mad."

Uncle Danny leaned out of the room and looked at the boy. "'Scary mad'? You mean our Liberty?"

Colin nodded emphatically.

Uncle Danny looked back at her. "I'm sorry. I was going to surprise you, but time got away from me. If you need to hit men, use my right arm. Dr. Tagg drew blood from my left yesterday."

"Oh No!" cried Colin in sympathy, but then he railed to support. "Dr. Tagg is…. well, he's trying his best."

Danny smiled at the boy. "I know. He'll get the hang of drawing blood, probably soon. Hopefully soon." Then he offered his right arm to the Librarian.

Liberty held up a hand. "It's okay." But she vowed to herself that she had to tell Tagg how the boy had stood up for him. Instead of punching, she looked at the small room that he was in. It had wooden racks for holding wine. "Why are you in the wine cellar, or whatever it's called."

"Well, I couldn't sleep…," started Uncle Danny.

"Again?" asked Liberty with pointed concern. "You should ask Tagg about that. Maybe he can prescribe something like Ambien."

Satisfied that no blood would be spilt, Colin wandered up.

"That's what my mama took," said the boy. And at the mention of his mother, the boy's face fell. Neither he nor his father had known where she was, even before everything fell. Colin continued in a hollow voice. "Until she had a fit and said she couldn't handle it."

Liberty reached out and pulled the boy into a side hug. When he did not object, she looked back up.

"So, yeah," she said. "I mean, you Do have a doctor, so you..."

Danny interjected. "*Ni modo.* Dr. Tagg's job is to keep my zombie virus at bay."

"He's not going to see it that way," insisted Liberty.

"Maybe," shrugged Uncle Danny. "I... I just...I hate to take medicine."

"But a good night's sleep is important too," said Liberty, using—without realizing it—her 'Mom' voice.

"True," agreed Danny, a little reluctantly.

"But really, you're my friend, so if you don't want to, I'll back your play," said Liberty quickly. "I just..."

Uncle Danny smiled warmly. "It's okay *Mija.*"

"Okay! So anyway," she said. "What started you thinking about my books and the wine cellar?"

"The sea air," replied Uncle Danny swiftly, with mounting excitement. "Not being able to sleep, I thought about borrowing one of your books. But! Then I realized that the sea air is literally gonna to kill'em."

"Oh my Gosh," hissed Liberty. "I didn't even think about how moist the air is."

"And this," said Uncle Danny and he waved at the wine cellar. "Is climate controlled."

"But the wine?" asked Liberty.

"At first, I wasn't sure if this would work," admitted Uncle Danny. "I mean, if this cellar had been stocked with Domaine de La Romainee-Conti, Vinaltura Malbec, or Vina Cobos, then...well, I'd have to think of something else...but this..." He gestured at the wine. *"Por Dios*, this is lucky to be in the hallway."

"Can I have some?" asked Colin.

"Maybe a sip later," said Uncle Danny. *"But*...only if it's good wine."

"What's the difference?" asked Colin, curiously suspicious.

*"¡No manches!* I can't give you crappy wine," insisted Uncle Danny. "That'd be like feeding you horse meat."

"And you know wine?" asked Liberty curiously. She suspected that he'd been naming various wines, but it had all been Greek to her.

"I was a sommelier in a past life," smiled Uncle Danny.

"A what?" asked Colin.

"Someone at a fancy restaurant, who helps the guest pick their wine," explained Uncle Danny. "I only did it at first to help my friend Pepe, and because it paid more, but then I really got a real taste for it."

"You'd be a scary waiter," said the boy.

Liberty looked down. "Colin! That's not nice."

"He's right though," said Uncle Danny.

"See!" cried Colin with vindication.

Liberty gave Uncle Danny a hard look. "You're not helping," she said.

"You're right too," admitted Uncle Danny. He looked at Colin. "She is right about you saying that I look scary. I mean—I like it! —but some people might take offense."

"So, you just want me to just shut up then?" asked Colin with a pout.

"No, no," said Uncle Danny quickly. He took a moment before continuing. "*Mi Abuela* explained it this way. She said that there are 'outside thoughts' that you can share, and then there are 'inside thoughts' that you really shouldn't share, maybe ever."

"So... saying 'you're scary' was an 'inside thought'?" asked Colin.

Liberty looked at the boy. "Well, what you're really saying is that, because of the way he looks, that he can only do certain jobs."

"Like robbing places," added Danny.

"And making assumptions can lead to trouble," said Liberty.

"Like what?" asked Colin.

"Pepe!" said Uncle Danny quickly.

"Your friend right?" asked Colin.

"Yeah. He was out of work when I was doing chemo..."

"Chemo sucks," grimaced Colin.

"Absolutely! But, since Pepe was free, he drove me to all my chemo visits," explained Uncle Danny.

"Wow," said Liberty.

"Exactly, so that's why, when he asked me to help him open a restaurant, I didn't even hesitate," said Uncle Danny. "But, getting back to my point…"

"You had a point?" asked Liberty with mock surprise. "How unusual for you."

Uncle Danny glowered at her for a moment. "Anyhow! Before Pepe had the restaurant, he was a security guard. And he really wanted to do a good job. So, when he saw someone in a tattered coat come in, he thought they were a bum. So, he kicked them out, maybe a little too enthusiastically."

"Oh no," said Liberty with wide eyes.

"What?" asked Colin in confusion.

"It was the CEO, who always dresses down," explained Uncle Danny, and Colin chuckled. "Luckily, the CEO had a sense of humor, or Pepe would've been in big, big trouble."

"You know," said Liberty thoughtfully as she looked at the bottles. "Having this wine might open some doors with other ships. In case we need their help or want to trade."

"Maybe," said Uncle Danny, and she looked at him questioningly. "If it's an okay wine, that'd be fine. But I don't want to give anyone bad wine." He looked at the boy. "Giving bad wine is just terrible etiquette."

"What's ed-eh-cat?" asked Colin.

"How we behave with each other," explained Uncle Danny. "How we treat others is important." He looked

220

back up at Liberty and beamed. "However, when we're on the Coast, we might want to get some of the good stuff."

Uncle Danny suddenly blinked. He leaned back slowly and inspected her dress like an overprotective father on prom night.

"And why, *Mija pequeno* ...?" asked the Big Mexican slowly. "...are you dressed to the nines?"

"What?" asked Liberty and Colin as one.

"I mean, why are you dressed...," began Uncle Danny, when they heard a voice call out from on deck.

"H... hello?" it said tentatively.

Colin cried out. "That's Tagg!" And he was off like a shot.

With a giant grin, Uncle Danny looked from the disappearing boy to Liberty.

The Librarian scowled at the Look.

"Shut up," she replied, and she went after the boy.

However, Uncle Danny followed right behind.

"I thought you had a project to work on," grumbled Liberty repressively.

"Oh yes," agreed Uncle Danny. "I have very important work to do. I need to see if this *cabron* is not just some bum, unworthy of you."

"It's Tagg," she growled with exasperation.

And, as Uncle Danny walked beside her, Liberty found herself oddly embarrassed. It was like having her father check her prom date's wallet for condoms. Luckily, her dad didn't check the cute, little, sparkly purse that she had.

Before they had even reached them, she could already hear Colin chattering excitedly to Tagg.

"...an' Liberty got scary mad, but then she saw that Uncle Danny was putting them in the wine cellar, except it's not in a cellar, so I don't know why it's called it that, but Uncle Danny wants to put her books in there, but..." said Colin breathlessly.

Coming up behind him, Liberty put her hands on Colin's shoulders, and the boy stopped to look up at her.

"Take a deep breath," she encouraged warmly. "You're going to pass out, talking so fast."

"It's okay," said Tagg, good-naturedly. "I'm used to it."

The Scientist's white, button-down shirt looked like it had been poured over his barrel chest. And around his neck, he wore a textured-knit tie, possibly from the 70's.

The Scientist was about to say more when he really saw her outfit. Dr. McTaggart's jaw dropped open. "Oh! Um...ah..."

Suddenly, a booming voice demanded. "¡Oye! ¡¿Qué haces?! What're you looking at?"

Everyone turned to look at Uncle Danny in shock.

Colin hissed. "See! He *looks* scary."

"Hush sweetie," replied Liberty, though she absolutely agreed.

But Danny's hard eyes were focused on the doctor.

"Wha...what?" asked Tagg.

Uncle Danny moved forward slowly—inextricably—like the tide coming in. "You. You got a job?"

222

"Wha...what?" asked Tagg again in confusion.

"A job," continued Uncle Danny. His voice full of iron. "A source of income. I need to know that you're not one of those guys, who's gonna lay around on the couch all day, expecting his woman to wait on him, hand and foot."

"Wha...," started Dr. McTaggert. "Um, besides being...well, the doctor for each one of you, I mean, I am trying to find a cure for the zombie virus. Is... that what you mean?"

"Humph!" said Uncle Danny. "Do you have a car though?"

"Um, I borrowed a boat to take us today," said Tagg.

Uncle Danny suddenly asked. "Did you know that you have shaving cream on your ear?"

Tagg tried to wipe away the cream but got the wrong ear.

"Okay, that's enough," said Liberty to Danny. "You've had your fun."

"Hey," said Uncle Danny defensively. "Excuse me for trying to make sure that he's an okay guy."

"He's a very okay guy," smiled Liberty warmly. "And he's taking me to lunch on the carrier."

"Not even dinner," sniffed Uncle Danny with disapproval.

Liberty just gave him a dark look.

Uncle Danny suddenly grinned at her and then looked at Tagg with a pleasant demeanor.

"The Carrier, as in the carrier of our little fleet?"

whistled Uncle Danny. "Fancy living."

Liberty spoke up. "The Rear Admiral invited me and Tagg to a little lunch...mostly to get the skinny on Dr. McTaggert's research." Then, she lowered her voice conspiratorially. "It'll probably just be food out of a can."

"Well, that's okay," said Uncle Danny, relaxed. "Me and *El Cobayo* can see how many books we can fit into the wine cellar. But next time that we're on the Coast, I might need to drop by Home Depot."

"Whatever you need," smiled Liberty indulgently, and she stepped around to face Colin. "And you be good!"

"Hey!" replied the boy indignantly.

After giving him a quick, warm hug, Liberty went to Tagg. She wiped the shaving cream off his ear.

"Ready?" she asked of him.

Not trusting his voice, or even his smile, Tagg just nodded quickly. Taking his arm, Liberty left with him.

Colin's brow furrowed. "What was that?"

Uncle Danny grinned happily. "Come on *Cobayo*, it's boy's night, or boy's day at least. Maybe we'll even watch an action movie. Something with Bruce Lee."

Colin blinked. "Who's Bruce Lee?"

With feigned shock, Uncle Danny froze. "Who's Bruce Lee? *¡Qué horror!* You wound me when you talk like that!" But he said it gently and carefully, so Colin knew that he was joking. "Come on, we're going to watch 'Enter the Dragon' right away. We'll worry about the wine cellar later."

"But I'm supposed to finish the '*20'000 Leagues Under the*

*Sea'* today," said Colin.

"Bruce Lee is more important," said Uncle Danny.

"Will Liberty see it like that?" asked Colin tentatively.

Uncle Danny stopped the boy and looked down at him with a grave expression. "I'll take the heat for you *Cobayo*."

Colin stood a little straighter and a smile danced across his face.

"Now come on," said Uncle Danny. "We can't EVER let Bruce Lee be forgotten! And Brandon Lee too! Hm, I wonder if they got 'The Crow'." But he harrumphed. "Actually, considering their taste in wine, we're lucky that they got any good movies at all."

**Volume Three**
*Chapter Ten*

UNCLE DANNY RACED around the corner, and his feet skidded a little bit on the wet concrete. Smacking into a brick wall, he pushed himself off to dive deeper into an alley.

And he almost plowed right into a knot of zoms.

"Ahhhnnng?" declared the closest zom, who looked like a Paris Hilton clone. Thankfully, the zom was sans dog.

Uncle Danny spun around the creatures like a footballer.

The zoms reached out, but their reflexes were dull and sluggish. Still, they followed him deeper into the alley.

Once clear of them though, Uncle Danny knew that he'd be safe, as long as he didn't get cornered. Which made the big truck, wedged into the alley ahead, a bit of an issue.

There wasn't enough room for a flea on either side.

Closing in on the mouth of the alley, there was a rending scream. It sounded like a bird, but it definitely wasn't terrestrial.

Hearing that sound poured adrenaline into Uncle Danny's legs.

The wedged truck was pointed towards him, with a fire escape right above it. Setting his shotgun on the hood, he managed to haul himself up, a little slower than he'd have liked.

"Ungh," he grunted, suddenly feeling very old. He grabbed his weapon and climbed up onto the roof of the cab.

Crawling on top of the semi-trailer, he heard something.

"*Guk fowe*," called out a voice from the mouth of the alley.

Luckily, Uncle Danny resisted the urge to drop immediately down. Instead, he slowly laid down.

Behind, he heard something race into the alley. There was a short scuffle with the zoms, but he soon heard footsteps moving closer to the truck.

Not daring to breathe, the Big Mexican started to lift up his shotgun, but the stock scraped lightly against the metal roof. Just a tiny noise, but he heard his pursuer stop moving.

"*Hun kulong*" hissed a voice by the front bumper.

Unbidden, a thought crept in his mind, of one of these birds kicking so hard that they instantly broke a man's femur. Carefully moving his shotgun, he pointed the barrel towards the front of the truck and tried not to breathe at all.

The front of the truck waggled a little, as if someone were testing the bumper to see if it was safe to climb up on.

Uncle Danny could hear the device in the alien's head buzzin insistently, incessantly. The very same device that made them walking woodchippers when it was active.

And that sound, a low buzzing, came from the front of the truck.

From the mouth of the alley, another voice bellowed. "*Riesss!*"

"*Inck,*" snapped a voice from the front of the truck.

"*RIESSS!*" insisted the other voice.

Muttering disgruntled, unintelligible words, the voice from front of the truck stomped away.

Danny waited a moment. Then carefully, he peeked over. The alley was empty of anything dangerous, just the faux Hilton zom and her entourage. In the clear, Uncle Danny went to the rear of the semi-trailer to see if the coast was clear.

Something dropped from the fire escape on top of the semi.

Uncle Danny swung around, but a hand grabbed the barrel of his shotgun.

"It's me," hissed Liberty and she let go of the weapon to take a step back. "What the hell were you doing?"

"Where were you?" asked the Big Mexican.

Liberty nodded her chin upwards. "When you took off, I found a fire escape."

"Up high? But they can fly," said Uncle Danny worriedly.

"I know," said Liberty. "But, chasing after you blindly would've gotten us both killed."

Uncle Danny straightened up, ready to argue, but then he stopped and slowly deflated.

"I'm sorry," he said.

"Just...just don't do it again," she said. He could see the deep concern on her face as she kept speaking. "Was it that one thing...alien...whatever?"

"Rakduson," supplied Uncle Danny softly.

"Yeah. That's what it's called, right?" asked Liberty. "The one with the red tuft on its head."

"Yes," he said.

"But the ones out there are looking for blood," she said urgently.

"I think it's that thing in the back of their head," said Uncle Danny.

"That device? Are you sure that the alien-birds didn't put it there themself?"

"When I found the alien-birds trapped in the sand," he said thoughtfully. "They seemed...intelligent."

"Not homicidal?"

"Exactly...at least until that device went off."

"But *it is* going off...," started Liberty hotly, however she caught herself. "And you apologized. I know. I just don't want to see you get eaten."

"Me too!" grinned Uncle Danny, which produced a little

chuckle that made everything good, as it passed between the two of them. Okay, let's get moving," said Liberty.

Carefully, they climbed off the back of the semi-trailer and kept going.

"I don't think we're ever going to find a phone book," grumbled Liberty softly.

"We'll keep looking," encouraged Uncle Danny. "I just used my phone to find stores, and to call Pepe on Sundays, so we both knew the other was alive." He paused, and then he added sadly. "I hope Pepe is okay...but, things never seemed to go his way. No matter how hard he tried."

Liberty saw his worry and had to speak up. "*Hey!* You never know. This might be the event that he was waiting for."

Uncle Danny nodded. "That's true! Maybe." But then he said in an excited whisper. "*¡Fíjate!* Look over there!"

"Book Store?" asked Liberty, a little desperately.

"No," huffed Uncle Danny, with a little roll of his eyes.

"Oooh, a pharmacy!" moaned Liberty happily.

The Librarian was about to say more when she noticed two zoms shambling towards them. "We got admirers."

"It's hard to be as beautiful as me," said Danny with mock sadness.

"Time to power-walk," said Liberty. "Heel first, then toe. Heel, toe. Heel, toe."

With her back ramrod straight and her arms pumping tightly next to her chest, she walked in an exaggerated fashion which made Uncle Danny chuckle. He, of course, had to copy her movement which made them both chuckle.

231

The front door to the pharmacy was unlocked.

"Lucky!" grinned Liberty. Slipping inside, they both froze just inside the door and leveled their weapons. But there were no zoms inside. The pharmacy was really a postage stamp with walls. They walked past a few front-of-store items to the counter.

"This could be a problem," muttered Uncle Danny.

"Yeah," replied Liberty softly. She tapped the thick glass which covered the counter, like at a bank teller. Only small slots allowed the meds through. And even Liberty's smaller hands could barely make it through.

"Door?" she suggested.

But that was not an improvement.

"Now, *that's* a door," muttered Uncle Danny.

"It looks like it's something out of a bank, or something that holds state secrets in a government building," said Liberty.

"Maybe Smalls?" suggested Uncle Danny.

"A Navy Engineer may be the only one who can get...," began Liberty.

Reflexively, Uncle Danny moved in front of Liberty as the front window exploded.

A hailstorm of glass showered the front.

The Big Mexican held up his coat to protect them.

Liberty saw the alien-bird's feet hit the pharmacy floor. Dropping to a crouch, she brought up her rifle as glass pelted his coat.

"*Hie Tah!*" screeched the alien-bird with a white tuft

upon their head.

Liberty fired right into its midsection, and it stumbled back in surprise. She jumped up.

"Time to go!" said the Librarian.

However, she noticed that Uncle Danny was looking hard at the alien-bird, who was trying to get up, despite their mortal wound. She grabbed his arm and he turned in surprise.

"It's not your bird, let's go!" said Liberty more loudly.

Uncle Danny nodded, quickly and fired his shotgun. He did not want to leave the White Tuft bird in agony.

Out the front door, they turned back towards the alley with the truck.

Two more alien-birds tore around a far corner and ran towards them. The alien-birds kept colliding into knots of zoms, who did not stop them, but slowed them down just enough.

Back in the same alley, Uncle Danny saw that they were facing the back of the truck with its high end. Pulling a little ahead, he stopped right behind and threw his shotgun up and over. It clattered noisily. Inside, he cringed at the sound, but he cupped both hands together.

Liberty understood and put her foot in. With a power-lift from Uncle Danny, she got up on top of the semi-trailer. After a quick check for danger, she gently put down her rifle and lay, reaching down to him. With verifying degrees of success, Uncle Danny started to climb up the back as the alien-birds tore into the alley. He didn't dare look back.

"Hurry!" grunted Liberty, worriedly.

233

Scrabbling, Uncle Danny got one leg on top of the semi-trailer, but the other still dangled. An alien-bird opened its beak, closing in on him. Danny yanked up his leg, and the alien ran smack into the metal door of the truck with a clang.

"Comeoncomeoncomeon!" she chanted atop the truck, grabbing her rifle. They moved towards the front of the truck. "You're heavy. No pudding for you tonight."

"Hey," hissed Uncle Danny as he looked for his shotgun. "Don't even joke about that."

The Big Mexican saw a zom pick up his fallen shotgun, off the hood of the truck.

Scrambling down, he kicked it in the chest. It stumbled back, but it still had his shotgun.

Liberty jumped to the ground. Uncle Danny took a moment longer because he was feeling his age. The alley zoms were closing when a huge shadow fell over them.

One of the alien-birds dropped into the alley, almost on top of Liberty. And the bird lunged at her, beak open.

With no time to turn it, Liberty jammed her rifle sideways into the open mouth, right at the hinge. It tried but could not bear down.

Uncle Danny saw that the alien-bird, with madness in her eyes, and a red tuft on top of her head. His stomach knotted, but Danny did not stop moving. That one zom still had his shotgun. Snatching it from the creature, he lifted it and aimed.

Sorry, he thought with a sorrow that went right into his bones.

The alien-bird aimed a powerful leg at Liberty's femur.

Unconsciously, with shaking hands, Uncle Danny fired.

The deer slug missed Rakduson's head, and instead smashed through the metal device at the back of her head.

The alien with the red tuft suddenly reared back and let out a shriek of utter agony. The bird pitched backwards.

"What the...," started Liberty.

Eyes watering, Uncle Danny grabbed her arm and led her towards the mouth of the alley.

Rakduson's scream no longer had words and she started attacking everything around her in a mindless frenzy. The zoms didn't stand a chance. But the moment that they were down, the alien immediately scrabbled after Liberty and Danny.

Just as the two reached the mouth of the alley, reinforcements were closing in, but not the humankind. Several more alien-birds were running in their direction. However, the angry buzz from the devices in their head began to taper off.

"*¡Corre!*" cried Uncle Danny, pointing away from the birds.

"No kidding," replied Liberty with light sarcasm.

Sprinting away from the alley, the alien-birds had just reached the mouth when Rakduson tore out in a frenzy. Pecking and kicking, she whirled around, but with no real aim. Baffled, the other aliens quickly backed away.

Rakduson's device gave one last pop of electricity and went dead. The alien collapsed to the ground, shaking uncontrollably.

235

With the sound completely gone, the other alien-birds slowly came to their senses and stared at Rak with startled concern.

"Hun kion?" asked one of the alien-birds with a Magenta Tuft.

Uncle Danny glanced back and almost stumbled. However, Liberty helped him keep moving.

"*¡Oye!* Rak's fallen," he said with horror. "I think...I think she's in pain."

"It's not your fault," said Liberty.

"But...I shot her," responded Uncle Danny as they reached a side street. He looked back at Rakduson trying to get up, but she was obviously hurting terribly. Magenta Tuft stepped close to help.

"And she would have killed me," reminded Liberty. "Thank you."

"I...," started Uncle Danny.

"You didn't know that shooting that device would do that, did you," said Liberty urgently. Glancing right, she saw a knot of zoms heading towards them now.

"I... I was shooting for Rak's head," said Uncle Danny guiltily. "To kill her."

Liberty grabbed him and tried to whip the Big Mexican around but outweighed her. However, he did turn towards her.

"*¿Mande?*" he asked, confused.

"We need to go," ordered Liberty. "Now!"

Uncle Danny slowly nodded and followed her.

"I wonder though...should I have shot her again. To put her out of her misery?" he asked so softly, that Liberty almost did not hear him. "'*¡Por Dios!* What have I done?"

***

At the shore by Malibu pier, Smalls was waiting at their small fiberglass boat.

"Any luck?" asked the Navy Engineer.

"Yes and no," replied Liberty as they got into the boat and headed away from shore.

"Well? Which one is it?" asked Smalls.

"Some yes, but kinda no," said Liberty.

Smalls looked to Danny, who was hunched over his shotgun.

Liberty continued. "We found a pharmacy, but the door looks like a bank vault."

"Ah, yes," said Smalls. "That is a problem."

"A pirate's life is not always easy," said Liberty and she patted Uncle Danny on the shoulder, who just nodded.

***

"So!" grinned an Army officer with no small amount of glee. "What you're saying, is that if we hit the device in the back of their head, it really hurts'em?"

"No!" said Uncle Danny sharply. "We can't do that!"

237

The Big Mexican and the Librarian were aboard the Fleet's carrier, the Theodore Roosevelt.

The face of the Army officer, Major Todd Princey, twisted with hate. "They killed one of our soldiers."

"I know!" replied Danny archly. "I was there when they killed him. Remember! And I'm also the one that killed it! But that's…"

"We need to stop these bird-things, however we can!" snapped Princey, pounding his delicate fist on the table.

"It's just…," started Uncle Danny. Suddenly, he felt exhausted, and he stopped to rub his lined face.

Once back on their own ship, they had called in their encounter to the carrier. But before they could even put their weapons down, a call came back requesting that they come in, straight away. But it had been a real request.

Liberty and Uncle Danny were not soldier's at Cirilo's beck and call. But, unfortunately, 'needing a nap' hadn't sounded like a reasonable argument to either of them.

So now, Uncle Danny was trying to think on the run. "I really could use a trenta coffee, with a shot of espresso. Maybe two. And a little raspberry, just for taste."

"Sadly, the Carrier ran out of coffee a few months ago," said Rear Admiral Cirilo, who had been mostly silent as everyone bickered. "So, I couldn't even offer you a cup of good ole Navy coffee."

Liberty looked at the Rear Admiral in surprise.

"No coffee? Wow! That must've been a hard transition."

"For me especially," chuckled Cirilo. "But yes, my XO

still argues that that was the hardest transition for the crew."

"Maybe we can see if we can find some coffee for you," suggested Liberty.

The Rear Admiral shook his head. "As much as it pains me—And it does!!—medical supplies must have priority."

"Will you stop gabbing!" snapped Princey. "In case you haven't noticed, we're at war with these things. We need to use every advantage we got."

"But do the birds know that we're at war?" asked Uncle Danny thoughtfully.

"What do you mean by that?" asked Cirilo, and he leaned forward curiously.

"What do I mean?" asked Uncle Danny, blinking in surprise. He wished Liberty could distract them with coffee for a few more minutes. He looked at her.

"You could tell them what you saw on the beach," she suggested gently.

"The beach...?" asked Uncle Danny at first. "Oh yes! The beach."

"You said that you had captured some," prompted the Rear Admiral.

"*Pues*...they kinda captured themselves," said Uncle Danny.

"What're you talking about?" demanded Princey in exasperation.

"Well, they dug a hole in the beach to hide in," cut in Liberty.

239

"But wouldn't they get stuck in the wet sand?" asked Princey in confusion.

"That's exactly what happened," nodded Uncle Danny. "Trapped like amber."

Major Princey's eyes bugged out, as if the Big Mexican was mentally challenged. "Then...why didn't you shoot'em?"

Uncle Danny reared back in shock. "But they weren't going anywhere."

"Best time!" said Princey. "I'd have put a bullet in them, brought them back and cut 'em open to see how they tick."

"Shooting prisoners? Dissection?" asked the Rear Admiral coldly. "Not exactly the Army way."

"What?" started Princey. "But sir...there're just animals."

"*No!*" declared Uncle Danny loudly. "There're not."

Everyone looked at Danny in surprise, so he lowered his voice and continued, but with an earnest tone.

"They communicate. They have names," said Danny. "They also understand danger, and cooperation."

Princey blinked in disbelief. "Cooperation?"

"I gave them some water while we waited...," began Uncle Danny.

"You...gave...them...water?" asked Princey in abject disgust.

"They were thirsty," shrugged Uncle Danny.

"You can catch more flies with honey than vinegar," nodded the Rear Admiral, and he focused on Danny. "Think we might be able to communicate? They could have valuable information about what we face."

"What?" asked Princey. "A good beating usually gets the info, that's what my old captain used to say."

"Best way to get information out of a prisoner is with a pack of cigarettes and a bottle of water," replied the Rear Admiral.

"That's soft thinking, and it'll get you killed," grumbled Princey.

"Beating up someone often gets bad information," piped up a National Guard captain. "I saw it when I was deployed in Afghanistan. When I was In Country...."

"Don't use 'In Country' please," interrupted the Rear Admiral.

"What?" it's a normal term," snapped Princey.

"It's short for Indian Country," said Cirilo in a hard voice. "New age. Let's start it off right."

"Oh, sorry Sir," said the National Guard Captain.

"It's okay," said Cirilo quickly. "Just a pet peeve of mine. Please go on."

"Oh okay, so when I was In... deployed, we caught this...," started the National Guard Captain, but he stopped before using the word 'Hajji'. "...this guy, and my CO tried to beat the information out of him...but the guy just told us everything."

"See!" said Princey triumphantly.

"No, I mean—like—he gave us anything and everything to stop the pain," said the National Guard captain quickly. "And the information was no good. And, after my CO got reassigned—Thankfully! —they couldn't get another peep out of the prisoner."

"But…," started Princey.

"That's enough," said the Rear Admiral repressively. "No one is to do anything to a prisoner that we wouldn't want done to one of our people. PERIOD. Now! Let's get back on track. We actually called them here for a different matter."

"What's wrong?" asked Liberty with concern, leaning forward.

"Not sure if anything's wrong," said the Rear Admiral. "But…" He put a device in front of him, which was flat and rectangular. To Liberty's surprise, it was a cell phone. It felt like forever since she had used one.

Cirilo continued: "I'm going to play a small portion, because there's a lot of audio. But this call came in while you were on the Coast. And they only want to talk to you. They said it's a delicate matter. It's some hairdresser that took refuge in a science building."

Surprised, Liberty and Uncle Danny turned to each other.

"Is it…?" she wondered.

"How many could there be *Mija?*" replied Uncle Danny with amusement.

The Rear Admiral pressed a button.

"This is Renoir, we met at the Dyson Science Building. I call for Liberty Schn…aagh, I am so sorry, I can't remember her last name, but I call for her and The Uncle Danny for help. Help that could mean life or death. Okay, maybe that dramatic. But please, please can she call?"

\*\*\*

"Ah! *C'est génial!* It is you, is it not!" cried the voice of Renoir over the ship's radio. "You are alive, and the world is a much happier and *Brighter* place."

"Hello Renoir," replied Liberty. Unconsciously, a great big smile spread across her face. "And Uncle Danny is here too."

"Ah! The Great Zom Hunter!" said Renoir with his Parisian accent.

"Well, I don't know about that," mumbled Uncle Danny self-consciously, but he let out a small smile.

"Tsk! I speak truth," replied Renoir. "You two are formidable. And that is why I must call on you, though I have no right to do so."

"Is...is something wrong?" asked Liberty with dread.

"Not wrong...per se," said Renoir dodgeily. "Are we alone? It is rather...delicate."

"The Rear Admiral of the Fleet is the only other person with us," explained Liberty.

"But I can kick him out if you need me to," declared Uncle Danny, without looking back at the man standing behind them.

Amused, the Rear Admiral raised an eyebrow, but didn't say anything.

"Are you on his ship?" asked Renoir.

"Yes, the carrier Theodore Roosevelt," replied Liberty.

"Then *No!* We cannot throw a man out of a room on his very own ship," declared Renoir. "That would be rude. Hello Admiral-Type-Person!"

"Pleased to meet you," replied Cirilo.

"Thank you very much for letting me talk to them like this," said Renoir.

"Well—really—I was kinda wondering what all the fuss was about?" replied Cirilo pleasantly.

"Ah, that is fair, for I have been a bit cryptic," admitted Renoir.

"Just a bit," smirked the Rear Admiral.

"So, you...and to this I refer to Liberty and The Uncle Danny...you know that I am with Dr. Milton," said Renoir. "And... well...um, preventative measures ran out several months ago..."

"Preventative measures?" asked Liberty with genuine confusion.

Uncle Danny cleared his throat and leaned a little forward to mutter sheepishly. "Um, condoms."

Liberty looked up in surprise at the Big Mexican, who blushed.

"Oh!" she said at last.

"Yes," said Renoir over the radio, as if he could guess what was happening. "And Nature. Well...Nature, being who she is…"

"Wait! Do you mean…," started Liberty.

"Dr. Milton is in her first trimester. *Ma souris* is having trouble keeping down her food," said Renoir, but then he

244

added happily. "Which means, I will be a Papa, if only *my* Papa were here to see." However, his voice grew serious. "But Dr. Milton, she is...very worried about bringing a child into the world sealed in this...cage, as she calls it."

"What do you mean?" asked Liberty fearfully, and her mind raced to a worst-case scenario.

"Can we get to the Fleet?" asked Renoir. "Can you get us to a safer place?"

Relief flooded through Liberty. "Oh yeah! Of course!"

"Really?" asked Renoir with excitement.

"Well.," began Liberty, but some uncertainly went through her. She quickly glanced back at Uncle Danny, who just nodded wholeheartedly.

"¡*Orale!*" he said in affirmative.

Her heart did a happy dance as she turned back to the radio. The Librarian spoke now with absolute assurance. "Yes. We will come and get you."

"Besides, I could use a haircut," said Uncle Danny. "Liberty can't do a good haircut."

Liberty gave him a sour look. "Hey! I warned you that I had little experience."

"Very little indeed," bantered back Uncle Danny.

"And! I only had a knife," said Liberty.

"This will not do!" declared Renoir and his laugh came over the radio. There was a healing nature to it because it was so filled with joy. "I will fix it. I swear if you get me to safety, I swear here and now on *ma mère et mon père* that I will cut your hair properly."

245

"It's a deal," replied Uncle Danny with a solemn nod, even though the hairdresser could not see it over the radio.

"Ah! Sooooooo, when can you be here? And then we can see...OH!" began Renoir hopefully. However, he suddenly let out a few words in French that Liberty assumed were naughty. "I almost forgot to ask after Dr. Tagg and the boy. That would've been dreadful." He continued earnestly. "Are they okay?"

The Librarian chuckled. "They're great."

"In fact, Liberty's been seeing *a lot* of Dr. Tagg lately," replied Uncle Danny slyly.

Whipping around, the Look from her eyes could have melted steel. But the Big Mexican just looked as angelic as a newborn lamb.

Unable to see this, Renoir replied with joy. "Oh really! *Amore* is always excellent news. I look forward to seeing them soon." He paused a moment and then added, hopefully. "Maybe even...in the next day or so...hmmm?"

Liberty was still glaring at Uncle Danny when she blinked. She looked back at the radio, and then turned to the Big Mexican, who shrugged.

"Um, this might take more planning," said Uncle Danny.

"To get you out safely," continued Liberty, thinking back to their discussions of Danny's niece.

"Mr. Renoir, this is the Rear Admiral again," said Cirilo. "Is there any concern of your safe area getting breached?"

"Breached?" asked Renoir with confusion.

"I think he's asking if the zoms can get inside the building?" translated Liberty.

"Oh no!" chirped Renoir. "We are still quite safe."

"And are you running short on any water or food?" asked Cirilo.

Liberty looked at the Rear Admiral in confusion, and Uncle Danny turned with a sharp eye. Cirilo saw the looks and stiffened, minutely, but he did not do anything else, except wait.

"Food? I think we are good on food and water, pourquoi?" asked Renoir uncertainly.

"Pour-wha...?" replied Cirilo.

"I think he's asking why this is germane," suggested Liberty.

"Germane?" asked Cirilo.

"Oh sorry. It means, why is shelter and water relevant to... *Oh!* I see," said Liberty.

"What?" asked Uncle Danny and Renoir together.

"I am assessing the situation to see what kind of timeline this needs," said Cirilo in an authoritative voice.

Renoir said, a little sadly. "That sounds like tomorrow is out."

"Let us be clear," continued Cirilo with authority. "I want to get you two out. But we need to do this safely."

"That is true," admitted Renoir a trifle reluctantly.

"No child should be born under such conditions," continued the Rear Admiral. "Though to be truthful, I'm not sure where you will go once you do get here. We do not have a lot of extra space."

Uncle Danny glanced at Liberty, who looked deep in

thought, and then he said. "Let's get them here first."

"True," agreed Cirilo. "I can ask our fishermen, and women, to look for abandoned boats too."

"Maybe we'll get lucky," said Uncle Danny.

"So, this is a 'maybe'," said Liberty, still pondering. "*But* it's dangerous to move people around the city on foot."

"And we could get a truck...," suggested Uncle Danny thoughtfully. "But we run into the same problems we find when trying to save my Tessy."

Liberty added, almost absently, but firmly. "Our Tessy. *And*, what if more people want to go? What if the whole science building is ready to go as well."

Uncle Danny's eyes grew wide with excitement. "I know where a school bus is! I thought about trying to get it running. But, even if all the tires are still inflated, there's still a chance of getting a flat. And I'm not a member of Triple A if we need a tow."

"*Also*, there's that mob of zoms around the science building," said Liberty.

"True," said Uncle Danny thoughtfully. "I've seen Day of the Dead parties with less people."

The Rear Admiral stood up even straighter. "So, you can locate this bus quickly?"

Uncle Danny looked at him. "*Si*. It's actually not too far from the Armory."

"Then let's talk with the Army," announced the Rear Admiral.

Liberty's eyes widened with concern. "Again?"

Cirilo explained, "I have an idea. But first, I need to talk with someone. Can you come with me?"

"But...Army help? *Pollas en vinagre,*" asked Uncle Danny, who had noticed Liberty's unease right away.

Liberty tried not to make a face. "Um...does this include...Major Princey."

Cirilo looked at her, and the Librarian swore that she saw a hint of a smile there.

"We might—Accidently, of course! —forget to invite Major Princey," replied the Rear Admiral dryly.

After saying *au revoir* to Renoir, Liberty and Uncle Danny followed Cirilo deep into the carrier.

After they had walked for a little while, Liberty leaned close to Uncle Danny.

"Where the heck are we?" she whispered.

"It's not just you *Mija,*" replied Danny with a soft smile. "I'm kinda worried that we're going to run into a minotaur."

Without looking back, the Rear Admiral said dryly. "Oh, don't worry. The minotaur's shift ended at 0600. He's probably on deck right now getting some sun, as we speak."

Liberty let out a snort of laughter and immediately brought her hand to her face.

"Sorry, I snorted," she said automatically.

But Uncle Danny's grin was focused on the Rear Admiral's back.

"I take it that you know where we are?" asked the Big

Mexican.

The Rear Admiral glanced back. "To be fair, back when I was a little ensign. It took me a while to get the hang of navigating a ship like this. Even with a cheat sheet. But the good news is that we're here."

Before they could ask where 'here' was, Cirilo turned and walked into a room. A captain with an extremely neat beard and a dark US Military turban shot up out of his chair. He went ramrod straight, as if ready for inspection.

"Rear Admiral in the room," bellowed the captain. He snapped off a crisp salute and held it. The other men and women in the room jumped up at his direction and stood tall. Uncle Danny got the impression though that they were really just humoring their captain.

With flinty eyes sparking, Cirilo glared at the captain who he kept up his salute.

"There's no need for that here," said the Rear Admiral repressively.

"Sir don't know what you mean, Sir, Rear Admiral Sir," replied the Captain with a quick, staccato speech.

Looking back at Liberty and Uncle Danny, Cirilo just shook their head in exasperation.

"This is Captain Deep Singh," explained the Rear Admiral. "Who is cheesed off at me right now."

"Sir, I don't know what you mean, Sir," barked Captain Singh.

The Rear Admiral turned back to the Captain and saluted smartly himself. The moment Cirilo finished, Singh stopped saluting, but stayed stock still.

"At ease captain," said the Rear Admiral.

"Sir, Yes Sir, Sir," replied the Captain, and he went into parade rest, which was still perfect. But Uncle Danny did note that the Singh looked at his people and gave an almost imperceptible nod, that they could relax again.

The Rear Admiral himself stopped, as if trying to keep his temper, however Liberty never saw his face change from bland authority. Instead, he turned to Liberty and Uncle Danny.

"Captain Singh here had an audacious plan to rescue people from the Coast," said the Rear Admiral. "But I had to shoot it down, because keeping the Fleet together was almost too much for us."

Singh's eyes stared straight ahead, but now Uncle Danny could tell that he was curious.

"Captain," continued Cirilo. "Tell them your plan."

Singh momentarily glanced at the Rear Admiral before remembering himself. His eyes shot straight ahead.

"Sir?" he asked cautiously.

"Captain!" said Cirilo with a soft bark. "Consider that an order."

"Sir, yes Sir," said Singh automatically. "When I was on the last helicopter to try to get Representative Kim, I saw an abandoned M1 Abrams tank, not too far from a small harbor. So, I wanted to use it to go through the streets and rescue people."

"And you even went to all the trouble of figuring out how to get fuel for the tank," explained Cirilo. He turned to Liberty and Uncle Danny, and suddenly sounded like a proud Papa. "He *even* found someone in the Fleet who had recently repaired M1 Abrams tanks."

Captain Singh looked taken aback.

"You squashed the plan, right off the bat," he said cautiously. But then he added hastily. "Sir!"

"Well First, we *were* having huge difficulties keeping the peace within all the boats on the Fleet," said the Rear Admiral.

"True," admitted Singh, a little reluctantly.

"And Second, I did not want to bring new people into a volatile situation," continued Cirilo.

"We could have found them boats," countered Singh.

"True, but it would have been just more ships to keep an eye on," said the Rear Admiral.

The Captain nodded. "Annnnnd, it *was* a little touch and go there for a while,"

"But *You*, and Your Whole Team, rose to the occasion. You kept people safe, alive," said Cirilo, proudly.

"Just doing our job," shrugged Singh, but Liberty could tell that he was pleased by the compliment.

"And lastly, when you found refugees on the Coast, how were you going to transport them?" asked Cirilo.

"Oh...we were just going to have them sit on top of the tank," replied Singh.

"Which I felt was too risky," said Cirilo. "Still do!"

Uncle Danny suddenly exclaimed, excitedly. "The bus!"

The Rear Admiral grinned at the Big Mexican. "Exactly!"

But the Captain looked understandably confused.

"What bus?" he asked.

Cirilo looked back at Singh.

"What if your tank was towing a school bus behind it?" asked the Rear Admiral.

"A... bus," replied the Captain, and a smile grew across his face. "A bus could work. At least, I think it'd work. I'd have to ask Bath, who is the tank mechanic, but yeah, it should work."

"Wait!" said Liberty to Cirilo. "You're proposing that we take a tank to the science building?"

"We could go to the Old Armory too," interjected Uncle Danny softly but firmly.

Excited, Liberty turned to him. "Yes! Tessy!"

"Tessy?" asked the Rear Admiral in confusion, and the Librarian looked back at him.

"When I first met Uncle Danny," she explained. "He was dropping off his niece at the Old Armory, to keep her safe."

The Rear Admiral turned to Danny. "This was after you'd been bitten, right?"

"*¡Orale!* And I did not know that I had some kind of immunity," shrugged Uncle Danny with a heavy heart. "So, I abandoned my poor Tessy there." He whispered sorrowfully. "*Mi Mariposa Unicornio.*" But then his voice rose. "And, if we can get her out, I can take her someplace even safer now."

Liberty whipped around. She fixed Danny with a stern look and said in her You-Cheesed-Off-The-Librarian voice.

"*YOU* didn't abandon her. *And* it would've been dangerous to bring her out on foot…"

"IknowIknowIknow," said the Big Mexican quickly.

"We talked about this," continued Liberty.

"*Si, si!*" he said apologetically. "You and I looked at it. Even with a vehicle, they break down. And even with two of us…" His voice trailed off.

Softening, the Librarian reached out and touched her best friend's arm. "We're going to get her too."

"Well, *first*," said the Rear Admiral. "We need to make sure this is going to work in the first place. *Then* we'll go from there."

# Chapter Eleven

*Present Day*

Uncle Danny let Captain Singh lead the Soldiers and Marines through the marina, towards the parking lot. It was one thing to follow Liberty—who was Awesome! —but he still wasn't sure about this guy. But he and Liberty had agreed that it was better to take a back seat, for now.

Besides, Danny was helping keep the former Army mechanic, Tricia Bath, safe, and she seemed like a nice young woman. She was probably in her 20's, but to a man like him in his 50's, she could've been his niece. And inwardly, he vowed to himself to protect her, like a Good Uncle would.

"Wish we could go faster," grumbled Singh.

"You don't!" said Uncle Danny quickly. "Really, you don't. You do not want to catch the attention of these birds."

Just in front of Danny, Private Collins started to look around more quickly.

"I'm...," started Bath, hesitantly. "I'm still having trouble with the idea of 'alien-birds'." She looked at some zoms as they moved past. "I mean—Sure! —I never thought I'd see zombies, but...aliens."

"They are very real," said Uncle Danny with somber earnestness. "I'm shocked that I've made it this long against them."

A soldier suddenly leapt forward. Private Frankline body-checked a zom on the dock. The zombie lost its balance and fell into the water, but not before it smacked hard into the side of a decrepit boat. The sound made Uncle Danny wince in sympathy.

"Okay," said Singh to Danny, though it sounded like he only half-believed him. "So, let's check out the parking lot first to...borrow some cars."

Yesterday

"So first, we steal some cars," said Singh.

*"Borrow!"* insisted Uncle Danny quickly. "Borrow. We're not thieves."

"What's the difference?" asked Singh.

"Uncle Danny doesn't like the idea of theft," said Liberty to the Captain, but then she turned to her best friend. "Pirates."

Uncle Danny opened and closed his mouth. "That's True."

Singh's brow furrowed. "What're you talking about?"

256

Turning to the Captain, Uncle Danny gave a little shrug. "*Mi Abuela* was very…"

"*Abuela?*" asked Singh.

"His grandmother," interjected Bath, without looking up from her reading.

"Yes. My grandmother made sure that my brother and I were 'Good Kids'," said Uncle Danny. "Even if she had to break us in half to do so."

"So…what…," began Singh.

Uncle Danny cut in. "Liberty and I consider ourselves 'pirates' for the fleet."

"Well really, we should be called 'privateers'," explained Liberty academically. "But it doesn't sound as cool."

Uncle Danny glanced at her and, with a nod, scrunched up his face. "Yeah. Privateers sound like some d-bags corporate guys."

"Yeah! Definitely suggests d-bags," agreed Liberty with feeling. "Not sure why, but…"

"¡Neta!" agreed Danny. "But then again, we're Bad Pirates." Liberty looked at him, puzzled. "Well, we have a ship with no name. That makes us bad pirates."

"Oh! I never thought of that," smiled Liberty. "We really do have to find a name for that ship. I've heard that it's bad luck to change the name of a ship, so it's probably bad luck to not name it at all."

"Isn't everything bad luck to sailors?" asked Uncle Danny with mock seriousness. "Like, it's bad luck to have a woman onboard a ship?"

"Okay," said the Captain, a little loudly. "Nautical

superstitions aside. First, we're going to try and 'borrow' some cars, and then to try and 'borrow' a tank."

"Hey, that tank is ours," said Uncle Danny. "Finders keepers."

"Wouldn't your *Abuela* object?" asked Liberty curiously.

"Naw. She never said nothing about no tanks," shrugged Uncle Danny.

Liberty gave a little chuckle.

"Again, back to planning," grumped Singh, but he was not even cheesed at them.


### Present Day

Uncle Danny tried to get a powder-blue pickup started. He didn't like the color, but what could you do? He did like pickup trucks. For a moment, the pickup truck vacillated on the idea of starting. However, it finally turned over.

Not daring to shut it off, he hopped out of the truck and moved to another car. Without slowing, he put the butt of his shotgun right through the passenger window.

Private Frankline saw this and sneered.

"Huh! You plannin' on being a passenger?" smirked Frankline as he took out the driver's side window with his M4 Carbine rifle.

As Frankline brushed the glass off the seat, Uncle Danny reached through the vehicle and undid the driver's side door. Quickly, the Big Mexican circled around and dropped into the driver's seat.

Just as he was sitting down, there was a yelp. A quick

glance saw Frankline jumping out of his car. The soldier was pulling a small sliver of glass out of his butt. He whipped around to glare at Uncle Danny.

But Danny was concentrating on trying to hotwire the car, all the while trying not to let a smile appear on his face. Oddly, keeping a straight face was one of the hardest things he had done in a long time. The car roared to life.

Jumping out, Uncle Danny waved Singh over. "I got another one going."

"You know," said the Captain thoughtfully. "For someone who didn't want to 'steal' cars, you start them up pretty good."

Uncle Danny smiled genially. "That's a fair question. My brother always had back problems, but it got a lot worse in the last five years. I came in on a Visa to help him at his garage for a few months, but...he didn't get better. At least, not enough."

"Ugh, poor guy," said the Captain. "I hate back troubles."

"*¡Orale!* And so, I kept the bay doors open these past few years. Plus, I've had to borrow more than a few cars to keep my niece and I alive since the Z Went Down."

"Yeah, I guess I've had to do a few things myself since that day as well," admitted Singh good-naturedly.

The Captain was giving Danny a companionable smile when a shot rang out. A zom ambling towards them dropped bonelessly to the ground.

Neither Uncle Danny nor Singh gave it more than a glance.

But the Big Mexican touched his earpiece. "Good shot."

"Thanks," chirped Liberty from her position.

"And I'm Loving these earpieces," he said to her.

"I know! Right!" replied Liberty with glee. She had climbed up on top of a nearby building to cover them. "And I was able to climb across a few buildings here. I want to see if I can get a clear view of the tank. Then, I might not have to climb up and down."

"Careful though," said Uncle Danny. "If those aliens are flying..."

"I know," said Liberty with gentle patience. "I'm keeping my head down, so as not to present a target."

"Okay," smiled Uncle Danny softly. "Sorry to fuss."

"It's okay," replied Liberty. "Hey! Friendship keeps you alive out here."

"Sure does," agreed Uncle Danny happily.

"I'm going to move a little ahead—Carefully!!—to find a better place to cover your route," said Liberty.

After saying goodbyes, the Big Mexican looked back to Singh.

"You all heard that too?" asked Uncle Danny.

"These earpieces transmit to everyone on this channel," said Singh. "So, you do have to be careful about what you say." But then, he added quickly. "Not that you were saying anything wrong."

"'Friendship saves you'?" scoffed Frankline from nearby.

"I seem to remember someone talking about something embarrassing when he first had one," said Singh to

Frankline with an arch tone.

"Someone had an itchy butt!" called out Sergeant Ruiz.

"It was One Time!" cried Frankline.

"Everyone quiet!" ordered Singh. "We still need to finish getting those gas drums, and the cables for towing the bus, off the boat."

"I'd help," said Uncle Danny, a little apologetically. "But Dr. Tagg doesn't want me lifting more than 50 pounds. Not the zom virus, but I have..."

"It's okay sir," interjected Singh with a smile. "We got this. If you can help cover us...?"

"That, Dr. Tagg would not complain about," smiled Danny. "And then once we're set, we...what do they say in those Transformers movies, 'Let's roll'?"

"Close enough," nodded Singh. "Now, I want everyone back to the boat. We're going to need that gas when we get to the tank.

### Yesterday

*"Do we need any kind of special fuel?" asked Liberty.*

*"Nope," replied the former tank mechanic, Bath, without looking up from her reading. Some magician had not only scrounged a bunch of technical manuals for the tank, but also the Haynes "M1 Abrams Main Battle Tank Owner's Workshop Manual" as well.*

*Everyone around the meeting table looked to her for more. But Bath was completely engrossed in reacquainting herself with the tank.*

*Finally, Singh said. "An M1 Abrams can take gas, diesel...and even kerosene!"*

*"Great. So, we're good there," said Liberty.*

*"Well, except for the fact that we're going to have to transport at least a few 55-gallon drums to the tank...," started Singh.*

*"And an M1A2 Abrams only gets .06 miles to the gallon," added in Bath without looking up.*

*"Sounds like my first car," nodded Uncle Danny.*

*"So, no joy riding," said Singh. "Once we have the tank running, the clock starts ticking. Hard! Because I really don't want to run out of gas out there."*

## Chapter Twelve

*Present*

Once the last drum of gas was levered onto the back of Uncle Danny's pickup, he frowned.

"Those tires look almost flat, with all that weight," commented the Big Mexican.

"Then we best start...," began Singh when he stopped and smiled. "Okay! Everyone in your cars. 'Let's roll out'!"

"¡Oye! But! Be careful driving," urged Uncle Danny fervently as he looked around.

"Yes Mom," said Private Frankline sarcastically.

"No, I'm serious," said Uncle Danny earnestly.

*Yesterday*

*"Even if we find enough vehicles, we're going to have to get there," mused Singh with measured concern. On the table before him was a diorama made out of anything they could find.*

*"Are the roads obstructed?" asked Sergeant Ruiz.*

*"Most traffic jams are headed out of town, and the highways," said Uncle Danny. "No, my worry is running over zoms."*

*"What're you worried about?" smiled Ruiz. "That the cops'll get pissy with us for a little vehicular homicide?"*

*Present*

Frankline's car tore out of the parking lot and clipped a zom as it went.

"Private! Slow down!" ordered Singh over the earpieces.

Which the soldier did—for exactly 2.3 seconds—but then he jerked the wheel left to sideswipe another zombie.

Uncle Danny, on the other hand, moved at a more sedate pace. Of course, he had 55-gallon drums of fiery death in the bed of his pickup. That did make him more cautious.

Meanwhile, the Big Mexican was largely able to tune out Singh yelling at the private. To Danny, it seemed like Frankline had played too much of that violent video game that the kids liked. For the life of him, he couldn't remember the name of it.

Singh barked over the earpiece. "Private! This isn't Grand Theft Auto!"

'Bingo', thought Uncle Danny.

"Just one more!" cried Frankline, aiming for a zom in a

costume. "Superman for 10 points."

The car went over the Creature of Steel, and immediately one of the back tires blew.

Frankline fought for control and almost lost it. But he managed to find a little oasis, in the midst of all the zoms.

Half a block back, Captain Singh stopped his borrowed car. Just a little way behind, Uncle Danny, and the other vehicles, slid to a rest.

Sergeant Ruiz had erupted into a blistering commentary, centered around the abysmal depths of Frankline's intelligence.

"Sergeant, I got this," said Singh.

A little reluctantly, Ruiz relented to the Captain and let it go.

Singh continued. "And Private, stay in your car."

But Frankline was already halfway out the door. Though he did to take a potshot at a zom with his handgun.

"What're you doing Private?" growled Singh.

"What? He looked at me funny," grinned Frankline, a little defensively.

"No," said Captain Singh, trying to keep his cool. His words clipped, staccato. "Why are you out of your car?"

"Just going to change the tire," said Frankline. "Aw damn. One of Superman's bones is sticking outta the back tire."

To himself, Uncle Danny murmured. "Which is why I said not to run over them."

"It's okay," said Frankline off-handedly. "I should have

the spare on in a jiffy, once I get...what the..." Suddenly, he cried out. *"Bird!"*

Tearing down the street, an alien-bird with a raspberry tuft barreled towards him.

"Get In! Now!" ordered Singh.

Too busy to answer, the Private scrambled towards the open car door. The alien-bird was already upon him. Frankline dove inside, and only just managed to pull the door shut behind him.

The alien-bird with the raspberry tuft kicked at the door, leaving a huge dent in it.

"What the hell is that?" cried out Frankline.

Raspberry Tuft started to move around the back of the car, as if stalking.

"What do I do? What do I do?" asked Frankline over his earpiece, and people started to respond.

"Shoot it you dum..." began Sergeant Ruiz. But then she remembered her orders and cut off the rest.

"Why the heck did you get outta your car?" demanded Private Mullins though.

But Uncle Danny's world slowed down. He knew these aliens. They were not stupid.

*"Ya te cargó el payaso,"* hissed Uncle Danny. He called out. "Everyone! Watch out!"

"It's just one," said Mullins.

"Eyes peeled people," ordered Sergeant Ruiz with a bellow over the rest of the chatter.

That's when Uncle Danny saw before him another alien-bird run up to the Captain's car. The bird's beak punched right through a side window, shattering it. There were screams over the earpieces.

Uncle Danny put the pedal to the metal.

Unfortunately, the pickup only shuffled along against its haul, geriatrically.

However, as Danny went forward, he did hear something collide with the side of his borrowed truck. If he had not started driving, they would have been right at his window. A little smile came across his lips.

Steering around the back of Singh's car, he aimed straight for the bird attacking it. The alien's head was partway inside the rear passenger window. But his truck was too damn heavy to go very fast.

An alien with a Magenta Tuft popped her head out and easily stepped out of the way. It waited just beyond Danny's passenger door, and the Big Mexican could swear that the bird looked smugly through the passenger window.

At least, Magenta looked smug until she saw Uncle Danny's shotgun in his outstretched hand.

The deer slug missed the alien-bird by inches, but it came with a shower of tempered glass.

Pelted fiercely by the shards, the Magenta Tufted bird cried out and scampered away.

Driving forward, Uncle Danny glanced left at the Captain's car. In the back seat, a uniform torn open, and in the passenger seat Collins looked as white as a sheet.

Over the earpieces, and guns were going off behind Danny. But the noise from the shotgun had been so loud.

So, Uncle Danny looked forward. Raspberry Tuft had completely circled and shattered the driver's side window. The alien was trying to climb inside, struggling against the size of its wings, oblivious to everything else.

This time, the pickup had enough time to get some speed as it swung around Frankline's car.

"She wore a raspberry beret...," sang the Big Mexican absently.

Uncle Danny's truck slammed into Raspberry Tuft's bottom half, dragging the alien out. Stopping a little way past, Danny put the truck into reverse and backed away from Raspberry's body. Swinging around, he stopped next to Frankline's driver side door.

The Private looked up in surprise.

"Get in!" cried Uncle Danny. "¡Andale niño!"

Freaked out, Frankline scrambled out the door and jumped into the pickup clutching his hand. A swift, knowing glance told Danny that the Private had superficial wounds, nothing of immediate concern.

The moment the passenger door shut; Uncle Danny continued to drive backwards towards the rest of the convoy.

A bird with an off-blue tuft lay dead by Captain Singh's car, and the captain had his window down firing with his M4 Carbine. Most of the aliens were in retreat, scampering away, as the angry buzzing in their heads died away.

However, one bird tried to charge Singh. But a sniper's bullet pierced it's back. The alien collapsed into a heap.

Breathless, Danny pulled around the alien and stopped.

Hurriedly unbuckling his seatbelt, the Big Mexican scrambled across the cab of the pickup. He leaned right over the private.

"What?" protested Frankline, weakly.

But Uncle Danny—heart pounding—stuck his head out the window to look at the fallen bird. At a distance, the bird looked like she had had a red ruft.

But this was not Rak.

Danny's chest unclenched.

From her perch on the rooftops, Liberty called over the earpieces.

"What's wrong?" she asked with concern. "Are you okay?"

At the same moment, Frankline, trapped below the Big Mexican, weakly asked. "Why're you on me dude?"

Uncle Danny touched his earpiece and said to Liberty. "I'm good, *Mija*. Nothing."

Moving back to the driver's seat, he buckled in and started to drive backwards again. However, he soon encountered a knot of zoms. They stood there, softly moaning.

Danny tried to back up a little and his truck bumped into one of them. But, after the zom righted itself, Uncle Danny decided that the creatures were not going to move anytime soon.

"Why aren't we going?" whined Frankline, starting to feel himself again.

"The zoms behind me aren't moving," explained Uncle Danny with a patience that he did not feel.

269

"Well, just run over 'em!" said Frankline.

And that worked out so well for you, thought Uncle Danny. But he decided that it was not worth it.

For a moment, he was nearly giddy that Rakduson hadn't caught that bullet.

But then the memory of Rak writhing on the ground, flooded back through him like a Tsunami. Writhing in agony because Uncle Danny had shot that metal device in the back of her head. His breath came short and fast.

However, before he could be pulled any deeper into that rabbit hole, Singh came over the earpiece.

"Danny?" called the Captain again. "You okay there in the truck?"

"*¿Mande?*" blinked Uncle Danny.

"Yeah, we're alive," replied Frankline happily.

"Private Frankline," said Singh with a cold voice. "We will talk later. Now Liberty, are you okay up there?"

"None came up here. I'm wondering if they can strategize much when that buzzing is going on,"

"That would be something," said Singh with a heavy voice.

"Anyway, they ran far and fast," replied Liberty.

"Liberty...?" began Uncle Danny softly.

"No birds with a red tuft," she replied right away. And then she added uncertainly. "If that's what you were going to ask...was it?"

"*Si*, and thank you," he said with relief.

Singh spoke up. "Okay then, let's get moving towards

the tank."

"Wait?" said Uncle Danny. "Is everyone okay back there?"

"Let's...just get moving," said Singh heavily.

Uncle Danny felt a pang of sadness, but he put the truck into gear and drove.

The zoms, in typical fashion, stood in knots on the street and sidewalks. Weaving in and amongst those knots was tight sometimes, but they were getting closer to the tank at least.

"Stop waving at them," grumbled Uncle Danny repressively.

"What's the matter?" asked Frankline derisively. "Scared they'll wave back."

"*Neta*, I wouldn't be surprised right now," he muttered. And thanks for that thought, he added in his head.

Danny began to slow.

"What's wrong?" asked Singh from behind.

"Need to clear a path ahead," said Uncle Danny, a little heavily.

"You want me to take the shot?" asked Liberty from above.

"No thank you," said Uncle Danny. "We'd just have to drive over it."

The truck sped up and veered left.

"Hey! What're you...," started Frankline.

Uncle Danny smacked right into a zom. It had been standing by itself in the only open space between two knots

271

of zoms. The creature bounced off the front of the truck, breaking a headlight. The collision propelled it into one knot of zoms, some of which were knocked down.

"Man! That was like human bowling!" grinned Frankline.

"Let's just go, before they start spreading apart," muttered Uncle Danny, ignoring the Private.

Straightening the truck, he drove through the gap, and soon the other cars followed. Up ahead though, he saw something.

Uncle Danny called out. "I see the tank. Lots of zoms around it."

The tank was facing away from them, almost on top of the sidewalk.

Up above, Liberty waxed poetic. "It's almost as if they know—deep down—that it symbolized protection."

"Could be," replied Uncle Danny noncommittally.

"You don't agree?" asked Liberty, cautiously.

"I... I just don't know," admitted the Big Mexican. "Any more sightings of the alien-birds?"

"*Nada,*" she replied.

Uncle Danny called out. "Captain Singh?"

"Let's do this," replied Singh. "We're one car short, so we're going to have to try and compensate."

"And don't get out of your cars until it's clear," added Uncle Danny in a strict voice.

"Right, we got a lot of lives depending on us," said Singh. "Danny, you need to be as close as you can to the left side. That way we don't have to move those drums too far." However, he remembered that he was talking to a civilian and added. "If you could."

"I will," replied Uncle Danny as he drove towards the tank and sped up.

"Um, aren't we going a little fast?" asked Frankline with concern.

Focusing ahead, Uncle Danny did not answer, though he did wince in pre-sympathy. *"Perdón por esto."*

"What?" asked Frankline.

Uncle Danny slammed the truck into a pack of zoms clustered along the left side of the tank. The creatures were violently thrown forward into other zoms. Some that he hit were now broken, and Danny's heart ached. He didn't like causing unnecessary pain, even if they didn't feel it, which they were pretty sure they didn't', but still.

At the impact, Frankline shot forward with a cry of surprise. He and Danny's backpack tumbled into the passenger side well.

Glancing over, Uncle Danny confirmed that the private was not broken.

The Big Mexican then immediately called over the earpieces. "We're alive."

Looking forward again, Danny shook his head. "Should've worn your seat belt."

Okay, he admitted to himself, a little guiltily. Maybe a little unnecessary pain.

"You didn't warn me," snapped Frankline as he tried to climb back into his seat. "I could've broken something."

*Always wear a seatbelt*, thought Danny. *Didn't your Abuela teach you anything?*

Out loud, Uncle Danny said. "We'll go out through your window."

"Seriously, you got to warn people before purposely getting into an accident," complained the Private.

"Watch out," said Uncle Danny, dryly. "We're going to get into an accident."

Bug-eyed, Frankline glared at Danny, who was still not looking at the private.

"I said 'Before'!" snapped the private.

"Private Frankline!" called out Singh over the earpieces. "Get onto that tank and cover us!"

Eyes forward, Uncle Danny did not say anything. There was just enough room for someone to climb out, but hopefully not enough for a zom to squeeze through.

Frankline turned from glaring at the Big Mexican to reaching for the open window when he stopped.

"Anytime now," said Singh, restless.

However, Frankline looked around the cab.

"Just need…," said the Private.

Uncle Danny saw this and asked with genuine concern. "What's wrong?"

"Um…," started Frankline, but then he gestured to show that his hand had a nasty cut on it.

"Oh!" said Uncle Danny over the earpieces. "Give us a second."

"What's wrong?" asked Singh.

"Private got hurt," replied Danny.

"Zom?" asked Sergeant Ruiz swiftly.

"No, No!" said Frankline quickly. "That damn bird."

"Just a cut," said Uncle Danny while he looked over the wound. "I bet it's not even going to scar."

The Big Mexican took out a med kit and quickly—expertly—cleaned the wound, which made Frankline involuntarily hiss in pain. But the Private did not cry out, which raised his Standing some, in Uncle Danny's opinion. Wrapping a bandage around the Private's hand, the Big Mexican taped it down.

"Okay, he's good for the moment," said Uncle Danny over the earpieces, and then he looked at the Private with a smile. "And you, no swimming for an hour."

Frankline let out a chuckle.

Singh began sincerely. "That's great." Then he barked. "Now get out there Private!"

"I'm going, I'm going," grumbled Frankline, though wisely without any noise.

Uncle Danny pretended not to hear and instead watched a zom come over to the driver's side window. It began to paw at the glass. The zom had been an attractive woman, once.

Frankline levered himself out the passenger window and climbed onto the M1A2 Abrams tank. Uncle Danny noticed some drying blood, which the private had left behind. He felt a sudden surge of annoyance that Frankline had messed up his truck. But then, as he swiftly reminded himself, this was not his pickup, which made him chuckle

275

softly.

Atop the tank, Frankline called out. "There's a bunch of zoms. But not that bad."

"Okay people," said Singh. "We're going to form a half ring around the tank. It's going to be a little loose since we're down a car."

Uncle Danny could not see Frankline's face, but he imagined that the Private winced.

Singh continued. "Then, we're going to have to clean up inside the circle. No one be a hero. Go slowly and get this done right the first time. Frankline, if any zoms start crowding the vehicle, I want you to aim for the knees. Get them on the ground."

"Yes sir," said Frankline as he drew his sidearm.

After a moment, Singh asked in a voice, which sounded more disappointed than angry. "Private, where is your rifle?"

"Oh! Um...," started Frankline. "I might have left it back in the car."

"Are you kidding?" called out Ruiz over the earpieces.

"Liberty, can you cover us?" asked Singh.

"I'm in a good position," replied Liberty from the rooftops.

"Then cars, get into your positions," ordered Singh.

Since Uncle Danny could not look out the back window, he had to wait until Singh's car appeared in front. It stopped near the front of the tank with the nose of his car really close to a brick storefront.

Soon, another car came in from behind, expanding the barrier. The vehicles soon created a semi-circle around the tank.

"Everyone set?" asked Singh.

In turn, each car called out their assent.

"Actually, it looks pretty solid," said Liberty from above.

"Then the next part is more dangerous," said Singh. "Frankline, you might want to crouch down, just in case. And Liberty, you should pull your head back."

"Already done," replied Liberty.

"Team, roll your windows down, just enough," said Singh. The driver's side window dropped down only enough to leave a small space open. Zoms started moving towards the cars, pawing at them.

"Shitshitshit," muttered Sergeant Ruiz over the radio.

"What's the matter?" asked Singh, concerned.

"Nonono, it's okay," said Ruiz. "My window just wanted to roll down all the way down. It's all good now."

"You sure?" asked Singh, who could only see Uncle Danny's truck, the tank, and the car behind.

"Yes sir," replied Ruiz with chuckled confidence.

"At least those bird-things weren't around," said Private Collins with a shaky laugh.

"Okay then, aim correctly, and take your time," ordered Singh. "AND *Don't* shoot the gas in the truck."

"I second that," called out Uncle Danny as he ducked down into the cab of his truck.

In Singh's car, a zom tried to get its fingers in. The

Captain pulled his sidearm, a M9 Beretta, and put a bullet through the zom's eye. The creature dropped, only to be replaced by another.

"Fire at will," called out Singh.

Uncle Danny heard the shots, but they came sporadically as the soldiers found their targets. It took less than five minutes.

"Everyone sound off," ordered Singh. There was a chorus of voices as the squad announced that they were all healthy and hale. "Frankline. I need you to do a slow circuit around the perimeter of the tank and look for movement. I don't want any ankle-biters."

Sidearm steady, a serious and focused Frankline started to look for zom survivors. As he found one, he'd quickly and expertly put it down.

For his part, Uncle Danny opened his window and leaned out.

The beautiful zom girl had moved towards Singh, and she was now laying—quite still—upon the ground. The girl's short skirt had flipped up exposing her underwear, that declared that it was 'Friday'. He did not know why, but that made him really sad. Maybe it was because the young woman had looked even younger than Liberty.

Shaking it off, Uncle Danny scanned the ground for movement.

A man in golf clothes was still wiggling so Uncle Danny fired his shotgun.

All the nearby zoms looked very dead, so the Big Mexican opened the door to his borrowed truck. He hopped out just far enough, so that if anything was underneath, it couldn't snag him.

"I didn't say that people could leave their vehicles," grumbled Singh repressively.

There was a gunshot and Frankline called out. "Clear."

Uncle Danny saw Singh's look of displeasure.

"Just going to make a quick circuit," said Uncle Danny with a conciliatory tone as he stopped. Using his boot, he gingerly pushed the zom girl's skirt to cover her decency.

"Well...," started Singh.

"Actually, he's best suited," injected Liberty from above. "He's already been bitten, so he has—at least—a partial immunity."

"And my doctor has me on a medicine that appears to have stopped it," said Uncle Danny absently as he started moving.

"But still," said Liberty with her 'Mother' tone. "Be Careful!"

Without looking up, Uncle Danny replied seriously. "I promise *Mija*."

After the Big Mexican had confirmed that all the zoms were indeed dead, or at least really dead now, Singh ordered everyone out.

Every car opened but one. Noticing that, the Captain started to walk over to it.

In the driver's seat, Private Collins saw the Captain and jumped. Quickly, the soldier scrambled out with his rifle. His eyes darted quickly to all the zoms beyond the cars.

Singh decided to let it go when there was a single rifle-

279

shot behind him.

"We got a gap over here," called out Ruiz behind him as she lowered her M4 Carbine a bit.

"I got another one over here," added Mullins.

Captain Singh looked around quickly. "Okay. Frankline, get down. I need everybody on sandbag duty, except Bath. Bath! I need you to start looking over the tank. But don't go inside until someone else has looked in first and made sure that it's clear."

"I'm okay with that," replied Bath.

"Sandbag duty?" asked Mullins.

Singh gestured at the zom bodies all around.

"Oh," said Mullins with distaste, but she did not argue.

"Improvise and overcome," said Frankline. "Or whatever it is."

"That's the Marines dummy," said Ruiz. "We're Army."

"Actually, I'm a Marine," said Mullins.

"Yeah, but Frankline is Army," said Ruiz. "And he's still a dummy."

"He probably wouldn't have survived our training anyhow," sniffed Mullins.

Ruiz suddenly turned to face Mullins and spoke with a dangerous tone. "Do not pick on my team."

Mullins opened her mouth to retort.

"That's enough of that," snapped Singh. "I can't believe you're arguing over which is the best branch right now."

"Army!" muttered Ruiz under her breath.

280

Singh gave her a flinty look. "You know, this question has been coming up more and more since we found ourselves on the Carrier." The Captain looked up at the sky for a moment and then back down at them. "Okay, so as far as I'm concerned, you are all part of one fighting force now. And, to make it fair since we're both Army and Marines here...then we're all part of the Continental Navy, as of *Right Now!*"

"*Navy!?!*" cried Ruiz and Mullins, united in horror.

"That's enough," bellowed Singh. "Get back to work! *Now!*"

The newly branded Naval soldiers scrambled to look busy, each quickly grabbing a corpse.

"Grab the farthest ones away," ordered Singh. "That way it'll be easier towards the end."

"I can check inside the tank," offered Uncle Danny.

"Thank you," responded Singh sincerely.

The Captain and his soldiers began to wedge zom bodies into the two spaces left open, because they had been down a car.

Uncle Danny walked over to the tank, though he did glance underneath, just in case. Thankfully, it was clear.

Bath was by the back of the tank as he got close.

"I can't believe that I agreed to come back out here," hissed Bath softly, and he could hear the strain growing in her voice.

"It's going to be okay," said Uncle Danny with earnest confidence.

"You...you've been here before?" asked Bath. "I mean,

281

back on the Coast before."

"Actually, I and my niece had been living in and around this city since this all started, until recently," said Uncle Danny.

"Your niece?" asked Bath.

"*Si*, she's at the Old Armory," said Uncle Danny.

"So, you know how to stay safe," said Bath.

"And Liberty," said Uncle Danny, and he nodded his chin towards the rooftops. "But I'm hoping it won't come to that."

"If we can get the tank started," said Bath in a soft voice.

"It's okay," said Uncle Danny and he declared. "You're going to be fine."

Bath smiled at that. And while the smile was still tinged with fear, there was more confidence in it.

However, Uncle Danny did need her help getting up onto the tank.

"This getting old business sucks," he grumbled.

While Bath started to assess if the tank was still viable, Uncle Danny went to check inside. He, Liberty and Singh had all wondered why anyone would leave a tank in the middle of the street. They had all come to the same conclusion: You only left it if you had to.

Opening up the loader hatch, a former soldier stood up and out of the tank, making terrible noises. It blinked at the sunlight. Then it saw Uncle Danny. Before it could say anything, Danny put a deer slug through its head.

"Gahh!" cried Bath behind him and a tool dropped.

Uncle Danny whipped around. "Sorry. I forgot to tell you that the tank might be loaded."

Despite herself, a small chuckle escaped Bath.

There were no more noises from inside.

Sighing, Uncle Danny moved around the tank. He pulled the one soldier out and onto the front of the tank. Then, he lifted up his shotgun, but no one else stuck their head out.

With a sigh, the Big Mexican looked down at the zom soldier. "*¡Oye! Güey!* You couldn't tell me if you had any friends in there, could you?

The extremely dead zom did not reply.

"*Me cago en la leche,*" muttered Danny. He climbed up to see if he could get a view inside.

"Careful," said Liberty.

"I will," replied Danny, not taking his eyes off the hole. He aimed his shotgun inside, but there was no light, except for the sun streaming in. He contemplated getting a flashlight or something.

A hand reached up and grabbed his collar. He was yanked forward and tumbled into the tank. He landed hard onto his back, but he was more worried about the zom who climbed on top of him. Uncle Danny brought up his shotgun between them, but he could not aim it. It only served as a fancy stick to hold the creature back.

Teeth, festering with grime, snapped down, and they nearly took off Uncle Danny's favorite nose. He tried to lean his head further back, but it was solid behind him. Letting out a roar, he used the shotgun like a weightlifting bar. He pushed the zom's head up towards the hatch. Still snapping, the zom tried to get at him, but it was too far away.

"Danny!" called out Liberty over the earpiece.

"I'm okay," he grunted. "Mostly."

In the claustrophobic interior of the tank, Uncle Danny was trying to figure out how to get away, safely. Zombie virus aside, he fretted. Who knew what germs were in those teeth?

A clank came from above.

This was followed by a wet clank and blood started to drip from the back of the zom's head. The creature's eyes crossed in an almost comedic fashion, and then it went boneless.

Past the dead zom was Bath, looking stricken. The bloody wrench in her hand shook hard.

"The clues show that it was Ms. Bath, with the wrench, in the tank," grinned Uncle Danny.

"I...I... I...," began Bath.

"You're awesome. And if you need to throw up, you might want to go to the edge of the tank," said Uncle Danny gently.

Without a word, Bath disappeared and soon there was the sound of someone being sick.

"Hey! You almost got me," cried out Frankline.

"Sorry," replied a sad voice, and then there were more wet noises.

Over the earpieces, Liberty said, a little breathlessly.

"Help is on the way."

"I'm good," said Uncle Danny because he knew that she would be worrying. Fair enough, he'd been worrying about her, if the roles were reversed.

Singh appeared atop the tank and looked inside.

"You alive?" smiled the Captain.

"Peachy, though not quite keen," replied Uncle Danny cheerily. "Just let me...." He stopped and pushed the zom body to one side and patted his pockets. Finally, he found a small knife.

"What're you...?" said Singh.

The Big Mexican quickly cut off a decent piece of the zom's sleeve and wadded it all into the creature's mouth.

"Just in case," he told the captain.

"Thank you," replied Singh sincerely.

"*De nada,*" replied Danny absently.

Uncle Danny lifted the zom up. The Captain grabbed the dead creature and hauled out the zom. Unfortunately, the wretched smell did not go with it. Turning in the cramped space, he quickly looked over the controls.

"Hope I didn't break anything," he muttered, a little guiltily. To his relief, nothing looked damaged.

Uncle Danny was rapidly overcome with an urgent and overwhelming need to not be in here, Ever Again. Scrambling up, he found delight in the fresh air. Or, at least fresher air, considering the delicate '*Eau De Toilette Of Zom*' that still hung in the air.

Turning, he waved to Liberty above, who waved back

enthusiastically.

Climbing out, he went straight to Bath, who was still at the side of the tank.

"Thank you," he said.

"I thought you were supposed to take care of me," chuckled Bath, sadly.

"Out here, we take care of each other," smiled Uncle Danny kindly. "You did good."

And Bath stood a little straighter at that. A small smile came across her face.

"We better go though," said Uncle Danny. "There're not paying us by the hour."

Sergeant Ruiz, who was standing nearby, heard this exchange.

"Hey Captain!" she called out with a mischievous grin. "What is our pay for this job?"

"Room, board, 2 square meals a day, and the exquisite honor of serving in the US Arm...," started Singh. But then he caught himself. "The United States Navy." His face suddenly turned to granite. "Now, I want everyone protecting this tank. Move!"

The squad immediately turned to make sure that their car barrier was holding. Singh climbed off the tank and quickly sorted out who was standing where. Once done, he pulled one of the soldiers aside.

Satisfied that they were safe enough, Uncle Danny went to help Bath when something shot up into the air. It was a quad-drone. After orienting itself, the drone zipped off.

Detouring, Uncle Danny crouched near Singh and

286

pointed up.

"New toy?" asked Danny.

"New? I wish," muttered Ruiz as she flew the drone.

Singh squelched a remark and looked up at Danny.

"Scouting actually," said the Captain. "Instead of a LRRP, we use…"

"Sorry, a what?" asked Uncle Danny.

"It's cool. Sorry, a Lurp is a Long-Range Reconnaissance Patrol," explained the Captain. "This way we can make sure that the path to the bus is safe…or at least safe-ish. "

"I got the school bus," called out Ruiz.

"Close?" asked Singh.

"About 4 or 5 klicks," reported Ruiz.

"Huh. 3 miles. I wish it were closer, but that'll have to do," said Singh. "I want you to fly around it and see if there are any obvious problems."

"Damn," moaned Ruiz. "The battery light is already on."

"Then just get it back," said Singh.

"If I can," muttered Ruiz with concern.

While they did that, Uncle Danny put down his shotgun and helped Bath. He had never repaired a tank before, but he knew how to hold a tool until someone needed it.

Uncle Danny also found himself amused by Bath as she worked. She talked to herself the whole time in a barely audible mumble until the tank was fueled up and ready to go.

"Okay," said Bath. "I'm going to get her going."

"And you drove tanks before?" sniffed Frankline.

"She repairs them," said Singh repressively. "She probably took one out for a spin."

Bath kept out of that conversation and went to the hatch. But she hesitated. Uncle Danny moved a little closer.

"It's clean," he said softly. "No more zoms."

The tank mechanic gave him a shy smile. "Just...just being overly cautious."

"Good," he replied. "Seriously, that's the best way to be out here."

Bath smiled at him.

"Okay," she nodded with more confidence. But she stopped at the Loader's Hatch on top and her face twisted up.

"When I meant 'clean'...," said Uncle Danny. "Sorry. I didn't have any time to get any Febreze."

Bath straightened her spine. "It's okay. I had brothers, so I can take this." She climbed inside and into the driver's seat.

At first, the M1A2 Abrams didn't start, and almost everyone's stomachs seized up.

"It's okay," said Bath, though there was an anxious flutter in her voice. "Give her a second. She's been asleep for a while."

As time wore on, Liberty looked up nervously from her perch atop the roof. She checked to see if the path back to the boat was clear.

At the same time, Captain Singh was also deciding on the safest method of retreat. That made losing Private Sonde, who had been killed during the bird attack, burn. And the idea that this had all turned out to be a fool's errand—*especially* after all the grief he had given the Admiral—compounded his misery.

But that, he would deal with later. Right now, the best thing to do would be to cram as many people as they could into the truck. Use as few vehicles as possible to get everyone, and Private Sondes, safely back onto the boat, he decided.

However, while the others anxiously planned, Uncle Danny just waited with a patient smile.

The tank suddenly roared to life. It made a throaty, self-satisfied noise.

Singh blew out a breath of relief.

"Okay then," he said, turning to his Navy Soldiers. "We're going to ride on the tank to get there."

For half a second, Uncle Danny almost raised his hand, but he immediately squelched that.

"Hey Captain?" he said. "I'm going to keep my pickup, just in case."

"Not a bad idea since we gassed her up," nodded Singh. He turned back to his people. "And we need to get Private Sondes wrapped up and ready for transport."

"I got it," said Sergeant Ruiz. "I'll need a hand though."

Private Frankline immediately stepped forward. "He was an idiot, but..." His voice trailed off, and then he said stoically. "Let's get this done."

Ruiz watched in surprise as the Private went over to the car with Sondes.

"I think they've known each other since Basic," supplied Singh softly.

"Okay," said the Sergeant and she followed Frankline.

With that done, Uncle Danny looked down into the tank.

"You good in there?" he asked softly.

"Yeah," said Bath, though she looked a bit disappointed.

"Sorry, after I ended up in there with that zom...," started Danny.

"No, no, it's all right," smiled Bath. "I understand."

Uncle Danny continued with mock indignation. "It almost took off my favorite nose!"

Bath chuckled. "I wouldn't want to be in here after that." Her voice, a trifle reluctant, but then she added. "And that means you don't have to put up with this smell."

"Ah! You have figured out my master plan," said Uncle Danny warmly.

"And you'll be safe, right?" said Bath, reassuring herself.

"¡A Huevo! Absolutely!" assured Uncle Danny.

"Okay," smiled Bath, wanly.

Uncle Danny turned and saw that Captain Singh was helping to lift the dead soldier up onto the tank. Once Private Sondes was settled, the Captain came forward. Singh looked in on Bath.

"Wow! It's a bit ripe in here," commented Singh.

"I didn't do it," chirped Bath. "It was Uncle Danny."

"*¿Neta?* Throw me under the bus, why don't you," said Danny with mock outrage.

"Permission to come aboard?" asked Singh of the mechanic.

"Permission granted sir," replied Bath quickly, almost saluting out of habit.

Uncle Danny turned to Singh and said. "I'm going to get Liberty, so that we can…"

"I'm coming!" cried a voice from above.

The Big Mexican looked up and saw the Librarian repelling down on a rope.

"It's about time," grumbled Danny loudly, with mock annoyance.

With playful dismissiveness, Liberty sniffed. "Yeah, yeah yeah. You're always complaining."

Liberty bounded over to the tank and scrambled up with a youthful speed that Uncle Danny envied. Not that he begrudged her.

"Okay," declared Liberty. "I totally wanna ride in the tank."

"Just to warn you *Mija*, there's a bit of a smell," said Uncle Danny.

"Still, it'll be worth it to ride in a tank," grinned Liberty. But then she looked at Singh. "If…that's possible."

Out of the hatch came Bath's voice. "Room for a 4-person crew. But-- Just to warn you! -- no cup holders."

"Darn, no Starbucks then," said Liberty jokingly.

From beside the tank, Ruiz cried with horror. "ARGHH!

291

It Burns!"

Liberty and Uncle Danny whipped around, startled.

However, Singh looked sympathetically down upon his Sergeant.

"I know," said the Captain gently. "It's hard."

"What's wrong?" asked Liberty with great concern.

Singh looked at her. "The sergeant is still mourning the passing of Starbucks."

"It's not fair," whined Ruiz as she put the quad-drone in its carrier. But then, she straightened up and put her game face back on. "Okay. I'm ready Captain."

"Never doubted it for a second," smiled Singh. He turned to Liberty. "You're welcome to join us in the tank." He turned back to Ruiz. "I want you up top, navigating."

"This is going to be so cool!" grinned Frankline.

Singh's dark eyes bore down on him. "Private! Your job is to get in that first car that I was driving. I need you to open up our little half circle. I angled it so that you should only scrape the storefront a little. Collins! I need you in the second car."

Collins' eyes grew wide, but before the Captain could ask, he got distracted by the Private.

With a little whine, Frankline asked. "Why can't we just drive over the cars? We got a tank!"

"I really don't want to try that with people on top," called out Bath from inside the tank. "Just sayin'."

And the Captain looked hard at the Private.

"You have your orders," said Singh, and he climbed

inside the tank. With him and Liberty inside, Ruiz took a position near the hatch, while the rest of the squad quickly found any available space on top.

"This is so cool," said Liberty with a reverent whisper.

Singh touched his earpiece. "Frankline! Collins! Now!"

For all his protests, Frankline pulled the first car out of the half circle, and only scaped the storefront a little. His car drove into the press of zoms, but only enough to get out of the way. Collins did his part, but in the opposite direction.

The zoms started to shamble through the hole.

"Now Bath," ordered Singh. "Move through that hole."

"Okay," said Bath, and they could hear the cringe in her voice. "Oh, I can't look." However, she quickly amended. "But I gotta. I know!"

The Abrams tank moved forward into the hole and started to collide with zoms. However, the creatures did not move out of the way.

"Oh Crap! Oh Crap!" muttered Bath.

The tank rolled forward and the zoms went under. The noises were horrible and even Uncle Danny winced in sympathy. Both for Bath, and the zoms.

"When I did this," muttered Frankline over the comm. "I got in trouble."

"Let her concentrate, that's an order" said Singh, squashing any bellyaching for now.

Collins' car had not gone out quite far enough. The tank slid noisily across the side of the car.

"SorrySorrySorry!" muttered Bath unhappily.

"It's okay," said Singh soothingly. "There's not a cop in sight for miles."

Despite herself, Bath gave a desperate little chuckle. "Thank God. I don't want to get shot for taking a tank."

As the tank moved forward, Uncle Danny put the truck into drive and came up behind the behemoth. He tried to veer around the worst of the bodies. If the truck lost a tire, Uncle Danny was going to be running after the Abrams.

"*Padre nuestro, que estás en el cielo. Santificado sea tu nombre,*" prayed Uncle Danny fervently.

As he prayed and drove, he could not help but think of his *Abuela*. As much as he missed her, he was happy that she was not here. Not in this horrible place.

As he finished, Ruiz called out. "Amén."

Uncle Danny started. "Oh, I forgot I was live."

"At least it was a prayer," said Ruiz with a smirk in her voice. But Frankline did not rise to it.

The pickup stopped between the two cars, Frankline and Collins jumped out of their vehicles.

"Careful," called out Uncle Danny earnestly.

They jumped the short distance and climbed into the bed of the pickup.

"We're in," called out Collins, but his eyes were looking towards the sky.

Uncle Danny moved forward, watching the road.

Soon, to the right of the tank, the street opened up.

"Finally," muttered Uncle Danny.

Cautiously pulling out from behind the tank, and its grisly carpet of remains, the Big Mexican pulled up beside the Abrams.

"Hey Sunday Drivers?" called out Uncle Danny over the earpieces. "I want to try and get a little ahead. Make sure that it really is all clear."

"Sounds good," replied the Captain.

"Hey, don't we get a say in this?" asked Frankline from the back of the truck.

"You can try jumping," suggested Ruiz with a smirk in her voice.

"Stand down Frankline," said Singh. "You and Collins go with. Keep your eyes peeled out for those damn birds too."

"Always!" said Collins, a little too quickly.

After a moment, Singh said. "Private Frankline, you're going with Danny? Okay?"

"Yes sir," replied Frankline grudgingly.

"Bath, keep this speed," said Singh. "Ruiz, navigate Danny towards the bus."

"And be careful!" said Liberty, but then she added apologetically. "Sorry, couldn't help it."

"I will *Mija*," he replied indulgently. If he wasn't leaving her inside a *resistente* tank, he probably would've been worried about her too.

Uncle Danny pulled further along. The odd tendency of zoms to cluster close to one another helped. By the time the zoms noticed, they were usually past. And behind, the tank weaved a little, but mostly the Abrams made its own grisly

295

path.

"You're going to want to turn left up ahead," said Ruiz.

Following her directions, Uncle Danny pulled out of sight of the tank. He drove cautiously through the streets, looking for any sort of trouble. He wasn't sure why he was so nervous.

Though, maybe Liberty had been right.

### Yesterday

"What the hell?" snapped Uncle Danny as he slammed a drawer shut. He opened another kitchen drawer and then whipped it closed. "What moron brings a hundred bottles of wine on board and doesn't even bring a corkscrew!" He stalked to another part of the kitchen.

Colin started backing towards Liberty. But he went carefully, so as not to draw attention. He reached the little table where they always ate dinner. Liberty immediately put out an arm to the 11-year-old and pulled him towards her. She wrapped a tattooed arm around his middle and held him close.

"It's okay," she whispered to Colin.

"I mean...," growled Uncle Danny angrily. "What kind of..." But then he switched to Spanish and unleashed a torrent as he slammed more drawers and cabinets shut.

Liberty let go of Colin to put her hands over his ears. The boy turned to look at her, perplexed.

"What're you doing?" asked Colin.

Suddenly confused, Danny saw this and—mid-screed—stopped. "What're you doing Mija?"

296

"I don't speak Spanish," said Colin to Liberty. "Well, not that much."

"Yet," said Uncle Danny, who was tutoring him in the language. However, while his demeanor was calmer, he still looked enraged.

Liberty put down her hands to wrap her arms around the boy again. This time in a gentle hug.

"I didn't know what those words were," she said primly. "But I could guess."

Uncle Danny looked like he was going to snap, however he stopped. He deflated a bit and leaned against the kitchen counter.

Liberty said gently. "It's going to be okay."

Uncle Danny looked up and furrowed his brow. "¿Mande?"

After a long day of planning, they were back on their unnamed yacht and pulling away from the Fleet for the night.

It was Uncle Danny's turn to cook.

"Tomorrow," she said patiently. "We got this."

"Oh...I know," said Uncle Danny off-handedly. "Just...need to get ready. Can't have any mistakes."

"The plan will not go according to plan," said Liberty.

Colin blinked and then looked at her in confusion. "Why do you say that?"

"Because it's impossible to plan for everything," continued Uncle Danny, a little calmer.

"But we'll improvise, and figure it out," said Liberty, really to the both of them.

"Oh. Okay...sure," muttered Uncle Danny.

*Liberty looked at him for a long moment. "Or are you worried about seeing her again tomorrow?"*

*"Hmmm?" asked Uncle Danny in confusion. "Who?"*

*Colin, having been hugged enough—he was almost twelve! — squirmed out of her grasp. He went to sit down in one of the other chairs.*

*Liberty reluctantly let him go. Maybe she had needed a hug too, she decided. But she continued to look at her partner-in-crime.*

*"Your niece," she said simply.*

*Uncle Danny looked at her oddly. "What're you talking about Mija?"*

*"Who?" asked Colin.*

*Liberty turned to the boy. "You know, Uncle Danny's niece. We told you the story of him dropping her off."*

*"Oh yeah, Tessy, right? She's at the Old Armory." said Colin to Liberty. "That's where you were before you got me."*

*"What does my niece have to do with some...," began Uncle Danny and then he used a Spanish word before continuing. "...corkscrew?"*

*"You know, I'm going to start looking up these words that you're using in front of Colin," said Liberty in her best You-Cheesed-Off-The-Librarian voice.*

*"He doesn't know what I'm saying," said Uncle Danny, a little defensively.*

*"I know what 'pendejo' means," said Colin, defensively.*

*Uncle Danny's eyes widened.*

*However, Liberty let it go and kept on. "Little pitchers have* big ears, as my Mom used to say."

"Hey," squeaked Colin in annoyance. "I can't help it if I got big ears." And he cupped his ears defensively, which were a little big for his adolescent head.

"You just need time to grow into them," said Uncle Danny soothingly. "It'll happen. Will Smith had big ears, and he was the coolest cat on the planet."

"That's true," said Liberty. "And what 'little pitchers' is really saying is that, just because someone is a child, it doesn't mean that they aren't listening."

"I'm not a child," protested Colin quickly.

"Sorry, a 'pre-teen'," replied Liberty gently. "And you want to say, 'if I have', not 'if I got'."

Colin made a distressed noise and looked at Uncle Danny.

"She's picking on me," whined the boy.

"Naw," replied Uncle Danny. "She just wanted you to understand that the 'little pitchers' wasn't about your ears, and she wants you to speak properly."

"But who cares?" huffed Colin.

"It's one of the few things that we had left," said Liberty primly. Her brow furrowed as her mind raced. "We have less now, out here on the ocean in a found boat. Our language is one of the few things that we do still have, which is ours."

The Librarian blinked, and then looked at the guys who were watching her curiously.

"Sorry, I got really deep there," she finished, a little awkwardly.

"No, no, it's okay," said Uncle Danny sincerely, and then he *looked at the boy. "She needs to teach you proper English, but I need to teach you proper* Spanish." *He looked at Liberty. "I don't want my language dying either."*

*Colin put his face in his hands and wailed melodramatically. "Ugh! I got saved from aliens, only to be dropped into First Period English."*

*"And Second Period Spanish," grinned Uncle Danny unsympathetically.*

*"It's not fair," wailed Colin.*

*Liberty bounced up and hopped over to him. "I Know! It's totally unfair." And she gave him a quick hug. Before he could protest, she moved back and turned to Uncle Danny. "And you. It's going to be okay."*

*"I'm fine," he said quickly, but he could hear the defensiveness in his voice.*

*"You were slamming those drawers like they'd stolen your girlfriend," replied Liberty with a little smile.*

*"I was just trying to find the corkscrew," said Uncle Danny defensively.*

*"I know you've been bothered by what happened to that alien," murmured Liberty.*

*"That's just guilt," said Uncle Danny. "Should've done more."*

*"But now it feels like something else," said Liberty. "What's really the concern? Is it tomorrow?"*

*"We've gone to the Coast before," shrugged Uncle Danny.*

*"But not to get your niece," said Liberty gently.*

*"We tried to figure out a way to get her off the Coast," said*

*Uncle Danny quickly. "No plan was safe enough."*

*"As opposed to leaving her in a veritable fortress," nodded Liberty.*

*"Why would that bother me?" asked Uncle Danny.*

*Liberty thought for a moment, and she said at last. "You didn't abandon her,"*

*Uncle Danny started. "What? I know."*

*"Do you?" murmured Liberty. "You had been bitten, and you didn't know that you had an immunity." The Big Mexican opened his mouth, so she kept going quickly. "Even a partial immunity."*

*"I got her somewhere safe," nodded Uncle Danny sadly.*

*"And she has been," finished Liberty kindly.*

### Present

"But...should I have gone back sooner?" whispered Uncle Danny as he drove. He remembered Tessy leaving with Liberty and there was a sharp pain in his gut. The little girl had not wanted to go, and he didn't want to lose her. But that zom bite should've been the end. Instead, he was here.

Should he have come back sooner though? Would that have endangered her more? And he knew that the answer was 'yes'. Borrowed vehicles can break down. And walking out was dangerous, even without those birds.

Tessy had been safer in the City of Angel's Old Armory. But still, he felt bad.

Suddenly, he saw his cross street. Already in the middle

301

of the intersection, he hit the brakes. Frankline and Collins almost tumbled into a drum of gasoline.

"Sorry!" he called back through the truck's slider window.

Looking forward, Uncle Danny turned the truck left and soon saw the school bus up ahead. He was casually observing that all the tires looked flat, when a new, dreadful thought came over him. *"Ya te cargó el payaso."*

"What's wrong?" asked Singh over the earpiece.

"Oh, nothing," lied Uncle Danny. "I'm just going to check out the bus before you get here."

"We'll be there soon," replied Singh, with a tone that showed that he heard the lie.

Uncle Danny was not paying attention though. He propelled the truck towards the yellow school bus. Pulling aside, it was almost flush with the vehicles while he slowed. The Big Mexican was coasting when they reached the door. Turning the truck, a little away from it, he could now open his door.

Leaning out the door, Uncle Danny saw that the rear of the truck was pretty tight against the back and his door made a semi-barrier the other way. It was a reasonable short-term solution.

"What're we doing?" asked Collins.

"I'm going to go check out the bus," replied Uncle Danny.

"You want us to come with?" offered Frankline, and Collins quickly glared at him.

"No," said Danny quickly. But then, he realized how

dismissive it had sounded and added. "No, no Thank you. Should only take one. But can you look from where you are to see if there's anyone in there?"

Uncle Danny carefully stepped between the pickup and the bus. Nothing grabbed him from underneath.

"I don't see nothing," reported Frankline.

Collins turned and eyeballed all the zoms nearby and spoke more rapidly. "On second thought, maybe we should all go in."

"Please just stay here," asked Uncle Danny gently, and he took a quick moment to look in the back of the pickup truck.

"What'chu doing?" asked Frankline.

"Just taking inventory of what we have," said Uncle Danny without looking up. He saw junk, heavy-duty cables, junk, tools, junk, at least one old tarp, and more junk. "Out here, always take inventory, when you have a second. Never know what's going to come in handy."

"You probably don't think we can handle the bus," grumbled Frankline.

But Uncle Danny ignored him and started towards the bus door when he stopped himself.

"Almost forgot," muttered Uncle Danny. He took out his earpiece and left it in the bed of the truck.

Now off the network, he turned towards the bus. It took him a minute to lever the door open and, as he did, he kept thinking about how much closer the tank was. He reminded himself that there might not even be a problem.

First question, 'Why do you abandon a vehicle?' he

303

remembered.

The door finally opened, and he brought up his shotgun. But there was nothing. Slowly, he stepped up into the bus, and he felt better that his ankles were no longer exposed to anything underneath.

"You make one little mistake," said Frankline grumpily. "And suddenly everyone thinks you're an idiot."

Collins took this time to guard the truck, and not to answer. Mostly not to point out that Frankline had left his rifle behind. A panic-sweat broke out on his back. He didn't know why Frankline wasn't worried about those damn birds, which might come back at any……

A shotgun went off.

Collins nearly jumped out of his skin.

After a moment, Uncle Danny came out. He tested the ground to make sure that no ankle-biters had crawled up in the meantime. Once he was sure that it was safe, he went to the truck and reached into the bed.

"I'm sure you don't need our help now," muttered Frankline snottily.

Not responding, Uncle Danny grabbed the blue plastic tarp and disappeared back into the bus.

"Tired of sitting on the sidelines," grumbled Frankline.

A moment later, Uncle Danny reappeared. The plastic tarp was now wrapped around something. Someone who had not been big enough to be an adult.

Frankline went pale.

"If the tank comes, tell 'em…," began Uncle Danny in a quiet voice. "Tell'em I had to take a piss, or something."

"Yes sir," said Collins, wide-eyed.

"And make sure that nothing else gets in there," ordered Uncle Danny, who turned and moved around his truck door. He walked down the street and weaved between the knots of zoms.

"Who is he to give us orders?" asked Frankline.

"Shut up," muttered Collins, and he jumped into the bus. Swiftly, he did a sweep, but it was clear. However, at the back of the bus, there was a small blood stain on the floor. The soldier moved swiftly to the front and closed the door.

"What the heck?" called out Frankline, but there was no response from the bus.

Through the front window, Collins was watching Uncle Danny move down the street. The Big Mexican was heading right for a storefront. Collins could not see what it was from here, but he saw Danny put a deer slug through a big window, which collapsed.

Uncle Danny disappeared inside. Collins watched while Frankline bitched about something. What if those bird-things were in there? wondered Collins with a pounding heart.

Just as Collins was about to call the tank for help, the Big Mexican reappeared. At the same time, the sounds of the tank came from the opposite direction. In a moment, Danny was back.

"It's all safe," sniffed Frankline snottily.

"Good," replied Uncle Danny distantly, then the Big Mexican knocked on a bus window.

"Why'd you close the door?" asked Uncle Danny.

"With me still out here," grumbled Frankline.

Collins opened the door partway. "You told me to protect the bus."

Uncle Danny grabbed the door and pushed it open.

"Can you leave this open?" asked Danny with a gentile tone. But he waited until Collins had taken his hand off the manual lever, which opened and closed the door. Then, the Big Mexican went to the truck bed.

By the time the tank arrived, Uncle Danny had replaced his earpiece and was back on network.

The tank pulled up past his truck and the bus. He did wince a little as the Abrams ran over more zoms. Shortly, the tank's rear was parked directly in front of the bus.

Once still, the Captain climbed out of the tank, followed by Liberty and Bath.

"We need to do this fast!" said Singh. "Bath, I need you to secure the bus, so that we can tow it. Frankline and Collins, put those cables from the truck down behind the tank. Then, you two make sure that there aren't any ankle biters under the tank or bus. And keep Bath covered!"

After laying down the cables, Frankline and Collins wearily crouched between the tank and the bus.

"Clear under," reported Frankline with relief as they looked under the vehicles.

"Thank God," hissed Collins.

"Hate being down here," grumbled Frankline.

Collin looked up. "Better than up there."

The mechanic, Bath, dropped down behind the tank and started to work to hitch the bus.

"I can help," said Uncle Danny to the Captain.

"Cool," said Singh. "In a moment, I need you to see if your truck can block the bus door and the gap between the tank and bus?"

"But...in a minute?" asked Danny, uncertain.

First, the Captain ordered Lieutenant Washington and Private Locke to carry Private Sondes' body into the back of the bus. As they passed Uncle Danny, he grabbed the last blue tarp from the pickup and followed them into the bus. At the back of the bus, he heard the soldiers.

"Who cares if that's a fresh blood stain," muttered Locke.

"Aren't you wondering?" asked Washington.

A heavy voice came behind them.

"Nothing to wonder about," said Uncle Danny. Washington's head whipped around. The Big Mexican held up the tarp. "Let's get this *hombre* wrapped up, so that he doesn't scare anyone we're rescuing."

For a moment, Washington wanted to say more, but then he heard the Captain, distantly giving orders.

"Yeah," agreed Washington. "Let's wrap him."

"Yeah!" grinned Locke. "We got some zombies to fight."

They worked quickly and the other two now-Naval-soldiers soon went back to the tank. Uncle Danny, for his part, jumped into the truck.

Danny called down to Frankline. "Could you move over a bit? I'm worried that I'm going to run over you."

307

"Hey! No problem," smiled the Private. And he moved over towards the middle of the bus while Danny maneuvered the pickup to cover the gap between the tank and the bus. The bed of the truck only just covered the bus door.

Just as the Big Mexican stopped, something slammed into the passenger side door. Danny immediately thought it was a bird and grabbed his shotgun.

But it was just some broke down executive. The zom reached through the broken window, but it was nowhere close to Uncle Danny. He was tempted to shoot it, or even disable it, but after having to clear the bus, he decided that it was not enough of a threat.

With the truck door partially blocked by the front of the bus, Uncle Danny had to climb out the driver's side window, a little awkwardly. As he did, Liberty caught his eye and silently asked if he needed a hand. Feeling way too macho, he shook his head. He might be old, but he wasn't infirmed.

Regardless, Liberty kept an eye on him until he was safely down onto the pavement. Uncle Danny carefully stepped over Bath, and then Collins, to cover the tank's left side, right beside the storefronts. Liberty caught Danny's eye.

"This street's more crowded than we hoped," she said, shouldering her rifle. She fired from atop the tank and dropped a zom. But more were wandering over to visit. "We don't have much time."

As Liberty took another shot, Captain Singh walked across the tank and called out. "Everyone else. I want you to shoot only if they get too close."

"Bring 'em on!" growled Private Locke eagerly.

"Don't get overeager," warned the Captain.

"I'm waiting. I'm waiting Sir," replied Locked defensively.

"Actually, there're already pretty close," commented Ruiz.

"I know," said Singh, and he decided that they should've kept a couple cars. But it was too late for that now.

"Maybe we should've run over more with the tank," suggested Ruiz.

"Next time," said Singh calmly.

"If there is a next time," muttered Collins out loud over the earpieces.

Singh heard and glanced towards the soldier.

"Stow that talk," said the Captain with authority. "We will cover Bath until the bus is ready to go." He saw someone else about to comment. "No matter how long it takes!"

Liberty took another shot.

"Okay people," called out Singh as the zoms reached within five feet of the tank. "Use sidearms and aim for the head."

Drawing his Beretta, Singh put a bullet right between a zom's eyes. But two others came into that space.

On the other side of the tank, two zoms came around the back of the bus and moved towards the tank. A zom came out of an open storefront right near Uncle Danny. He put it down, but another was already wandering out. Flicking the safety switch, he took a deep breath and focused on the problem.

Up on the tank, Liberty let out a breath slowly and then squeezed her trigger. An old man zom fell backwards. She saw more creatures starting to move around the tank to Danny's position. Turning her attention there, she started to cover that way.

The tide of zoms reached the edge of the tank as Singh ordered his people to begin to pull back.

However, Private Locke moved closer to the edge with a big grin on his face. He popped them, one after another. A spray of blood came out towards the soldier.

"Take that," crowed Locke. "Oh, you want one too."

"Get back private!" ordered Singh.

But Locke was either not listening or did not hear.

Private Mullins tried to pull Locke back, but the private shrugged her away, leaning over, he put his gun to the temple of someone who might've been on game show. Locke happily squeezed the trigger.

Click.

Before Locke could pull his hand back up, the TV star tried to bite him. Turning the gun at the last second, the zom chomped down on it.

"Ha-ha!" grinned Locke. "I'm too fast for…"

That was when the private slipped on something and tumbled forward into the crowd of zoms.

"OhShitOhShit," cried Frankline watching through the small space between the truck and the tank. "Man down! Man Down!"

Singh jumped towards the edge of the tank but stopped just short of it.

"H... help!" cried Locke, but then he uttered a horrible cry.

"We should...," started Ruiz, but she couldn't finish.

"No," said Singh with a dour voice. "We shouldn't." Aiming his gun, he started to kill the zoms crowded over Locke. The TV Star collapsed on top of the soldier's body. Underneath, a few neural impulses kept trying to move Locke's legs, but that was it.

"Everyone! Move away from the sides!" barked Singh as he backed up. He stalked the tank, which now felt like a claustrophobic little island.

"We need help over here!" called out Liberty. She was now on the left side of the tank by the storefronts. More zoms were moving that way. She picked off a wandering zom, while opposite her Uncle Danny fired down the length of the bus and killed another zom.

More came around the back of the bus, stepping over bodies with a single-minded predatory thought.

"I need to reload," called out Danny.

"Collins!" bellowed Singh. "Cover him."

"Su...sure, Sir!" replied Collins. He hopped out from between the tank and bus, firing his sidearm. Hands shaking a bit, he missed.

"Take it easy," said Uncle Danny softly to Collins as he was shoving shells into his shotgun. "You got this!"

Quickly, Collins glanced at Danny, but then he looked back at the zoms. He fired again and this time the zom's

311

head snapped back.

"Good one," said Uncle Danny. He moved around Collins and started to fire again. In between, he called over his earpiece. "My ammo's not going to last forever."

Singh crouched over the back of the tank but said in a calm voice. "Bath? How are we doing?"

"Getting close," she squeaked. "Almost."

"Please hurry," said Singh, and then he stood back up.

"Oh shit!" cried Frankline. "One of 'ems trying to crawl underneath!" He flipped onto his stomach to get a better look at the zom crawling under the bus towards him and Bath. "Bath, get back!"

"What?" she muttered. On her back, she was too focused on attaching the cables underneath the bus.

Frankline crawled underneath the bus past Bath. His mind sang out, warning of ricochets. If a bullet hit a piece of metal and bounced back at the tank mechanic, he'd really be screwed. And besides, she seemed nice. The Private moved swiftly and cut across. The zom in a tattered shirt was crawling swiftly.

Stopping between the oncoming zom and Bath, Frankline tried to aim.

It's teeth looked like they had started to rot long before it had become a zom. The Private's hand was shaking in fear, so he rested his elbow on the asphalt.

"What are you...?" asked Bath absently. "Oh shit! Zom!"

Frankline fired once. He didn't miss. It wasn't hard at this range. The zom slumped down. It was so close,

Frankline could even see the beginnings of its bald spot.

Heroically, Frankline did not throw up.

"Good job," cried Bath. She stretched out and patted his back quickly before returning to work.

Still shaking a little, Frankline backed up and looked for more. He could see, from his vantage, more zoms walking towards the back of the bus. Reaching the open space between the bus and tank, he hopped to his feet.

"Captain Singh, there's more coming," said Frankline as he pointed past the rear of the bus. "A lot more."

"Thank you Private," said Singh with a nod. "Keep up the good work."

A little surprised by the compliment, Frankline sunk back down to watch for ankle-biters.

As the Private sunk out of sight, the Captain looked around. They were quickly running out of time. He wished that they had brought more cars. Or grenades. Starting with grenades from a healthy distance would've slowed the zoms down. Unconsciously, he glanced to where Locke lay.

Stepping to the left side of the tank, he looked at the space between the tank and the storefronts. Uncle Danny and Liberty were stopping the press, but they couldn't hold forever.

"Done!" cried Bath as she hopped up.

"It going to hold?" asked Singh.

"I think so," said Bath. She hoisted up her bag of tools— in its canvas tote that read 'PBS: Supported by Viewers Like Me'—and put it on the back of the tank. "Ugh. That's

313

heavy." Then she looked up at the Captain. "I used a lot of the cables that we brought. But I saved some in reserve, just in case. We need to try and not drive over too much stuff in the road. I don't want to strain the cables. Oh! And the bus is going to need to be in neutral."

"Done," nodded Singh.

Bath lifted up the remaining cables and Singh helped put them on the back of the tank.

Once she was up, Singh said. "Get in the hot seat. And get us ready to go. Start slow."

"Yep," said Bath. "I've towed stuff before."

"Good," replied Singh as the mechanic ran off. He watched her for a moment, worried that she might slip, but then he realized that he was being a Mother Hen and turned away. "Frankline! Get up on the truck!"

"Yes sir!" responded the Private happily.

"Collins! I need you in the bus," ordered Singh. "See if you can get it into neutral."

"Happy to!" replied Collins loudly, a little too enthusiastically.

The moment Collins was in the bus, he dropped into the driver's seat with visible relief.

"Danny!" called out Singh. "Fall back to the truck!"

"Don't mind if I do!" grinned Danny, who did not have to be told twice. Though he did have to climb back through the truck window. Frankline was there to help him. It made Danny feel like an old man, but he also didn't want to fall on his butt in front of everyone.

The moment that Uncle Danny was inside, he deflated a

little. Even with a busted passenger window, he felt immediately better. Looking up, Danny noticed Liberty looking worriedly at him.

The Big Mexican smiled and gave a giant thumbs-up. With relief, Liberty grinned back and then dropped into the tank. Knowing that she was safe also made Danny feel better.

As Singh began to give orders to move soon, Uncle Danny felt an urgent need. However, it had been so long, so he took out his earpiece. Despite his *Abuela's* best efforts, he didn't remember the words anymore, but he did remember the basics of the prayer.

Danny opened his hand and wiggled his thumb. "God, protect Tessy, Liberty, Colin, Tagg...Oh! and Smalls too. Actually, Colin should come after Tessy, because he's *mi sobrino*, and then Liberty. Sorry."

Wiggling his Index finger, he said. "God, I think the closest teacher I got right now is my friend Liberty, so maybe a double prayer."

Wiggling his tallest finger, he said. "God, Please help Captain Singh and Rear Admiral Cirilo make good decisions."

Wiggling the fourth finger, he said. "God, please give courage to those who need it." And he said it with Frankline's name in his head. "And help those who are sick."

Then wiggling the pinky finger, he said at last. "God, I am *definitely* not worthy...but then again, I have tried to help as many people as I could. I would appreciate any help to get us back to the Fleet safely."

Frankline banged on the truck slider window and made Danny jump.

"Hey! The Captain's calling for you!" said the Private.

The Big Mexican slid back in his earpiece.

"You ready Danny?" asked the Captain, but not with any heat.

"Oh...yeah!" replied the Big Mexican. "Sorry."

Danny drove the truck a little to the right, which gave the bus more clearance to get past.

"Just making sure," said Singh. On top of the tank, he turned and climbed inside. "Okay, Bath, take'er slow."

The tank suddenly jerked forward, and everyone held on tight.

"I said slow," muttered Singh.

"Sorry," squeaked Bath from within the tank. "Still getting used to it."

This time the tank started to move forward sedately, bumping aside some zoms, while other ones went under. The cables went taut, and the bus started to move forward.

"Collins! It's your job to make sure that the bus does not stray too far off course," said Singh. "And call out immediately if there's a problem."

"Yes sir," replied Collins. With the tires flat, the going was rough, but manageable. He gripped the steering wheel tightly, unsure if that would make any difference. They began to pass the furniture store, and Collins did a double take. That was where Uncle Danny had gone, but no one else on the tank glanced that way.

The bus pulled slowly past and on a white bed was a shape, still wrapped in the blue tarp. Whoever it had been, they had not been that tall. Collins looked ahead, a little sadly, and hunched in the safety of the bus.

Some zoms tried to follow the tank/bus, but the rest turned to look at Uncle Danny and Frank in their pickup.

"Time to go," muttered Uncle Danny. Shifting into drive, he pulled out around the zoms.

Really, he didn't want to run over what was left of that dead soldier. It was too dangerous to retrieve him right now. Uncle Danny realized that he couldn't remember the guy's name, which he felt oddly guilty about.

They were not more than fifteen feet ahead of the mob of zombies, when the truck sputtered, died, and began to drift to a stop.

Frankline cried out in alarm from the bed of the truck. "Um! What? What's happening?"

Uncle Danny did not answer. Instead, he hot-wired it again. The pickup roared to life, and he let out a sigh of relief.

"They're following us!" called out Frankline worriedly.

Once more, Danny pulled away from the zoms.

They almost made it 20.3 feet.

The pickup did not even sputter. It just went dead. Uncle Danny looked down just as the electronic dashboard became an inky darkness.

"That's not good," muttered Uncle Danny.

"Start it!" called out Frankline as his voice raised. "*Start it now!*"

The tank/bus was over a block ahead and, in that moment, Uncle Danny immediately weighed his options.

Grabbing his shotgun, Uncle Danny jumped out of the truck and put on his Avengers backpack. He turned towards the bed and glanced at the drum of gas. Thankfully, there had not been much left, because he wasn't carrying that big old thing. Dr. Tagg had said only 50 pounds max.

"Okay, here's where we walk," said Danny.

Frankline did a double take. "Are you…" And the Private peppered his sentence with a lot of swear words. Not very imaginative swear-words in Danny's opinion, but it got the point across as Frankline ended with. "…kidding?"

"Swearing wastes time on the street. Time, we don't have," said Uncle Danny calmly. "Come on. It's going to be okay."

Turning, Uncle Danny walked quickly after the tank/bus.

"Where the…" And again, more swear words. "…are you…" Even more—but still unimaginative—swear words. "…going?"

Danny ducked around some zoms that were lurching as fast as they could.

"You're just going to…," started Frankline when there was a wet thump against the back of the truck. The Private looked back and jumped, letting out a pretty high-pitched scream.

Finding a safe spot, Uncle Danny looked back. For a moment, he wondered if he should go back.

However, Frankline finally moved. The Private scrambled over the truck and hit the ground running.

Satisfied, Uncle Danny turned and kept after the tank/bus. He wasn't even going to complain about running, what with those birds around.

Looking forward, Uncle Danny wondered if, during all his travels with his niece, he had walked down this road. His stomach clenched a little at the thought. He would see her again soon, as long as Certain-People-Whose-Name-Will-Not-Be-Mentioned did not do anything stupid.

Frankline slowed to walk next to him with a host of bitter complaints. "You were going to leave me."

"Said that swearing slows you down," replied Uncle Danny drily, keeping an eye on the tank/bus.

"What did you do to the truck?" spat Frankline.

Uncle Danny felt a flash of anger. If he had been a young man again, the Private would've been in trouble. Maybe a little of his *Abuela's* grace had fallen down upon him.

Instead of hitting the Private over the head, Danny called out over the earpieces. "Hey Liberty? Captain?"

"You're ignoring me?" asked Frankline in disbelief. "We're going to get eaten out here."

Calmly, Uncle Danny said to the Private. "Not if you stick with me."

"Danny?" called out Liberty over the earpiece. Her voice was close to fear.

"You okay?" asked Singh a second later.

"Yes, we're okay," said Danny quickly.

319

"Speak for yourself," interjected the Private.

"But also, a little 'no'," admitted Uncle Danny.

"What is the 'no'?" wondered Singh.

"Our ride died, but we're good," explained Uncle Danny.

"We could turn around," suggested Singh.

"Definitely," interjected Frankline.

"I wouldn't Captain Singh," countered Uncle Danny swiftly. "Keep going and we'll catch up."

"Are you crazy?" demanded Frankline of Danny.

"Surprisingly, no," replied Danny to the Private, and his brow furrowed in thought. "And I wouldn't hold it against anyone if they were." The Big Mexican went back to his earpiece. "We'll catch up soon Captain. The mission is more important."

"Mission," scoffed Frankline.

"You wanted to add something Private?" asked the Captain over the earpiece with dread authority. Singh's voice was not loud, but it was firm.

Frankline's eyes went wide for a second, but then he barked out. "No Sir!"

"That's what I thought," said Singh firmly.

"This way," said Uncle Danny to the Private, leading Frankline around a knot of zombies.

"Why don't we just run up and catch them?" huffed Frankline.

"The alien-birds," replied Uncle Danny.

Frankline looked confused. "What about 'em?"

"Don't you remember the briefing?" said Uncle Danny, a little surprised.

Ruiz came over the earpiece. "The birds hunt by movement dummy! Go too fast and you're snack food."

"Ruiz," said the Captain with a warning tone, and she did not add anything more.

"Not a dummy," grumbled Frankline, but only so Danny could hear.

Danny assured the soldier quietly. "I'll get us to a safe spot." He motioned for them to go around another knot of zoms. They were going just a little faster than the shamblers.

Inexplicably, Uncle Danny saw someone jump off the tank up ahead, and he muttered. "*¿Mande?*"

The figure power-walked towards them, and across Uncle Danny's face came a big ol' grin.

Halting in front of the Big Mexican, Liberty threw off a smart salute.

"Captain Librarian, reporting for duty," grinned Liberty.

Uncle Danny returned the salute. "At ease captain. I'm Major Paininthebutt. Glad to know that you're on our side."

Liberty dropped the salute and pirouetted smartly to walk with them.

"I needed more exercise," replied the Librarian airily. "I'm not getting enough, you know, sitting around on the yacht."

Frankline's eyes grew wide at the mention of the yacht, but his mind was occupied with something else.

To Liberty, Danny continued with an uncle-familial tone. "You know, we do have an exercise room."

"*I know*," replied Liberty with a painful sigh. "I just...hate to exercise."

"I understand *Mija*," nodded Uncle Danny. "But we probably should go on our days off. We can't get slow, not now."

Liberty nodded soberly. "Not with Colin back home."

"And Tessy in that armory," added Danny with a gentle smile.

"Exactly," said Liberty.

Frankline cried out in sudden exasperation. "What I want to know is, WHY'D YOU JUMP OFF THAT TANK!"

Liberty and Danny looked at Frankline in surprise. But then they swiftly turned back to each other and burst out laughing.

"Not one of my brighter moves," chuckled Liberty.

Uncle Danny shrugged. "Actually, I know a shortcut to the Old Armory." As they reached an intersection, he pointed them down a narrow street. "The Tank is way too fat to go this way."

"We should tell the Captain," suggested Liberty.

"Oh! Good idea," nodded Uncle Danny. "We don't want them to lose time looking for us." He spoke up. "Hey Captain?"

"Singh here."

Uncle Danny was about to speak when he whipped around with his shotgun.

Liberty immediately turned, rifle up and ready. "What?"

"Danny? You okay?" asked Singh, suddenly concerned.

But the Big Mexican was focusing just past his old truck. "Thought I…"

Liberty said over the earpiece. "He's fine Captain Singh. Something just spooked him."

"I don't get spooked," replied Uncle Danny tartly as he snapped out of it.

"My mistake," said Liberty with lighthearted sarcasm. "He just happened to jump like a bunny rabbit, for no reason at all."

Over the earpiece, Uncle Danny grumbled. "Thought I saw something."

"Animal, vegetable or zom?" asked Liberty with a more serious tone.

"Maybe we should keep going," urged Frankline.

Uncle Danny nodded. "He's right." He led them down the narrow street. "Captain Singh, we're going to take a shortcut. Easy for people, not so for tubby tanks."

Bath called over the earpieces. "She can't help it. She was born this way."

"Got it," replied Singh ignoring that. "Be safe, and we'll see you at the Old Armory."

\*\*\*

323

After a moment, an alien with a red tuft peeked back out of the alley, which Uncle Danny had been watching. Rakduson saw that they had left again. However, before she could go any further, something sparked in the device embedded in the back of her head. She wobbled for a moment, nearly having another seizure. But she quickly found her bearings. Luckily, those moments were getting rarer.

Once Rak had her bearings, she shot out of the alley, stalking them from a distance.

*-End of Part 1-*

## About the Author

## Walter G. Esselman

*Apparently, I'm supposed to write this bio to humanize me.*

*It is bold of them to assume that I am a carbon-based lifeform from Earth, but regardless...*

I grew up in Michigan, practically on the campus of MSU. Not that I follow sports, humorously enough. I've been writing forever but never really sent anything out. So, I pushed myself to get short stories out there and became a regular contributor at World of Myth and Dark Dossier. I recently started turning my eye towards novels, which is the first step in that process.

My wife Amy and I still live in Michigan because it's the

most beautiful state. Not that I like to go outdoors, humorously enough. I mean, seriously, there are bears out there, Sharks! I even saw a Bearshark once. A chilling sight.

After tooling around the Commonwealth with Cait for many years in Fallout 4, I'm back in the land of Skyrim once again.

*Khajit will shoot arrows if you have the coin. Or, it's a dungeon with a lot of loot.*

I hope you have a wonderful day!